What I Carry

ALSO BY JENNIFER LONGO

Six Feet Over It

Up to This Pointe

What I Carry

JENNIFER LONGO

Random House New York

Text copyright © 2020 by Jennifer Longo
Jacket art copyright © 2020 by Spun Inthawong
Emoji copyright © Apple Inc.

Visit us on the Web! GetUnderlined.com

Educators and librarians, for a variety of teaching tools, visit us at RHTeachersLibrarians.com

Library of Congress Cataloging-in-Publication Data
Name: Longo, Jennifer, author.
Title: What I carry / Jennifer Longo.
Description: First edition. | New York: Random House, [2020] | Summary: "In her final year in foster care, seventeen-year-old Muir tries to survive her senior year before aging out of the system"—Provided by publisher.
Identifiers: LCCN 2019001923 | ISBN 978-0-553-53771-0 (hardcover) | ISBN 978-0-553-53772-7 (lib. bdg.) | ISBN 978-0-553-53773-4 (ebook)
Subjects: | CYAC: Foster children—Fiction. | Interpersonal relations—Fiction.
Classification: LCC PZ7.L8634 Wh 2020 | DDC [Fic]—dc23

Printed in the United States of America

10 9 8 7 6 5 4 3 2 1

First Edition

This one is for Maudi.

Only by going alone in silence, without baggage, can one truly get into the heart of the wilderness.

—John Muir, in a letter to his wife, Louie, July 1888, *Life and Letters of John Muir*

What I Carry

One

YOU WILL NEVER, IN ALL YOUR LIFE, meet a person who packs a better suitcase than I do, and I'll tell you right now, the secret is not organization—it is simplification. Get rid of your crap. Do not own things in the first place. Surrender the weight of what you carry and the wild, wide world is yours.

Pack. Light.

Which sounds easy—"when in doubt, go without" and all that—but to achieve true freedom you must be *brutal* as a consumer. Is dental floss on sale two for one? Don't fall for it—one extra thing taking up room to pack and repack, and, besides that, what if your teeth all fall out before you ever need to use it? Now you're the dummy hauling around extra floss for no reason.

Yes, *floss.* Insignificant weight until you add it to that pen you bought, the T-shirt you *had* to have, the non-travel-sized thing of shampoo, until one day you wake up dragging the weight of a rolling suitcase taller and heavier than your own body and you're exhausted trying to keep track of all these things you've convinced yourself you need—*Where did I leave that? Did someone take the other? Why can't I find my socks underneath all these stupid boxes of floss?* Trapped.

My packing credentials were passed to me from my name-sake and honed since my birth, straight into foster care and never adopted. The longest I've lived in any house is eleven months, and now I am seventeen years old, so you do the math.

At school people sometimes ask me what it's like to live this way, which, I suppose for kids who lost or were removed from a family they once lived with and maybe loved, is a legit question, but for me is like asking a person born blind what it's like to not see—it's not *like* anything. I've got no objective context because I was left newborn, nameless, cord still attached, and jonesing for meth at John Muir Medical Center in California. A "foundling." When no one came to claim me, the NICU nurses named me for him; Child Protective Services let them put *Muiriel* on my birth certificate, and I have grown into it.

On my eighth birthday my social worker, Joellen, picked me up, and we walked a wooded Seattle path along the shore of the Salish Sea, and she told me how lucky I am to carry the honor of this name: Muir, a Scottish naturalist, father of our national parks, a guy who slept outside nearly all his life. We sat beside the water, and I unwrapped her gift to me: not a toy or the glitter hair bar-rettes I'd secretly hoped for.

The Wilderness World of John Muir. A weighty, hardback an-thology of Muir's best writing about nature, curated by another naturalist, Edwin Way Teale, who arranged the essays in a way that makes them also a biography of Muir's life.

I mean . . . birthday dream of eight-year-old girls everywhere.

The transcendental nature and half the vocabulary of the book were beyond me, of course, because *third grade,* but Joellen has, all my life, been more about what I need than what I think I want. I skipped rocks, and she told me Muir's story like it was mine, his days a timeline of my own.

"Muir's whole life was about protecting the natural world because nature is vulnerable; it can't defend itself against people. 'Any fool can destroy trees. They cannot run away.'"

I nodded.

She read a passage to me, and marked it so I could find it again:

Standing alone on the mountain-top it is easy to realize that whatever special nests we make—leaves and moss like the marmots and birds, or tents or piled stone—we all dwell in a house of one room—the world with the firmament for its roof—and are sailing the celestial spaces without leaving any track.

"All living things, we are *one* family," she said, "together in one home, sleeping beneath the same stars."

With my pinkie finger I petted the illustrated black bears hiding in the forest trees on the cover. I did not know then what *first edition* meant. Joellen put her hand on my head and made me look up at her.

"Muiriel. Do you understand?"

Not that day. But Joellen planted the seed of Muir's wisdom that grew into the truth that comforts me now: he lived nearly all his life more at home outside than in, and I understand why. Every house I live in smells different; the rules and beds and people are never the same. But one walk outside and I am always home, beneath the same sky. Alone is not lonely. Nothing to miss, nothing and no one to wish or search for. John Muir set me free.

He walked thousands of miles over mountain ranges and forded rivers; slept in trees and deserts and forests; and carried with him only a washcloth, a bar of soap, a loaf of bread, a compass, and, oddly, a stack of heavy books he felt were as vital as the bread—which I think is ridiculous—so I see his books and raise him one library card. But as Muir loved Thoreau, I love Muir, so every move to each new house, I pack *The Wilderness World* in with the socks.

Socks are important. Warm, dry feet are key to movement, and therefore to freedom. Socks are packed pressed flat together and rolled, tight, like well-made sushi. Two pairs of shoes (indoor and outdoor), one raincoat, one lightweight warm coat, seven sausage-rolled shirts, three pairs of pants, one pair of shorts, two sets of pajamas, three bras, seven rolled-up pairs of underwear. Basically, your suitcase should look like a grocery store deli platter of cotton-pinwheel party sandwiches, exactly a week's worth of outfits—laundry on Sunday. No new item of clothing is allowed in unless an old one is removed; anything reversible is twice as welcome in any well-packed case. Seriously, I could give a TED Talk on this shit and, oh, let us not forget the Holy Grail of packing: the toiletry kit. Flat, water-resistant nylon and plastic, four refillable bottles for soap and shampoo, pocket for a nail clipper, razor, tampons, hair ties, toothbrush, toothpaste, and your *one* floss.

I can pack and be out of any house in four minutes flat.

Except this day: eight minutes, twenty-three seconds.

Dying in sweltering summer heat in a bedroom crammed with bunk beds the day after my seventeenth birthday, I kept Joellen waiting while I debated for the hundredth and maybe last time the merits of abandoning a secret I carry that renders my "John Muir Packing" TED Talk a bunch of hypocritical garbage.

Hidden among the sushi socks and sausage shirts is a stash of compulsion in a blue-and-white-striped pillowcase tied in a knot. A sieve of burden and humiliation that in each house catches new things I collect and carry with me year after year, and I don't know why.

Muir would be so disappointed. Or maybe he would understand.

When we try to pick out anything by itself, we find it hitched to everything else in the Universe.

"Little blackbird nest," Joellen said the one time she saw it, while helping me pack in fifth grade. I rushed to hide it. "Not everything has to be useful to be loved," she said.

In my experience, that's debatable.

Besides, these *things* I carry are not loved—a ship does not love the barnacles clinging to its hull. Still, even on this August day, I could not bear to let them go. I held the bag of worthless loot and agonized until Zola, the small girl who'd slept in the bunk beneath mine for the last few months, came in.

"Here," she said, and put a small metal thing in my hand. An Allen wrench.

"In case you get lonely," she said. "Okay?"

I nodded. "How was swim class?" I asked. "You put your head under yet?"

"Didn't go."

"Why not?"

She shrugged.

"Oh, Zola." I sat on the bed. "You *have* to remind her." This foster mom liked to think she was well intended, a white lady who, instead of providing kindness and understanding, had a penchant for calling the police for minor offenses. And she was forgetful as hell. Especially, it seemed, with Zola's very few activities.

"Will you come see me ever?" she asked. "Can I write you?"

I rolled the wrench around in my palm. "Not sure writing is allowed," I lied. "But you never know when you'll see someone again."

Zola's face fell. My eyes stung.

I didn't want to keep Joellen waiting, and besides, if she had her way, this was maybe the last of packing, unpacking, packing, unpacking, so I dropped the Allen wrench into the pillowcase, removed one of the things and slipped it into my pocket, retied the knot, and carried it all in my perfect suitcase to her waiting car. To one more—one last—foster house.

"You want to come out?"

Zola nodded and trudged beside me.

Joellen was in her usual spot at the curb to give the foster mom time to say goodbye to me because she always thinks parents will miss me, which is not entirely true; it's just the older I get, the more help I am around the house, and that is what they will miss. I don't blame them. Most foster parents are overworked and exhausted, and I am not only not a burden but often useful. Sometimes I feel bad for leaving, like I'm ditching a job knowing there's no new employee to take on my duties.

This foster mom hugged me, said she wished I didn't have to go. "Maybe you'll be back, though." She sniffed. "A bad penny always turns up."

I ran back into the house and fetched a wad of toilet paper from the bathroom because she was crying a little and the house tissue box was empty. On my way out, I added *Kleenex* to the magnetic shopping list on the fridge and *Zola Swim Class 8:00 a.m.* to every Tuesday square in August on the paper calendar tacked to the wall.

Zola hugged me around my middle, and I let her and felt my throat swelling tight, so I turned to the newest kid, a boy whose arrival this morning made my being here untenable—no more room at the inn; he's younger and needs it more; our ages and genders can't share a bedroom—who did not hug me because he is ten years old and scared and also doesn't know me, so I waved to him, alone on the porch swing.

I let Zola squeeze me a few seconds more. I put my hand on her head for a moment, then took the porch steps two at a time.

Joellen popped the hatch of her worn-out Subaru, the car I've ridden in since I was still in a five-point car seat, and I tossed in my suitcase. Leaning across the passenger seat, she—small white lady, permed brown curls framing her round, middle-aged but unlined face—unlocked my door and smiled up at me. She's shorter than me, and I'm barely five five. She sits on a pillow to drive. "Ready?" She smiled again.

"What's a bad penny?" I asked. "Why would it always turn up?"

She took her hand off the wheel. "Who said *that*?"

"No one. Just wondering."

"Well. It's like . . . bad decisions come back to haunt you. Or a bad person keeps showing up where they're not wanted. Like that. Why?"

I looked forward to the road, not back at the house. Not at Zola alone on the porch. *She'll be okay. She'll be fine. She'll go home soon.*

One more year, starting today. All I have to do is stay unnoticed and unadopted until my eighteenth birthday and I'm free.

"Let's go," I said, and buckled in.

Two

AT THE SEATTLE FERRY DOCK, Joellen bought a ticket for one car, two passengers. She saw me eyeball the ticket and passed it to me. "Here you go, Blackbird." I put it in my pocket and felt the thing I'd taken from the pillowcase, a tangled necklace chain I worked to unknot. *My first ferry ride.* A year from today I will buy my own ticket to go anywhere I want, anytime I want. Joellen pulled into the line of tourists' and commuters' cars leaving Seattle to cross the Puget Sound, thirty minutes over the blue-black water to what Wikipedia calls "a forested island the size of Manhattan, with a population equal to 0.4 percent of Manhattan's population." Thirty minutes from Seattle, where I've lived nearly my entire life, but I've never been to any of the islands because what foster parent has the time or gumption to haul a bunch of kids on a ferry across the Sound for fun?

This island, Wiki also tells me, holds the grim distinction of being the place where America's disgusting Japanese internment began but is described now as "twenty-seven square miles of land, much of it untouched forest, marked by thirty-two miles of trails, and farms and fields, and rocky shoreline." And houses and some schools. And now me.

Our line moved, and Joellen parked in the ferry's belly full of cars. It felt like driving on water. She led me up two flights of steps in a metal stairwell to the top deck, and we leaned together over the rail in the cold sea air and sunshine, Joellen wrapped in a blue down jacket, her short curls moving like mown lawn, me taller beside her in forgettable jeans and T-shirt, straight brown hair whipping around dark eyes in my nondescript white face. The ferry sailed from the dock, and Ivar's Fish Bar, the Ferris wheel, the Space Needle—all of Seattle—grew smaller on the horizon, water churning in the ferry's white wake. I breathed in the brackish sea air and tried to absorb the beauty of the water reflecting the summer sky, and the skyline, and I tried to exist in the moment, but electric nervous heat squeezed my heart.

"You can ferry back for a visit whenever; just call and I'll pick you up," Joellen said, and then, for the gazillionth time, "I'm sorry. I tried so hard to find something in the city—"

"I know," I said, and almost added, *It's okay,* even though it wasn't.

"There's just *nothing* for you right now. I mean, there's hotels, but I'm not doing that to you. Not one bed in a house in all of Seattle, and I wanted—"

"*Jo.*"

"*Muir.*"

Her *let's have a talk* tone. I love Joellen. I don't love *talks.*

"I need you to try," she said. "It's only twelve months. Think of it in weeks or hours, count them down, mark them off, do what you have to, but you've got to stay put. One house. Senior year matters for college, or just . . . for life. It's important. You need to concentrate, no moving around, just this last *one* school. Please. For me."

She barely ever pulls the "for me" line. Maybe never. Everything is always for *me*.

"I already said okay," I snapped, and instantly felt bad. "I will. I'll try."

"Okay, but I mean *really* try hard. Universities love a solid senior year."

Oh, Joellen. She thinks the fat file folder recording every moment of my life of "perfect" behavior and acceptable grades is me trying to get into college. The foster parents think it's me trying to get adopted. Both are so far from the truth it's a little sad. That file is saving me *from* adoption, and college is Jo's fever dream, not mine. The file is the only lever I control, and I have crafted it with painstaking care; clean behavior means more people are willing to let me live with them, which makes it easier for Joellen to place me somewhere new when, to preserve my freedom, I leave a house on short notice. Which I do. A lot.

Most kids in care are understandably sick of always moving, and conventional wisdom among us says that when you find a place and people that feel okay, you stay as long as you can. But that's for kids with their own families or parents, kids who had a true home and miss it. When *I* start to feel okay, when it's too comfortable or when it's bad—that's when I get out. I've never attended an entire academic year at one school. Every Seattle neighborhood seems to be a different district with its own schools, and I've been to nearly all of them.

This is a good time to say that I understand, and so should you: I am definitely *not* representative of all kids in foster care. I am an anomaly. Mine is not a typical life in care; which is not to say there even *is* a standard, because every kid's situation is our own; every birth family and foster family and CPS and social worker situation is its own universe, and laws change all the time. I am only one of a half million kids in foster care in America, one of twenty-five thousand who will age out—but I am a cradle-to-age-outer, which is kind of rare. It's given me time to accumulate the uniquely high twenty placements I've lived in. And I have unfair advantages that other kids do not; as a foundling, I am not in perpetual mourning for a family I remember losing or being taken from, and I am not escaping abuse or neglect at the hands of a relative.

Lucky.

I've also been fortunate with foster placements, never hit by a kid or a parent. And despite what you see in pretty much every TV show or movie about kids in foster care—and maybe this seems like a total fantasy—I am here to tell you it's possible to live a life in foster care and never get molested. Also, I am white, and I know that buys me a definite amount of privileged safety, because I've seen kids who aren't white get unfairly blamed and accused of all kinds of shit that never gets thrown at white kids. I have advantages in place for when I'm on my own: thanks to my flossing obsession, my teeth are healthy (so is the rest of me—oral hygiene is the key to good health); I'm not dependent on any expensive medications or booze or drugs; despite the meth-birth debacle, I can keep my head above water with acceptable grades (not exceptionally good or dismal, nothing worth drawing attention); and most fortunate of all, I have had one social worker, only Joellen, almost my whole life. These things increase my odds of survival when I'm out.

I've watched kids without my good fortune get dropped out of care on their eighteenth birthdays and become one of five thousand every year who are instantly homeless. Alone in the world with a Hefty garbage bag of clothes and no family. No job, no experience or education to get one, no home, no health insurance, and a file full of justifiably angry behavior with repercussions that follow them and make it impossible to live. They carry the blame for every mistake the adults in their lives made to put them in the situation in the first place. Not their fault, but they suffer for it all.

And listen, do not #NotAllAdults me. First of all, way to get defensive and yet again prioritize the bruised egos of grown-ass people who should know better over the lives of kids just trying to survive. Also, we aren't stupid; *obviously* we know there are adults trying to do the right thing. The system is mostly broken, but a ton of the people working in it aren't. I personally know really nice, dedicated foster parents, including kinship-care parents who are blood relatives (grandparents, uncles and aunts) taking care of kids. There have been social workers with huge caseloads who still made me feel safe, and I've met loving bio parents who just need some help. All of them are overworked and underpaid. Their existence does not change the fact that adults, and *only* adults, law-makers definitely included, are the reason kids end up in foster care. No kid is in foster care because of something we did. That's not how it works. And adults are solely responsible for the sorry state foster care is in. Until everyone understands and admits this, nothing will ever change for us.

Aging out is terrifying.

Still . . . I can't wait.

I can't help believing I will be okay. Maybe I'm setting myself up for spectacular failure, but all this time I've been so lucky; if I am as perfect as I can be, I bet I can stave off the likely possibility of being homeless within a year, or pregnant, or dead. Outcomes for kids who age out with no family are mostly a nightmare, and it makes me furious. I refuse to let the stupid circumstance of my birth ruin me. I am a *Muir,* for Christ's sake! Not in meaningless blood, but in what truly matters. I believe that the nurses who held me and named me could tell John Muir's singular life force is in me and in our shared name, and I will end my childhood the way it began: alone. Finally free to live and take care of myself in the wilderness of the wide world.

I hope.

When I was little and still thought I wanted parents, I used to ask Joellen all the time why *she* couldn't adopt me. She had no husband or kids of her own. I'd been with her since before I could remember, she always showed up, she kept her promises, she was never late, she never got mad at me, and she always had gum in her purse.

That was before I understood she stayed with me because she was paid to.

"If I adopted every kid I wanted to, I would have eleven base-ball teams," she always said, combing my little-kid hair with her fingers. "I can't, Muir. Not kosher with my job; I would probably have to quit. And then who would I be helping?"

"Me," I said. It was the only time I ever saw her cry.

Joellen has never asked me for anything, ever. Until today.

The thought of staying all year in one house, in one school, on an *island,* was giving me hives. John Muir would never camp in one spot for so long, not with unexplored wonders waiting over the next horizon.

The ferry engine went silent, and the boat floated still in the middle of the Sound. A voice came from deck speakers.

"Passengers, please offer a moment of silence for a memorial at sea."

The captain stood with a family at the bow of the ferry, a woman and two men and three little kids. Seagulls cried, and the family tossed ashes into the cold wind, and rose petals, which scattered and floated, pink confetti on the glassy dark water.

"I'll try," I said to Joellen.

She smiled.

Three blasts of the ferry horn and we were sailing again.

In my pocket, I worked the knots in the necklace chain.

*　*　*

I carry this tangled chain from a house in third grade. I was nearly eight years old, and Joellen says that house is the one I stayed in the longest, almost the whole school year. Back when parents decided how long I could stay, and I remember these parents liked me a lot. I remember I liked them.

Memory is a fascinating thing. Months and years can pass, uneventful and lost, but then certain tiny moments, pieces of conversation or feelings within the thousands of blank days stay sharp, clear like yesterday. I remember the dad worked at an office, the mom was home with us kids, who came and went in this house in the University District, except for me—I stayed and stayed. The parents were youngish, white; they took us kayaking on Lake Union, to matinee movies on weekends, to see the cherry blossoms at the university fountain, and to the library, and once, between kids, when it was just me, the three of us rode the fast elevator to the top of the Space Needle, and we sat in the restaurant for lunch.

"Are you happy here?" the dad asked.

"Yes!" I said, and put my hands on the glass wall and watched the mist move in a slow circle. "We're in the clouds."

"Are you happy with *us*?" the mom said. "Living in our house? Do you think you'd like to stay?"

I remember getting off my chair to climb in her lap—too big but she let me—and I put my head on her shoulder beside the wall of glass, all of Seattle beneath our feet, tiny and beautiful and *home*.

Alone in the top bunk at night without the sleeping sounds of other kids, I tossed for hours. I dragged a blanket from the bed and made a nest on the hallway floor outside the open door to their big bedroom, and that worked, until the morning the dad tripped and fell over me, banging his shoulder into the wall so loud he cursed. I stayed in the bunk after that, glad when other kids were in the house for a few days, sometimes a week or two. Joellen asked again and again if I was happy, and I told her I was. Because it was true.

At the park one afternoon two boys beside me on the swings saw me wave to the mom, sitting on a bench with some other moms, and she waved back. She did not look like me, and one said, "Is that your nanny?"

"She's my foster mom."

The kid frowned. "What is *that*?"

"It's when you steal something, your parents send you to some-one else," the other boy said, swinging high with authority, and turned to me. "What did you steal?"

"I didn't," I said. I wished Joellen was there. The swing chain was rusty, my hands were turning orange.

The first boy jumped from his swing and landed hard in the sand. "What do you call her?" he asked.

"I call her Linda."

"Right. So she's *not* your mom."

"She didn't have me from her body," I recited. "I live with her, and she takes care of me."

"Oh." The kid nodded. "She's *pretending* to be your mom."

"Sort of," I said. Wasn't she?

I dragged my toes in the dirt to slow myself and got off the swing.

More weeks passed in their house, which smelled perfectly neutral and was always a comfortable temperature. Other kids stopped coming, and one Saturday the mom and dad moved the bunk beds out of the bedroom and brought in one big bed, just for me. Brand-new white sheets and a comforter printed with flowers and leaves, with a pillowcase to match. I helped them make the bed, and we stood together, admiring our work.

"Are you going to adopt me?" I asked.

"Yes," the mom said. "That's the plan."

I jumped on the bed like a trampoline, and they didn't get mad.

My own big bed. We all thought it would help me sleep alone. Instead, I woke repeatedly every night, crying until one of them came in to turn on the light and begged me to try again, to please just lie down and close my eyes. They plugged a night-light into a low wall socket, and I played with toys in its pool of yellow light on the floor until the sun rose. I was tired, and so were they. I listened to them argue about how maybe I should sleep in their room with them—*She has to learn boundaries! The book says she'll get used to it; she is not in charge.*

I fell asleep on the school bus, in class, everywhere but in the bed in the room meant for me. I became, according to their side of phone conversations, *angry, demanding, unmanageable.*

I only remember being exhausted. And scared.

But when Joellen came each week, we all pretended we were fine.

"Yes," we said. "We're happy!"

Joellen smiled and smiled, scribbled her notes, and hugged me goodbye.

The mom was nearly always in tears, neither of them patient when I spilled my milk or missed the bus to school. It was probably weeks since any of us had slept a night through. We didn't go to the lake or to the library anymore. The mom slept in late on weekends, the bedroom door closed sometimes until lunch.

The mom's mom came to visit on a Sunday afternoon—an older white woman with a short, sensible haircut and perfume I could smell down the hallway. She shook my hand in greeting, and we ate the Subway sandwiches she'd brought for lunch. Afterward, they thought I was napping at last, but I lay in the bed and listened to them talking in the kitchen, the mom's mom's voice not at all modulated.

Beautiful room all to herself; she doesn't know how good she has it. This sleeping nonsense is only the beginning; it's all genetic—these kids are unknown quantities. You have no idea the kinds of chaos she'll bring into this house, into your life, into our family's life. Why are you punishing yourself? Why do this to us? I understand you're trying to do a nice thing and you feel sorry for her, I mean of course we all do, but she's just not capable of gratitude. This isn't your problem. Don't you deserve to be happy?

I lay still and listened hard, but the mom did not respond. She only sniffed and blew her nose again and again, and I wondered what new problems my "unknown quantity" would reveal. If my not sleeping was just the beginning, what kind of future was I in for? Was I a late-blooming werewolf? One more thing to worry about.

The next Saturday the dad took me for a walk to a nearby

jewelry store. He said we should bring the mom a present, that I could pick something out to give her and we could wrap it for her at home.

In a glass case crowded with gaudy bracelets and diamond earrings was a necklace, a simple gold chain that looked like something a mom could wear all the time, even to the park or the pool or riding bikes.

We wrapped the box in brown paper I colored with markers and crayons. We gave it to her after dinner, and the dad lifted her hair and clasped it around her neck, and she let me feel its delicate links.

"So pretty," I said. "You look like a mom. Real, not pretend."

She put her head on the table and cried.

A week later, Joellen came to help me pack.

The mom and dad waited in the kitchen, probably listening to Joellen tell me again and again as I rolled my shirts and socks, *Yes, they did want to adopt you. . . . No, you didn't do anything wrong. . . . They wish they could, but they can't. It's not because of you or anything you did. It's not your fault,* and I packed as slowly as I could, waiting for the mom and dad to come and say it was a mistake. I imagined a very dramatic rescue. The mom would rush in, maybe even pick me up or take my pajamas from Joellen's hands: *Stop packing! Don't touch her suitcase; she's staying here with us; this is her bedroom; she is our daughter.*

I folded and rolled and packed my pajama top.

They did not come.

I went to the bathroom to collect my toothbrush and washcloth but stopped first at their open bedroom door. The bed was unmade. Scared but curious, I stepped in. Quiet and dark. Her pillow smelled like shampoo, and on her bedside table, in a knotted pile, was the gold necklace.

My throat burned. What had she *done*? It had no charm, no pendant, how easy it would have been to keep it untangled. Just a simple, perfect chain. Ruined.

I did not think. I picked it up, slipped it into my pocket, walked fast down the hall and out the front door, my heart thumping, to cry on the porch and wait for Joellen to come out with my suitcase.

"Don't you want to say goodbye?" she said, trying to wipe my tears and also wrestle me into a jacket because it had begun to rain.

Didn't *they* want to? Still hiding in the kitchen. Cowards.

"I need a new toothbrush," I sobbed.

She gave up on the jacket and knelt down beside me. "Okay," she said.

"And a washcloth. A blue one."

"Okay."

"No. Pink."

"All right."

I grabbed the handle and lifted my suitcase.

"Muir," Joellen said, "let me help you."

"No." The bag was too heavy, but I dragged it to the car anyway, banging it against every single porch step. She stood, letting me struggle, and watched me heft it into the trunk of the Subaru, get in, and buckle my seat belt. I rolled down the window and let the rain in. "I'm ready," I called to her.

That was the last time a parent told me I had to leave.

Hand in my pocket, I worked the knots in the chain. I could fix it, and then *I* would wear it. "Let's go."

Ten years messing with this delicate thing, trying so hard to fix it, and it's still tangled. But not broken.

Three

JOELLEN DROVE OFF THE FERRY and onto the island, past a harbor full of white-sailed boats. The sun broke through low clouds, and the dark water sparkled. Over hills of farms and barns and houses, Joellen kept taking her eyes off the road to look at me. Monitoring my reaction.

"Beautiful, right?"

It *was.* Worthy of public television voice-over reverie extolling the virtues of small-town life. A world away from Seattle, no sidewalks, all these *trees.* I wished I could calm down and not just see but truly appreciate the beauty. I wished I could stop thinking of Zola's disappointed face.

Joellen turned onto a dirt road beneath a canopy of cypress and Douglas firs, and then it opened to a field of tall grass and wildflowers and pines.

"Ohhh . . . ," we breathed in unison.

The house was white and small with a metal roof, in the middle of the field, rock-lined path to the front porch, and raised garden beds.

She parked, and we got out and stood in the quiet. Wind in the trees.

The winds will blow their own freshness into you, and the storms their energy, while cares will drop off like autumn leaves.

Oh, John. If only.

"Muir," Joellen said, her face turned to the sky.

Blackbirds, a moving shape of black wings racing silent circles above the house and field.

Joellen smiled. "Good sign."

I nodded.

"Okay," she said, face still tilted up at the birds, "so it's only a mom, and just in time. She was a month from letting her license expire, but I begged her. And as always, it was your file that convinced her."

"Just when she thought she was free," I said. "Poor woman."

"No," Joellen said. "She's lucky to have you. You're good company."

I looked down at the grass, tiny white flowers and a few weeds pushing up through it.

"The high school here is excellent," she said.

"What colors?"

So many schools have aggressive colors, clashing in the hallways and on the lockers, maroon and mustard yellow, army green and gold; and all the stupid "spirit days" make it hard to disappear and be ignored.

"Blue and white," she said. "Spartans!"

Okay. That and the blackbirds. Good omens.

I hefted my suitcase from the car, and we stood together before the only house in all of Seattle and its surrounding islands that had a long-term bed for me.

"Muiriel." A woman came out to the porch, wiping her hands on a dish towel. Almost as small as Joellen, maybe in her sixties, a white lady with graying dark hair piled in a bun, wearing a plaid apron over a soft body in jeans and a gray sweater.

"Francine," Joellen whisper-reminded me.

I held up my hand. "Hello, Francine."

I picked up my suitcase, and Francine held the screen door open for us. We blinked the sun from our eyes and stood in the bright kitchen. Butcher-block countertop. White cabinets. Clean smell of dish soap. Through the wall of windows above the sink I saw a back field with a little wooden house.

"Chicken coop," Francine said. "You like chickens?"

"I do," I said. "Just not to eat."

Her head tilted. "You eat pigs? Cows?"

"No, sorry."

Bread without flesh is a good diet, wrote John Muir, confirming what I'd already learned on a field trip to the grocery store in second grade. A gutted pig hung from hooks by its back legs in the deli, and I figured out meat is *animals.*

"Muiriel," Francine said, "we are going to have us a time. I don't eat them, either. Here. Give." She took my suitcase and led us down a narrow hall to a stairwell that opened into an attic room beneath the A-frame roof. A braided rag rug and one big bed beneath a dormer window. Smelled like clean laundry.

"Are there—where are the other beds?" I asked.

"I donated the bunks to hospice just last month," Francine said. "Bought all new linens, too. Painted, repaired all the kicked-in doors and holes in the drywall; twenty years of fostering takes a toll on an old place," she said.

I nodded. Absolute truth.

"Joellen tells me you're not bound to make me have to do it all again, paint and all that. File says it, too. You set to prove them right?"

Not accusatory, not suspicious—just a matter-of-fact question.

"Yes," I said. "But, so I'm— It's only me? In this room?"

"Only you in the *house*. You're my last," Francine said.

"I told you it would be only you," Joellen said, low.

"Yeah," I said, just as low. "It's just . . . a big room." My heart sped up. So much easier to be ignored, helpful and hidden, *unnoticed* in a loud group of *many* kids.

"It's beautiful," Joellen said to Francine.

"Big bed," I said.

"It's a full," Francine said. "Smaller than a queen, bigger than a bunk. Never had a kid your age. Twelve-year-olds fit pretty well in bunks, but I thought you'd like a real bed, room to stretch."

I stared at the lonely expanse of blanket and pillows until Joellen nudged me.

"It's so pretty," I said. "Thank you."

Francine put my suitcase on a wide chest of drawers and went to the window to push it open. "Air this joint out a little," she said. And then something black flitted in, a fast, aimless bird with silent wings. "Oh," Francine said, "get!" She flapped her apron and shooed it back outside. "Bats," she said.

Joellen's face went ashen. "In the *daylight*? Doesn't that mean they're rabid?"

"Not necessarily," Francine said. "You girls like lemonade? Unpack and come get some." She made her slow way down the steps. I leaned out the window. Attached beneath the sill: a wooden bat house. Joellen was shaking.

We stood for a moment in that cavernous room, filled with

light and a wide-plank wood floor. The closet door with a brass handle, no keyhole. A perfectly nice room. I sat on the end of the lonely bed. White quilt with vines of leaves and blue flowers stitched, maybe by hand, all over it. This woman put a hand-sewn quilt on a bed for a foster placement? What the hell?

Joellen sat beside me. *"Bats."* Her voice was faint. "I can keep looking."

"Just mice with wings," I said, and worked the necklace in my pocket.

Later, I stood with my lemonade beside Francine on the porch and waved as Joellen maneuvered the car around granite boulders in the grassy driveway. The sun was really out now, and the grass and trees smelled fresh, different from the trees and lawns and forested parks I walked in Seattle, definitely better than the streets. Here, without the hum of freeway traffic, the quiet was nearly deafening.

Joellen finally got the car turned around; she waved out the window and was gone. The blackbirds rose again from the trees.

Joellen's leaving had never been a big deal. She'd always been so close, never more than a few minutes away. Now a half-hour ferry ride and a lot of water between us, and I couldn't breathe very deeply.

"You okay?" Francine asked.

I nodded.

"Hungry?"

I was. But instead I said, "Can I take a walk?"

She took my lemonade glass into the house and came back out with a folded paper map. "Trails," she said. "Joellen said you'd want to walk."

Oh, Jo. Breathe.

24

"Make sure your phone is on," Francine said.

I exhaled and got ready for a familiar, annoying battle. "Don't have one."

She frowned. "No phone?"

"No phone."

Her eyes went wide. *"Really?"*

"Really." Back on my freedom hobbyhorse; without a phone, I am not tethered to anyone having access to me anytime they want, with their texts and calls. Joellen has her phone; I can always find a landline to get to her. She and the parents can call the school if they need me, and outside of school I am always where I say I will be. Libraries and school have all the computers and interwebs I need. I am impeccably reliable and so have earned the right to not be under constant surveillance.

"Huh." I could hear her wheels turning, but she said only, "Walk near civilization for now. Need some money?"

"I'm okay," I said. *Never be needy. Never be a burden.*

"All right. See you in two hours, not a minute past."

"Two hours. From now. I'll be back here. Got it." I learned years ago that the best way to avoid getting accused of being late, missing curfew, misbehaving, was to repeat their words, exactly what a parent says, right back to them. Helps them remember.

"Can you find your way?" Francine asked.

I nodded through my swollen throat. *Could* I find my way back? What had I agreed to? Alone on an actual island. With bats.

"Joellen says I'm meant to be your last," she said.

"Yes."

"Okay then." She put the map in my hand. "Let's be each other's."

Her smile made my throat feel a little bit better.

Four

NO FOSTER PARENT HAD EVER let me just take off for a walk like that, and definitely not twenty minutes after arriving, especially not in a brand-new town. Francine was a puzzle. Maybe, since I was her last, there was no reason to be meticulous. Coasting to retirement.

The first thing I always do when I move into a new house is get back outside as fast as I can and walk beneath the open sky, where I am still and always home.

I only went out for a walk and finally concluded to stay out till sundown, for going out, I found, was really going in.

I walked the island that first day, across a quiet highway to a trail through a forest wilderness, back out to the road to a path beside the harbor, boats docked and bobbing in the ferry's wake, and then the main street. Shops lined both sides, not chain stores—candles and books and toys. A sign guiding me to the internment museum. Post office with a thousand paper cranes folded from express envelopes suspended in its branches. A candy shop. I ducked in and bought a pack of Fruit Stripe gum. Outside, people and dogs walked around me, and then in the sea air there was the aroma of baking bread.

Across the street. *Blackbird Coffee and Pie.* Like the four and twenty.

Joellen will love this.

I keep ten dollars with me at all times, strictly for emergencies and necessities like Fruit Stripe gum. Not frivolities such as eating in coffee shops.

But this day felt different. Anxious. And I was hungry. So, sort of an emergency.

Inside, Blackbird was crowded and too hot, but bread definitely was baking, and also pie, and coffee brewing. I stood in line before the glass case of cakes and scones, and on the bottom shelf, at toddler eye level, were baskets of the most intricately decorated sugar cookies I had ever seen—shapes of mice and owls and even ferry boats, frosted in perfect green and white just like the real boats, only with sparkling sugar and tiny frosted-icing words: *Washington State Ferry.* Works of art.

The line moved, but the girl in front of me, face in her phone, did not notice or step forward.

The girl at the register rolled her eyes. Black hair in a high bun, very pierced ears, black Sub Pop tank top. She was maybe Japanese American? And looked my age but couldn't have been, because inked across both her forearms and shoulders were elaborate, beautiful tattoos that would have taken years—ocean waves, birds, and words, and across her clavicles, a pine branch with cones. Her name tag read *Kira.* "Next," she called.

The girl in front of me also looked my age. She was taller than me, white, dressed in jeans ripped in a way that there was no point in calling them pants anymore. She wore a cropped shirt and had long, dark hair that reminded me of this one mom I lived with who was always getting Brazilian blowouts. This girl leaned against the glass and drawled, "Give me a latte, nonfat, no foam, like *none,* and let me see . . ." She took her time considering every single crumb in the case before deciding, at last, on "cookies."

Basicest of the white basics, Zola called girls like this one.

Kira sighed. "Which kind?"

"Um . . ." Line Girl texted some more and knelt down to take a picture of the cookies. "Boats."

"How many."

"All of them." Line Girl smiled.

Kira closed her eyes and exhaled. She made the latte, set it on the counter, and then assembled a paper box, lined it with tissue, and nestled all eight beautiful ferry boat cookies in two careful rows.

Ten years in nearly twice as many schools gave me sense memory for classic, run-of-the-mill mean-kid bullshit. This whole exchange had a familiar tone.

Here was the windup:

Line Girl paid with a twenty, Kira gave her the change in coins, and the girl dropped them into the empty glass tip jar beside the register.

The pitch:

Line Girl picked up the latte and the cookie box, smiled brightly once more at Kira, and turned to go.

The swing:

She paused at the trash basket beside the counter, dropped the box of cookies into it, took a picture of it in there, and walked out the door.

Home run.

Kira blinked hard, refusing to cry, and looked right at me. "What can I get you?"

I've seen that face in every house, school, and mirror I've known.

In the tip jar were three pennies and a nickel.

Whatever was happening, it was clear that even on this idyllic island, there were still dickhead kids. They are All. The. Same. Where does this uniformity come from? Are they taken aside to a special class where they memorize the techniques and voice patterns of Assholery 101?

Never one to jump into anyone else's battle, for some reason I shocked myself when, on autopilot, I went to the trash basket, where the cookie box lay unopened and lopsided on a pile of empty coffee cups and wadded-up napkins. I pulled it out and wiped dripping coffee from its side, otherwise perfectly intact. Kira watched me, wide-eyed, from the register, then looked away. I walked back to the counter.

"What can I get you?" Kira asked again, all business, clearly bewildered by what I'd done, and so was I, but she wasn't going to acknowledge or say anything about it, and thank God, because I didn't want to, either. Key to flying under the radar and therefore surviving in school or life is always, *always* staying out of anyone else's business; I *know* that, I live that, so what had compelled me to dumpster-dive and insert myself into this obviously well-established war?

Because the familiar look on Kira's face when those cookies went in the trash said it obviously wasn't a war. It was one-sided bullshit, and she was scared. That's why.

"Tea, please. And . . ." I hated to part with any more of my ten dollars, but I was so hungry. "What's the best thing?" I asked. "Your favorite?"

"Toast," Kira said, no hesitation. "With jam. House-made."

I got a little light-headed and put my hands on the counter. "Toast?" I said. *"With jam?"*

"It's life-changing," she said, expressionless.

"Okay."

"Tea and toast. Five dollars. Name for the order?"

"Muiriel."

"Got it. Next."

I paid and waited for a table to be free. Even in hot weather, tea is good. John Muir made tea from pine needles, which sounds to me like it would taste the way Pine-Sol cleanser smells, but you do you, man. Sometimes he purposely lived on nothing but tea and bread for months.

But *bread and jam.*

Near the coffee lids and napkins was a corkboard tacked with notices: apartments for rent, dog walker available, aural cleansing for seventy-five dollars (which I first read as *anal* cleansing, and it made me smile). One notice had pine boughs drawn as borders and was the only one printed in a font that wasn't Papyrus or Comic Sans, so it looked especially professional.

INTERNSHIP
Salishwood Environmental Education Center

High school seniors * Earn college credit helping elementary school groups learn about wilderness ethics and explore 250 acres of untouched forest

* No experience necessary *

Contact Jane at Salishwood

What. The. Hell?

Toast and jam. Blackbird. Wilderness, forest, internship. What universe had I stumbled—ferried—into? For half a second my worn-out brain entertained the notion of *Does Joellen have the power over time and space to create an entire town full of lures to keep me rooted all year?*

Beneath the worry in my anxious, rapidly beating heart, there was a tiny flash of something else. Unfamiliar but working against the fear. Hope? Excitement?

Maybe the big bed in the lonely attic at Francine's wouldn't be so bad. For a while.

I tore off an email address flag and put it in my pocket, then glanced around before tearing *all* the flags and stashing them. People left a booth beside a window, and I sat and thought about what Salishwood could be, and the delicious words *wilderness ethics.* I messed with the paper flags in my pocket and watched the sidewalk. Dogs on leashes met and sniffed and moved along. Kids on bikes. People pushing strollers. Lots of tourists. Island Harbor Book Company looked good. Grocery store. Barbershop.

Then my toast came.

Thick, buttered slices of sweet wheat bread, crisp outside, warm and mealy inside, and a dish of homemade raspberry jam. Kira was not wrong.

Life-changing.

I walked back to Francine's, past the harbor and through the trees, in kind of a daze. Twenty minutes early, as always. I thanked her for the map and excused myself to lie down.

"Think you'll want dinner?" she asked from the bottom of the stairwell.

"Probably not, thanks," I said from the top, watching bats

flit around their little house beneath the window. "Might sleep through it, anyway."

I nearly had the door closed, and she called, "Muiriel."

I peered down at her, pushing hairpins from her mouth into her messy bun.

"How was the walk?"

"Good. Thank you."

"See the town?"

"I did. It's nice."

"You okay?"

I nodded.

"Sure you're not hungry?"

"I went to Blackbird."

"Toast?"

"Yeah," I said, then, "Oh, wait!" I'd forgotten the box in my hands that I'd carried the whole walk back. "These are for you." I stepped down and gave her the cookies.

She lifted the lid and beamed. "Ferries. Beautiful."

"Yeah." They were too pretty to be thrown out. What a weird, stupid thing for that girl to do.

"Muiriel, thank you," Francine said. "I'll take them to the girls I volunteer with; we've got a meeting tomorrow. When you're up for it, let's go grocery shopping. Make sure we've got food you like in the house. Okay?"

"Yes, thanks."

"You sure you're all right?" She frowned up at me.

"Just tired." This was exactly the kind of attention I was trying to avoid; in a house full of kids, I could go take a nap and skip eating for days if I felt like it, and no one would even notice. Not that

I would; I love food more than life. But I mean, I could. If no one was paying attention.

"All right. Well, plenty in the fridge if you wake up and want something. Will you be able to sleep?"

I nodded.

"Phone's in the kitchen if you want to call Joellen. See you in the morning."

"Yep." I climbed the steps to the lonely room two at a time.

"Oh, and, Muiriel?"

I stopped and turned back, Francine still looking up at me.

"Unpack."

I nodded. "Good night," I said, and closed the door.

Everything I own could fit in the top drawer of the big dresser. I shooed the bats and shut the window.

It wasn't even five o'clock, but I unzipped my suitcase and put it on the floor, took my toiletry kit to the bathroom, where I brushed my teeth, washed my face, put on my pajamas, put everything in the kit, took it to the bedroom, and placed it into the suitcase. Shoes in their bag *in the suitcase,* dirty clothes in a plastic grocery bag beside the socks *in the suitcase,* the tangled chain in the pillowcase of useless treasures tucked in safe, all closed and zippered and snapped up tight *in the suitcase.* I lay on the beautiful quilt on the big bed. Left side.

I pulled *The Wilderness World* from my suitcase and read in bed until the sun turned the room gold, and faded to dark. Then I read by key chain flashlight and tried not to think about Zola. When it's time to leave, it's time to leave. And when I go, no one comes with me. Otherwise I won't make it.

It's not like I'm dead inside. It's that I am allergic to

manufactured, insincere emotion. A lifetime of people saying one thing but doing the opposite has inoculated me, and now I understand how to survive with my freedom and sanity intact until I'm eighteen: I can have friends but can't let myself "life or death" depend on them or let them "life or death" depend on me. I can go out with boys but not *date* them. I can have foster parents but cannot let them adopt me.

Joellen started worrying when I began refusing offers of adoption, that I'd become "emotionally detached." In truth, I prefer to think of myself as "emotionally prescient"—there are better ways to express love than through obedience and submission. People stopped surprising me a long time ago. Which kind of breaks my heart.

See? Not dead inside!

The flashlight flickered and went out. Old batteries. Bat wings tapped the window. No night-light. How was I supposed to find the bathroom or remember where I was if I woke in the night? No snoring, no kids breathing—how could a person sleep in all this silence?

Joellen was going to be so disappointed. I'd promised her. Then the most dismal thought—living in a hotel. There was nothing, no place for me. Even if I wanted to ask Joellen to come get me, she couldn't. I gave in and cried quietly as I could and tried to muster the hopeful feeling back into my heart. I thought about Salishwood—What was the deal with that? What if I could work there?—but alone in the loud dark, I knew: there was no way I could survive staying still, all by myself, for an entire year. Impossible.

* * *

I carry with me a thing I stole from a pile of tea bags in the trash at a house in the Queen Anne neighborhood during sixth grade.

Seventh? The parents were a retired couple, white and basic, with their own grown children, who never visited. Counting me, it was a rotation of four foster kids, and the parents made us all walk to church every Sunday, even though none of us kids were church people. The mom there had no patience for my not eating meat.

"God says, his own words right here in the Bible, man has dominion over every living thing. Men are the stewards and all living things were created for him, to use or eat or whatever. Don't be arrogant in God's eyes—eat that chicken. It's breaded with panko."

I thought of poor John Muir, whose own father beat the crap out of his son until, by the age of eleven, he had memorized and could recite *every word* of the Old Testament, and most of the New. Nothing infuriated Muir more than the hypocrisy of white men claiming God-given blessing and authority to kill his supposed own creations.

I kept my head down, hid the chicken in my paper napkin to toss over the fence later to the neighbor's dog, didn't say any of the snarky rejoinders I had on deck. Like how I was not a man and didn't care what the Bible said. Or that, if her actions were any indication, she didn't seem to, either.

The house was big, brick, lots of bedrooms and a huge kitchen with a wide windowsill over the sink. Lined up on the sill was a parade of little white ceramic animals: horses and elephants and cows. My very favorite was the polar bear. I love polar bears. They adopt orphan cubs.

A couple of months after I went to live there, the mom got home from shopping one day and I helped her unload the groceries. I pulled out a cellophane-wrapped box of Red Rose tea.

"Oooh," she said. "Let's see." She tore off the wrap, opened the box, and rummaged through the tidy rows of tea bags to pull out one of the ceramic animals. "Giraffe." She smiled, triumphant, and put it on the sill with its friends.

Then she picked up the Red Rose box, an entire brand-new package of perfectly good tea bags, and tossed the whole thing in the garbage.

"Muriel, fold up these grocery bags, will you?" She turned to organize the produce drawer.

I watched her do this every week. If she got an animal that was already on the sill, it wound up in the trash along with the tea. Poor little white hippos and tigers and pigs, helpless among the coffee grounds and orange rinds. It made my stomach hurt.

I started purposely hanging around on shopping days to help her unload the bags and then waited for her to leave the kitchen so I could rescue the tea and the wayward animals from the trash. I put them in clean Ziploc bags and surreptitiously dropped them into the donation bins at the church each Sunday.

I got home late from school once, a dark and rainy afternoon, and when I went to toss a banana peel in the trash, there were more tea bags, dumped loose and ruined in a pile of half-eaten breakfast scraps, and in the middle of the mess was a discarded polar bear.

I wiped him clean, hid him safely in the pillowcase, and dialed Joellen's number.

Five

I WOKE ALONE THAT FIRST MORNING in Francine's house after nine hours of unusually dreamless, sound sleep and found the sharp edge of the hopeless impossibility a little dulled. Maybe anxiety had exhausted my brain and body enough that they were forced to shut down for a while? And despite the lonely room, holy cats was it quiet in Francine's fiveish-acre wood. No middle-of-the-night emergencies or kids arriving, only me and the night wind and ship bells and the bats. Some completed REM cycles. It was disorienting. All that day I walked the island, ate some stuff, had polite but brief conversations with Francine, and then slept soundly again. And again. I clung to the renewed strength and hope the sleep was offering, resisted calling Joellen, investigated the Salishwood situation, and two days later I had an interview.

Technically—maybe legally—I should have told Francine about it, about wanting to work in general, but I waited. Some foster parents are not down with kids working. It interferes with school and makes the tether too long, but if we're aging out, how else are we supposed to build a résumé so we can get a job to support ourselves when we're out? I've played a long game, working a job in one way or another since the day I started dodging adoption.

I've been a barista, a grocery store bagger; I've pumped gas and cleaned car windows at a gas station; but my most recent job and very favorite in the world ever was tutoring and reading to little kids at the Seattle Central Library. Being alone on the island was making me miss little kids. I missed Zola. Sometimes I used to pick her up after school and take her with me on the bus to the library and let her color and read while I worked, and for that job I'd been fingerprinted and had security clearance with the Seattle police and with the freaking FBI. Salishwood, as it turned out, was looking for help with the little kids' summer camp and day hikes. Which required security clearance. I mean. *Magic.*

Aside from my Muir-based knowledge of the world as our home, I am the least "Kumbaya" person I've ever met, but even to me this felt like the universe *wanted* me at Salishwood, which Jane from the poster, when I spoke to her on the phone, described as "two hundred fifty acres of forested land beside the water turned environmental research and education center." Internship, so no pay, but internships can lead to jobs—*in a forest.* I hadn't wanted anything so badly in a long time.

Francine, three days in, was being really nice—leaving me mostly to myself; she let me walk and made me eat only when I felt like it, but I was scared to ask her stance on kids working. So I took ye olde "It's better to beg forgiveness than to ask permission" tack.

The sadness I'd felt pressed beneath lifted just a little with every step to the bus stop on the route to Salishwood. The driver let me off at the entrance to walk a one-lane road that wound through dense forest, and I made myself breathe in deep, exhale all I could.

Birds sang, sunlight streamed through the dense branches to clover and ferns on the forest floor. I'd never felt more *Muir*.

He was eleven when his father, seeking harsher religious doctrine, brought the family to America, away from the Scottish hillsides and rocky seashore young Muir loved and walked. His father made him work for years in a machine factory in Wisconsin, where Muir was blinded in an accident with metal tools. He hid for months in a blackened room, scared he would never see again. When he emerged, depressed but with his sight miraculously restored, he was so grateful and hungry to see every tree and mountain and river and lake and ocean and blade of grass, he swore never to live within walls again if he could help it. He walked outside and did not stop.

Made haste with all my heart, bid adieu to all thoughts of inventing machinery and determined to devote the rest of my life to studying the inventions of God.

He packed his bread and compass and books and walked a thousand miles, to the solace and beauty of the natural world, and lived to save Yosemite Valley from destruction; he saved the redwoods and sequoias of California and the alpine wilderness of Washington's Mount Rainier. He gave those places his life in return for saving his, with Joellen-level dedication to protecting vulnerable, innocent nature, emboldened by fury at his fellow white men who would harm it. He would have been an excellent social worker.

The Salishwood road widened into a small parking lot, and beyond it was what looked like a cathedral, made of cedar, with a glass ceiling that reached into the treetops and seemed part of the forest. Jane—white, with a long gray braid and a young, smiling face, dressed like me but with dangly beaded earrings—walked to me and took my hand in both of hers.

"Muiriel," she said, "come inside." She led me in, talking the whole time. "So, we're in the great hall." The whole wide cedar-wood room glowed in the sunlight streaming from the vaulted glass roof. I stared up into the trees.

"Beautiful." An understatement.

"Inspired by Suquamish architecture. Suquamish were the first people who lived on the island. The tribe has education centers and a museum near Agate Pass and the Port Madison Indian Reservation. Cut to: not how it should be, but now here *we* are."

I sat beside her on a wooden bench bathed in sunlight.

"So," she said, "want to help us teach a bunch of kids that the land and sea and sky are not now and never were ours and the least we can do is learn how to respect and care for them?"

"Yes, please."

She smiled and tucked her legs beneath her on the bench, buzzing like a five-year-old at Christmas. "I can't begin to tell you how thrilled we were to see your résumé, especially your experience with kids—that's the hardest part, and you've already got it. We'll get you trained for the wilderness ethics curriculum on the job. Starting with: hiking in jeans might not be the best idea."

My face flushed.

"Shorts are good, hiking pants if you have them. Have I said I'm jealous of your name? Your parents are brilliant. Speaking of, we'll need a signed parental consent and proof of school credit, and you'll be all set—you're at the high school in the fall, right?"

I nodded and silently worked out ways to put off the consent form signing as long as possible.

A school bus pulled into the circular drive over a thick carpet of pine needles.

"Here we go," she said.

She led me outside to a field of grass encircled by dorm-style cabins and, beyond, the forest. Two guys filled hiking bottles at a water spigot near a wooden picnic table.

"Men, introduce yourselves; this is Muiriel. I'll be back with the wildlings."

And she left me there with them. One looked my age, the other older, both white guys who stopped their conversation and stood looking at me.

"I'm Muiriel," I said, and raised my hand in greeting to their general direction. The older one was unreasonably tall, over six feet, and he grabbed my hand.

"Excellent," he said. "Finally some new female energy. Thank you, Mother Gaia!"

He put his palms together and tipped his head down, revealing long, stringy dirty-blond hair tied in a bun. "Welcome, sister. I'm Natan."

Good God. The other guy winced and stayed real interested in his water bottle. I side-eye noticed he was lean, he had well-defined arm muscles in a blue T-shirt, and he wore what were definitely actual hiking pants—lots of zippered pockets. I turned back to Man Bun. "Nathan?"

He closed watery blue eyes and exhaled out his nose. "Na*tan*," he said, in a way that he probably intended to show great patience and restraint over my admittedly failed pronunciation of his name but was instead super condescending, delivered through his over-wrought beard and complicated waxed mustache.

The other guy smiled into his water bottle.

A lifetime of people deciding they know all about me after two seconds of introduction and the words *foster care* has taught me to try not to prejudge anyone else, because it's total bullshit—but oh my God there still is such a thing as instinct, and Natan was making it difficult to stay neutral about him.

"Are you replacing Jason?" Natan asked, rocking on his heels, arms folded.

"I guess," I said, edging away from him and toward the table. "Was Jason the intern?"

He nodded. "My man J had to answer the call of duty."

"Oh, wow," I said, "he's in the military?"

Another wry, mustached smile. "Duty to his *soul*. He needed to wander this world to find his true purpose, honor the light within himself."

The other guy spoke up. "Jason got a job at the Honolulu Hilton handing pool towels to tourists."

"Sean," Natan sighed. "Our journeys are all our own."

Sean.

Sean smiled again, at me this time. I offered my hand, which he accepted, and gave one firm shake. Inches shorter than Natan, Sean stood nearly directly at my eye level, and I'm not real tall for a girl. I liked it. Dark eyes, tanned skin, blessedly close-cropped dark hair. "Sean," I said. "You"—*his eyes are so dark, they're almost black*—"work here all year?"

"Sean's our high school kid. Part-time come fall, right, little bro? I'm full-time," Natan droned on. "Salishwood's MS program with U Dub. Guess I'm the big man on campus—in every way, right, little guy?" He punched Sean's arm.

Sure thing, big jerk.

Sean just rolled his eyes, ducked out of Natan's punching range, and busied himself tightening the straps on a day pack. He looked up past the lodge. "Here they come."

Streams of little kids came screaming into the field.

A rush of familiarness swelled in me: raucous, hyper little kids. I felt my whole body brighten, then remembered these kids were my on-the-job interviewers. "Wait," I said. "Are we— What do I *do*?"

"Just stick with me," Natan oozed. He put his hand on my shoulder, and his long, bony fingers massaged my skin through my T-shirt.

I recoiled and ducked away, nearly knocking Sean to the ground.

"Sorry," I said, moving fast to put Sean between me and Creepy Fingers, who strode ahead of us.

"You hike?" Sean said, eyeing my jeans.

"I . . . walk," I said. "A lot. But in the city. On sidewalks. Sometimes in parks. But mostly on concrete . . ." I stopped walking. "Don't tell Jane. I really want this job."

He stopped and turned to me.

"I would never," he said. "Honestly, hiking is just a dirty walk—God, no, I mean a walk *in* the dirt."

I smiled. Muir hated the implied rush of the word *hiking*. He preferred to *saunter* through the forest, stroll into the woods.

"The kids are easy," Sean said kindly. "The trails are all marked; you'll figure it out as we go. Don't worry."

Had I only ever known super-tall boys? Because his eyes were just . . . still right there at mine, and sort of killing me. "Thank you," I said. "Sean."

"You're welcome. Muriel."

We walked together into the swarm of kids.

Three hours and a three-mile dirt(y) walk with a bunch of second graders later, I sat filthy, sweaty, and tired on the bus back to Francine's house.

Before I left, Jane took me aside in the lodge and offered me a cold fizzy water from the staff fridge. "The kids looked pretty happy. Did you have fun?"

"I did," I said. "Thank you. But did I . . . do it right?"

She laughed. "You did. You'll learn fast; I'm not worried."

"So I can come back? I can stay?"

She walked with me out into the sunshine. "Muriel," she said. "I think you might be just what Salishwood needed. See you Monday, first thing. Seven o'clock."

"Monday. Seven. Okay."

I walked back through the trees to the bus stop. Floating.

I have been "useful." I have been "not a problem." I have never been what anyone *needed*.

Sean sped past me on a bike, raised one lean, strong arm, and called, "See you Monday!"

On the bus I caught my reflection in the window. Smiling.

I could not remember a happier day.

The bus dropped me back at Francine's road. Three cats stretched in the sun on the porch, one gray striped and two black, and in the open doorway a dog stood and watched me walk to him.

"Hi," I said. It did not move. "What's your deal? You going to bite me?"

Same size as the cats, it was brown and black and kind of

mangy. It said nothing until I got to the porch steps and then of-fered one single bark. Like *Hey*. Then it turned and went into the house.

I dropped my backpack on the bottom attic step and followed the dog to the kitchen, where Francine stood at the sink, rinsing strawberries. The table was set with tea. Not the drink, but, like, a *whole tea*: sandwiches and cookies and fruit on little plates like on PBS shows where people live in manor houses.

"Hi," I said. "Do you have company coming?"

"You. And our neighbor's three hundred cats . . . ," she said, an apron over her usual jeans and a sweater, hair up. She looked at her watch. "Right on time again. Hungry? Nice walk?"

My heart sped up a little. Half lie—I *had* gone for a walk; there was just also the first day of an internship in the middle of it I hadn't mentioned, so more of an omission than a lie—but close enough. Not even a week here and I was already breaking a cardinal rule. *What am I doing?*

The teacups and plates looked fancy. Breakable. This was a *lot* of food.

"It was a really nice walk, thank you," I said. The sandwiches and cookies looked so good. "I *am* hungry."

Her face brightened. "You *are*?"

"But I should shower."

"Shower later; you're hungry now! Here, help me with these."

I washed my hands and started hulling berries with a knife, a skill I'd picked up a few houses ago. The dog clicked over to Fran-cine's feet and looked up at her, hoping for crumbs.

"So," I said, "is the dog visiting?"

"Oh, no, this is my Terry Johnson. Terry Johnson, say hello to

Muiriel. Got him back from the vet this morning. He was having his teeth cleaned the day you came, and then they found a weird lump they decided to remove, which turned out to be benign, but they kept him till they knew for sure—now here he is. Didn't want to overwhelm you with it all, in case things went south. You never can tell with older dogs. . . . I can't make out if he misses having a bunch of kids around or if he's enjoying the peace and quiet."

I looked down at him. "Hello, Terry Johnson."

Francine scratched his ears. "Joellen says you're not allergic."

"Not at all. Is he . . . named for someone? A person?"

"Nope. Let's eat!"

My heart slowed a little, and I smiled toward the berries in the sink. I liked that Francine said what she meant and no need to elaborate or apologize. Matter-of-fact. Maybe she would understand my wanting to work. About Salishwood, why the trees and kids made me feel better, and why I wanted the job so badly. I put the berries in a bowl and we sat down.

The table was crowded. Fruit and actual clotted cream and scones, and the sandwiches. I took a little of each.

"I've had these dishes in storage for years. Figured it was safe to bring them out: you don't strike me as a plate thrower. Now, remember," she said, spooning lemon curd beside my scone. "It's only you and me. Eat as much as you want and still we'll have leftovers. And then later we can eat those."

I missed a dinner table crammed with a bunch of other kids to disappear into . . . but eating as much as I wanted? And then *leftovers*?

Intriguing. I took a second scone before I even started the first.

"Well done with the strawberries," she said. "Aren't they

gorgeous? They're from the Sakamoto family's farm, and they've got pumpkins at Halloween, unless you're too old to carve a jack-o'-lantern?" She reached over to the sink and handed me a piece of cold bacon from a covered dish. "Dog's not vegetarian. He'll love you."

"I like Halloween," I said, feeling lighter every minute.

I put the bacon on my palm and Terry Johnson looked me in the eyes, swallowed the bacon without chewing, and trotted through Francine's open bedroom door to climb a set of dog stairs up to the bed and tuck his nose beneath his tail.

"Curls up like a cinnamon roll," Francine said. "Okay. Pour some milk in your cup, then the tea. That's how they do it in England. Also Oprah told me."

Paper tea bag tags hung on strings from the teapot lid. *Red Rose.* I stared, a little hypnotized.

A million kinds of tea—loose-leaf, Lipton, organic-green-goji-berry bullshit. Why does every middle-aged white woman love Red Rose tea so much? I glanced at the windowsill—all clear. No ceramic circus animals. *See,* I thought. *This is why you need to get rid of that pillowcase. Toss it all into the ocean and be here now.*

"Remind me to get you a bus pass," Francine said, bringing me back. "It'll take you to every trail head in every forest; there's a ton all over the island." She put another sandwich on my plate. "This one has goat cheese, can you believe it? Goats are adorable."

It was a perfect day—I looked at the table laden with food, at this nice lady who made it all for me and who let me walk wherever and whenever. Who seemed to trust me already.

I wanted her to like me.

I wanted this job.

I wanted to see Sean on Monday.

"Francine," I said. "I hiked at Salishwood."

"Oh, good! Isn't it beautiful?"

I swallowed. "It is. I'm—sort of working there." I spoke fast, terrified to ruin the best thing I'd had in forever but more scared of getting caught in a lie of omission. Aside from stealing, lying is the number one crime foster kids are accused of and ruined by, no matter the kid, no matter the situation. We are liars. Says everyone. I've practically killed myself keeping that one at bay.

"You've been here three days. How'd you manage that?"

I couldn't read her tone.

"I saw a notice at Blackbird and took a chance and applied. I didn't want to bother you unless I got it—"

"Or risk my saying no."

Note to self: Francine is not dumb.

"But," I said fast, "it's not paid; it's just an internship, so really it's not a *job* job. I'm sorry." And truly, I was. Because I'd maybe screwed myself out of my dream work situation. And Francine did not deserve to be even half lied to.

She squeezed a wedge of lemon into her teacup. "You tell Joellen?"

"I will. I swear."

"You need to tell me when you make a decision like this."

"I will."

She put a cucumber-and-cream-cheese sandwich on my plate. Was she worried I was malnourished?

"Well," she said. "Summer internships are good."

I clenched my toes tight in my shoes. "They said I could stay all year. If I wanted." My heart raced.

She took the tea bags out of the pot and *looked* at me. "Muriel.

My job is to help you do *your* job, which is to graduate from high school. School is your job; it is your *only* job."

"I've always worked, you have my report cards—I can do both, I swear."

We sipped our Red Rose tea. An impasse this early—she was probably working out how to call Joellen to pick me up.

For the first time in a long time, I didn't want to go. Not yet.

"Wait," I said. "They said I have to get school credit to work all year. Would that make it okay? You could come with me, meet Jane, the lady with the . . . school credits? Oh, and I heard they do a thing with U of W? So really it's a class; it's like independent study!" Thanks, Creepy Man-Bun Natan.

Francine sighed and got up from the table but said nothing. It was maddening. She opened the refrigerator and brought a shallow dish of custard to the table. She tossed a handful of sugar on top and fired up a little butane blowtorch. "Watch your hair," she said, and aimed the blue flame at the sugar, which melted into an amber glass sheet on the custard.

The hiss of the flame sent Terry Johnson skittering down his doggy steps and under Francine's bed.

"Oh, come on, you big baby," Francine called to him. She handed me a spoon and with her own, cracked the sugar glass and scooped it up with custard. She eyeballed me until I did, too.

Was this custard code for yes? Or no? I took a bite.

Holy hell. I closed my eyes. Otherworldly. This was the fanciest meal I'd ever eaten in all my life. It seemed likely she made every single thing from scratch.

"Crème brûlée," she said.

I took another spoonful. *What. About. Salishwood?*

"Want me to teach you how to make it?"

I nodded.

She put more strawberries on my plate. "Colleges like internships," she said.

I held my breath.

"I'm going with you next shift to make sure you're getting school credit, and I'll tell Joellen myself. Transferable *college* credit."

Whatever. I exhaled. "Okay."

"Your GPA has to stay where it is."

"Always does." Hope crept in.

"No more doing ambiguously not cool things and then apologizing after. It's exhausting and part of the pile of reasons I retired from fostering. Just *ask* first. Too soon for this nonsense if you're planning to stay with me all year. Agreed?"

Straightforward. Calling me on my shit. But still—kind. Refreshing.

"Yes," I said.

"Do I have your word?"

I smiled so hard my face hurt. "Yes. Thank you."

"Not for nothing, you're my last," she said.

"Same."

She laughed. And weak with relief I nearly did, too.

The brûlée was probably four servings' worth. We ate the whole thing.

"Francine."

"Yes?"

"Thank you."

She sipped her tea and smiled at me over her cup.

"I've never had a real tea before," I said as I cleared the table, and we stood together at the sink, Francine rinsing, me loading the dishwasher. "Is it supposed to be so *much*?"

"It is when it's for a welcome dinner," she said. "Do you feel properly welcomed?"

The bright warmth swelled tentatively in my chest again.

That night, showered and in my pajamas, I sat at the kitchen table and called Joellen on Francine's rotary dial landline. Which, if you haven't tried one, is kind of fun.

"Francine?" Joellen's voice was anxious. "Everything okay?"

"It's me."

"Muir! You okay?"

"Hi," I said. She was quiet. I liked the faraway buzz in the receiver. It felt like talking in an old movie, underwater and through a tunnel.

"Muir."

"I'm here."

She sighed. "You want me to come get you?"

The dishwasher, full of our high tea plates, shifted its cycle. Francine was in the living room watching TV with Terry Johnson cinnamon-rolled up in her lap.

"Ohhhh," Francine said to him in what I was learning was her special Terry Johnson voice, "you hate the new Bachelor, too, don't you?" Terry turned his belly up to be scratched. "Yes, you do, that's because he's a mansplaining dummy. Every one of those cute dental hygienists and marketing majors is too good for him, but it's all fake anyhow, so who cares? *We* do. That's right, yes, we do! Brittney better get a rose or else!" And she smothered his face in kisses.

"No," I said to Joellen, working the knotted chain I'd taken from the pillowcase, more because I was feeling lucky than to soothe my nerves, which were oddly still. I watched Terry push his nose up against Francine's face. "Don't come get me. Not yet."

Upstairs, alone in the empty room in the huge non-bunk bed, I lay awake past midnight watching the bats dive and swoop around the moonlit window until I gave up and took a blanket from the bed, crept down the stairs to the living room, and lay down on the narrow sofa. Better. Two distinct sets of breathing echoed in the dark from Francine's room. I closed my eyes and was nearly lulled to sleep until I was startled by trotting clicks on the floor. Terry Johnson jumped lightly up onto the sofa, wormed his way into the crook of my knees, turned around a bunch of times, curled up like the pastry he was, and fell asleep.

Every orphan needs a dog to rehydrate our dead, frozen hearts, symbolize the unconditional love we've been denied, and make us realize that *there really is beauty in the world, after all.* Ask anyone. Ask Annie. Ask Sandy.

Terry Johnson smelled gross and snored like a drunk guy.

But I was asleep in about a minute, awake at dawn and back upstairs in the big bed before Francine was the wiser.

✳ ✳ ✳

I carry with me a paperback copy of *Bread and Jam for Frances* by Russell Hoban, pictures by his wife, Lillian Hoban, from the third house I lived in. I was six, and Joellen says I stayed for nearly half the year. I remember the kids were fun and the foster people were nice and they had a lot of books, including *Bread and Jam,* which I loved so much I read it over and over and hid it in my bed so the other kids didn't take it. The pictures are pencil sketches in only black, white, and a little blue. It is a story about a family of badgers, nature's most vicious killer, an animal that kills for *fun*—but in the Frances books, the badger family stands upright and lives in a house and they wear clothes and talk, and they have manners, they brush their badger hair and badger teeth, they have birthday parties and bedtimes, and the mom wears an apron and runs a tidy, efficient household.

Frances is the older of two badger daughters, and she is having issues with trying unfamiliar food. Almost always, the new food does not work out; poached eggs are slimy, veal cutlet and French-cut string beans are complicated. Frances is sick of new tastes and textures being repeatedly forced on her, being told she'll love them if she'll just give them a chance, only to be disappointed again and again and again. So she takes matters into her own hands. She refuses any new food and eats only her favorite meal, bread and jam, all day. Bread and jam instead of slimy eggs for breakfast. She trades the chicken salad sandwich her mother packs in her school lunch for a friend's bread-and-jam sandwich. Dinner is more bread, more jam. Bread and jam make Frances happy, she always knows what she is getting, and it always tastes good, so she is never disappointed.

Every house I live in is different in every way. They all smell different, different median temperature, and the food is always unfamiliar; people buy a million kinds of peanut butter, milk, cereal, soup; some people cook only in Crock-Pots, or microwaves, or they fry everything that holds still long enough. Some people are really great bakers or barbecuers; some people buy a bunch of mixed nuts in bulk at Costco and call it dinner. Wonderful or horrible, none of it matters. I am a badger.

White, wheat, sourdough, rye, multigrain, French baguette—every house has bread. Homemade or store-bought; strawberry, grape, raspberry—every house has jam. And almost all of them have a toaster.

Everybody needs beauty as well as bread . . . strength to body and soul alike.

Even John Muir knew the greatness of bread.

Every new house I live in, bread and beauty are home. Toast and a walk. I always know what I am getting, and I am never disappointed.

When the parents at that house told me I couldn't live with them anymore, that I had to move again to a different house, I snuck *Bread and Jam for Frances* into the pillowcase. Joellen came to get me, and I did not say goodbye.

Six

IN THE MORNING IT WAS SATURDAY, day four at Francine's house, three weeks until the first day of school, and she insisted I attend the school district welcome-back picnic. "It's an island tradition, makes the first day of school so much easier. Meet some people, stay an hour—half an hour—and then you can leave."

I took the bus to a park near the water that was filled with kids from every school on the island, kindergarten through high school. A cloudless, seventy-eight-degree day, cooled by the breeze off the Sound. I stood at the bus stop to watch the little kids chase each other, screaming, and set my watch alarm to beep in thirty minutes.

"Toast and Jam," a voice called.

Kira. My age after all? She stood by herself just beyond the park fence, knee-length bright blue cargo shorts, black boots, black tank, and hair up, showing off her swirling tattoos, elbow-deep in a bag of popcorn.

I am excellent at engaging with new people, even crowds; that's basic foster care survival. But being good at it doesn't mean I like it. I walked, wearing the clean version of the same gray T-shirt and jeans I'd worn to Salishwood, to Kira alone in the shade of a stand of pines. "Hey."

She leaned against the nearest tree. "You *live* here?"

"I do," I said with my *meeting new people* smile. "Now."

"Going to school?"

"Yeah."

She crumpled the empty popcorn bag, downed almost an entire bottle of water, unwrapped two pieces of gum from her pocket, and chewed them into a giant wad.

"When'd you move in?"

"Few days."

"Where?"

For all my city navigation, I was still unsure where I stood on this forested island. I turned toward the water, where the sun was positioned in the sky, then to the road. "Um. That way?"

She nodded. "You'll figure it out. Might be near me. Where from?"

"Seattle."

"So. Muiriel."

"How'd you remember?"

"You took cookies out of the trash."

"Right." My face felt hot. "Sure. That was . . . You're Kira?"

She nodded again and snapped her gum, and to my relief, smiled. For real. "And the bitch with the cookies was Tiana. Just so you know. I'd say steer clear, but I think she saw you dumpster-dive, so it's too late for you now. What grade?"

"Twelfth. She saw me?"

"Same. Tiana, too, so that should be fun."

"Okay, but she *saw* me?"

Kira spit her gum out into a napkin, unwrapped another piece, and went to work on it. "I'd offer you some," she said, "but it's nicotine. Tastes disgusting. Don't worry about Tiana. She's all up-speak, no action."

Now I smiled. Kira tried to blow an unsuccessful bubble, but Nicorette is not for playing around. So many kids I lived with used that gum. No smoking in the houses. I leaned against a tree beside hers. One of us looked pulled from central casting to star as Pissed-Off Foster Kid on an especially touching episode of *Law & Order: Special Victims Unit*. As per usual, it was not me.

A group of younger boys ran past, screaming and using sticks like swords, and one of them waved at Kira as a man came running after them, yelling, "Boys! We've talked about this!" Kira rolled her eyes.

"My brother. Freshman and instantly popular. You have brothers? Sisters?"

I've answered this question hundreds of times, always without thinking, straight-up honest. *Foster care.* I never lie to new people. Lets people show me right away if they're going to be dicks about it, or maybe they'll be nice, though it doesn't matter anyway when I leave halfway through the year. So I was shocked when I heard myself say instead, "Just me. I'm living with my aunt. She made me come to this."

What am I doing?

"My mom and dad made me, too," she said, looking past me to the bouncy houses and food trucks. "We moved here last year from Los Angeles, and they are still shocked—*shocked,* I tell you—that starting a brand-new high school as a junior hasn't made me the most popular and well-loved student in a school full of people who've grown up together on a damn island and have known each other since kindergarten. They're *baffled*."

"Well," I said, liking her more every minute, "you need to understand, this picnic is the answer."

She chewed her gum, turned right to me, and smiled. "Nothing like carnival popcorn and egg-and-spoon races to create lifelong bonds of friendship with a bunch of idiots who would rather be hiding in the bathroom vaping and getting drunk at eleven a.m."

One more year. Just nine more months of school. Two hundred ten days.

That's a *lot* of days.

"Aren't there *any* sober non-vapers?" I sighed.

"I mean, in the world at large? Or . . ." She unwrapped another piece of gum. "Speak of the devil," she said. I followed her gaze.

Sean.

He came walking to us, across the field, in jeans and a faded Yosemite Valley T-shirt. Still those arms and eyes, dark and directed right at mine even while he hugged Kira hello. "Muriel?"

"What the . . . ," Kira said. "You've lived here five minutes. How do you know Sean?"

"We work together," Sean said. "Muriel, I figured you ferried from the city—do you *live* here?"

"You *what* together?" Kira said. "Five minutes and you know Sean *and* you have a job?"

I could not look directly at him. "I'm highly motivated," I said.

"And making some powerful-ass vision boards?" Kira shook her head. "Don't ever let me introduce you to my parents."

"Kira, how's your summer?" Sean asked. God, this guy was so . . . *sunny*? Genuinely cheerful. Or maybe I've just been living with sad, scared kids for so long I've lost the metric of normal emotion, and now baseline happy looks like a person living in a perpetual surprise party. *Ice cream! Sunshine! Hey, I know you!*

"Living the dream, schlepping toast and coffee," Kira chirped, and to me she said, "Explain the work situation."

"Salishwood," Sean and I said in unison.

"I saw the flyer at Blackbird," I told Kira. "I've only worked one day."

"Your first day was the best day I've had all summer," Sean said. "Jason was the worst, and Natan is . . ."

"Worse?" I offered.

"Exactly. Thank God you're there." He smiled. "And *here*—when did you move? You're going to school? Please tell me you're a senior."

Kira watched this exchange, nodding through her gum chewing. "She's with us," she said. "Class of *Get the Hell off This Island.*"

"I don't want the hell off," he said.

"You do," Kira said. "You want to live on a mountain in a Bob Ross cabin and, like, write poems about the sunrise. Don't lie to yourself."

"I could build a cabin here, and I don't write poems—they're called *sonnets*," he said. "Muiriel, do you like it so far? Want the hell off yet?"

"Not yet," I said, in a voice thinner and three octaves higher than my own. Jesus.

"Good," Sean said. "Please don't ever leave. Being alone with Natan every day was a nightmare. And the kids loved you."

"Sean-y!" A laughing voice pierced the crowd. "We *need* you!"

The three of us turned to see Tiana—of course, because that's how school goes for me—surrounded by a group of kids our age, the girls' long arms beckoning frantically for Sean to *Come on! Come here!* All of them admittedly beautiful, cute shorts and blouses, shining hair, perfect teeth. I ran my tongue over my own.

Not crooked, exactly, not like a jack-o'-lantern, and, yes, immaculately clean—but definitely not perfect. Braces, like phones and nonutilitarian clothing, are not necessities. They are luxuries I had no need for, no access to even if I did want them. It's possible to remain alive without straight teeth and stylish outfits. Alive is all that matters.

Still.

I felt my clothes on me. I was dressed, as always, in the colors of a bruise: blue, black, gray. My wardrobe was made almost entirely of things found at Goodwill or hospice thrift shops, which I take a needle and thread to, *Pretty in Pink*–style, so everything more or less fits me. Fashionwise, everything I wear safely represents the last half of this decade, a few splurges from Target once in a while, just neutral enough to not draw attention from mean kids at school. My face, my body, my wardrobe all perfectly nondescript, and all I had.

But right then, for maybe the first time ever, I wished I had more. Or something different.

Sean kind of grimaced at the girls' calls. He hugged Kira goodbye. "See you at Blackbird. And, Muiriel? I don't really write sonnets. Not that there's anything wrong with that. Or poetry in general. See you Monday."

Is he nervous?

"Sure thing, Seany," Kira said, snapping her gum. He ducked his head a little, and we watched him walk back into the crowd. "Don't hold it against him," she said. "His mom is friends with

Tiana's mom. And mine. Small island. Also, he's too nice for his own good. He's the only guy in the world who's super popular for *not* being a dick, and he's completely oblivious—I mean, can't he see those people are assholes to anyone who's not *in* with them who's not him? I think he thinks he can make them be nicer; he's the resident life coach or some shit. But sincere—I mean, he *means* it, he just can't see they'll never change. Douchebags gonna douche. Sean is kind of the one thing everyone can agree on; he's friends with *everyone:* the jocks, the stoners, even those basic bitches there, and he tutors the special ed kids. . . . He's Ferris Bueller without the narcissism."

Not friends with Natan, I thought. Good to know he had some kind of line. I watched him laugh with the girls. In my experience, both extreme kindness and hyper assholery in people are almost always born of tragedy. Something happened to this kid.

Right on cue:

"His dad died when we were ten," Kira said.

Knew it. God, how awful.

"He was a ranger, the dad. Like a . . . forest ranger? National park–type deal, wore the hat and everything."

Well. That explained Sean's love of the forest. Joellen would say, *He comes rightly by it.*

"Everybody loves him," Kira said.

"Oh." *Including you?*

"Except me. I mean, yes, I love him, but I've known him since I was little. He's a less annoying second brother."

Thank God. "Wait. Didn't *you* just move here?"

She unwrapped more gum. "My mom's family has lived on the island since my grandparents' parents. Same house, the next generation moves in when the one before it dies. We've been in LA since I was born, but we've spent every summer of our lives here. Grandma died last year, so now here we are."

Four generations. One island. One house. One family. Unimaginable.

"Why don't you ask Sean to get Tiana off your back?"

"No," she said, fast. "Not his problem."

"Sorry—"

She shook her head. "It's fine. Just don't need him in it making it worse. It's fine."

"Got it." Not my business. My own rule.

Someone in the crowd sent a beach ball flying. "This thing's been happening since 1945," Kira said.

"Yeah," I said, looking at my watch.

"No," she laughed, tipping her head at the mayhem of kids. *"This.* When the war ended and the internment camps closed, some of the families came back, their kids still school age, and the teachers thought the white students should get reacquainted with their Japanese pals who were back from prison before the school year started. Then they just kept doing it every year, so now it's a tradition. I bet not a single one of these people knows how it started. Or would give a shit if they did."

Nearly everyone on the field was white.

She was right. Why had Francine not told me? And why did every high school history class I took act like the internment never happened? *Oh, Wikipedia—please don't end up being the vital core of my education.*

We stood for a while, watching the littlest kids try to fly a kite in no wind, me wishing I could think of something not stupid to say.

"I *made* that flyer," Kira said. "The one for Salishwood."

I looked at her. "You did *not*." But there they were; the pine boughs from the paper, across her shoulders.

She drew the flyer. She drew the ink on her own body.

"Oh, Kira," I said. "The ferry cookies." No wonder they were so perfect.

She shrugged. "More where they came from." Tiana's laugh rang from the crowd. I tried to keep my burgeoning hatred at bay. A smaller girl, just as loud, also pretty, was buzzing near Tiana's side, laughing at something Sean said, trying to wrestle him into a selfie.

"Tiana and Katrina," Kira said. "Even their names suck. They share half a brain and a third of one personality, so I just Frankenstein them as one: *Katiana*." She spit her gum once more into a wrapper.

"Okay," I said, "so what happened to her?"

"Who?"

"Tiana. Someone die? Do her parents beat her up? Does she have a rare blood disease? Is she homeless?"

Kira's eyes were wide. "Uh . . . not that I know of."

"Because what's making her be like that?"

The girls tossed some guy's hat in the air and scrambled to take pictures of their own cleverness.

"Or," Kira said, "maybe her parents are fine, her life is great, and she's just awful because she can be."

Joellen always reminds me that mean kids who seem to have perfect lives may very likely be enduring some unseen tragedy. Which is obviously true of anyone, everyone has sadness they don't go around blabbing about. But my sympathy has worn thin, because the meanest kids I've encountered in the nearly twenty schools I've attended in my life were never *us*. Kids in foster care aren't having the greatest time in life, but we are never afforded leeway to be assholes; we are expected to be perfect every god-damn day or we're instantly and indelibly labeled out loud and in our files: *Trouble*. No longer people. We are *problems*. Kira wasn't wrong. It seemed equally as likely to me that at least some kids like Tiana have known, instead of unseen tragedy, nothing but comfort and safety their whole lives, and they simply feel entitled to hold on to their flimsy self-esteem and high school social status by humiliating anyone they feel superior to. It's not like they'll get kicked out of their house for run-of-the-mill bullying. In fact, bul-lies' parents typically roll up to the school to defend their unsavory offspring, no matter what. Makes it pointless to ever ask for help from an adult.

"I don't know," Kira sighed. "I'm trying to do better with . . . people."

I watched Sean make his way among the crowd. "What'd they do?" I asked. "Katiana?"

She shook her head. "Nothing. Nothing I haven't done to myself."

Interesting.

She pulled her phone from a black backpack at her feet. "Well. Back down in the mines. That toast isn't going to butter itself." She held up her hand in a sort of wave and walked through the trees to the road, where she stopped and turned.

"Muriel?"

"Yeah?"

"Boys your thing?" she asked, matter-of-fact.

"Yeah."

"Because he likes you. Sean."

"*No.*"

"*Yes.*"

I tried not to smile. "Okay."

She turned and kept walking.

"Hey," I called. "Do you take the bus to school?"

"I walk."

All the best people do.

"Do you want— Could I walk with you? On the first day?"

She faced me and walked backward. "What's your number? I'll text you."

"Don't have one."

She stopped. "Don't have what?"

"A number. No phone."

A car passed.

"Okay, just come to Blackbird later, we'll figure it out."

"All right."

"Muiriel?"

"Yeah?"

"Can I call you Muir?"

"Sure. Yes."

She walked away, down the street and to the water, back to Blackbird, and yelled to me, without turning around, "Not having a phone is fucking weird."

It was that, more than anything, that made me want to be her friend.

Seven

THE NEXT THREE WEEKS became a routine of sitting and reading at Blackbird before my shifts at Salishwood. Kira brought secret free toast with jam to my window seat. "Until they raise the minimum wage, I'll take it in toast," she said, and pretended to wipe the table while we talked.

"How's the woods?" she asked every time.

"Woody. How's the math?"

"Mathy."

She was spending her summer afternoons with a math tutor, trying to get through algebra, let alone geometry or precalculus, before graduation. "My parents are horrified by the fact I may not get into college because of it, and I keep telling them to calm down, because I'm majoring in art, so I'll be fine."

I noticed a big square bandage on her shoulder.

"Nicotine patch," she moaned. "Gum's giving me TMJ."

"Maybe because you chew fifteen pieces at once?"

She sighed. "Maybe."

"How long did you smoke?"

"Year? Fifteen months? Don't ever do it. I'll be nicotine's bitch the rest of my life." She rubbed the patch.

"Well. Is it helping?"

She shrugged. "Not as much as horking gum. I need to find a better spot; it's covering my waves." The swirling inked ocean spilled from beneath the patch.

Each of her tattoos, as I suspected, was her own design: the waves, birds, whales, the pine branches across her shoulders. I could not imagine anything in the world worth putting on my skin, part of me *forever*.

"Do your parents have tattoos?" I asked, nosy but not rude enough to ask what I really meant: *What kind of parents let a fourteen-, fifteen-year-old kid start collecting so much ink that they're practically sleeves?*

"God, no," she said. "They'd rather die." She stood up and wiped the table for real. "Want tea to go? On the house," she whispered. Like Francine. Said what she needed and nothing more. I walked, full of toast and jam and tea and intrigue, to Salishwood.

Salishwood, Jane had told me in the lodge when I arrived, slows down considerably during the school year. She and Man-Bun Natan and the other grad students would work with the school-day visits, but she asked me to come on Tuesdays and Thursdays after school and Saturdays. "You and Sean," she said. "Okay?"

Twist my arm.

She gave me my official name tag and smiled longingly as I pinned it to my shirt. "Still jealous," she said.

This sunny Monday I wore new-to-me hiking pants I'd found at the Humane Society thrift shop—they fit pretty well, gray and lots of pockets—with my best T-shirt, blue and the newest I had. I was worn out trying to look . . . *pretty* . . . around Sean, and simultaneously berating myself for caring to do it. I walked outside and leaned against the edge of our unofficial "counselor picnic table" to tie my shoes. Two busloads of summer school fourth graders arrived from a district I once was in, a school I attended. I recognized one of the teachers, but she either didn't know me or was too busy trying to herd the insane ten-year-olds whacking each other with their backpacks and water bottles to notice me.

"Hey," I called to two boys climbing a tree beside a really big wooden sign clearly painted with twelve-inch letters: *Do Not Climb.* "Your reading skills suck! There are trees to climb on the trail we're taking. Cool it for ten minutes."

The boys dropped to the ground, panting and red-faced, eight in the morning and full of bottled energy from the ferry and bus ride to get here, tearing around full-throttle.

"Are we going with you?" one of them asked.

"Maybe," I said. They looked at each other and sprinted to the teacher.

"Ms. McKinstry," they screamed. "We want to go with the girl!"

"I would, too," Sean said, tossing his pack on the picnic table. "If you'd let me climb trees."

I wished so badly I didn't like his voice, his . . . everything so much.

Be. Cool. "I'd let you," I said. "The ones you're allowed."

All his T-shirts seemed worn and faded: this one blue with *REI* in block letters and, like the rest, humbly revealing his defined arms.

"The kids always like you best. Got a lot of brothers and sisters?" he asked.

"Hundreds," I said, and right then small hands grabbed my arm.

"Muir?"

I looked down, disoriented, at a familiar face.

"Zola."

"Muiriel!" Her arms wrapped so tight around my hips that my circulation slowed.

"What . . . are you . . . ?"

"What are *you*?" she squealed into my side. She would not let go, she nearly knocked me off balance, and I reached to steady myself against the table. Sean was watching the scene unfold, and I tried to not see him seeing us. "Why are you with this school?" The bad-penny house was not in this district.

"This is *my* school," she said. "I'm home. With my mom."

I couldn't pretend to not be relieved. "Oh, Zola," I sighed, and untangled myself from her python arms to put one hand on her head to keep her still so I could see her face, her beautiful hair braided and beaded the way it was when I first met her, the way she liked it best. There is a pervasive lie born of the corporatization of adoption that insists birth parents are bad, adoptive parents are good, kids get "bad" traits genetically and learn "good" behaviors from adoptive parents. And worse, the disgusting additional lie that kids of color are better off removed from their families and stuck with white foster parents who can't keep track of one goddamn swim lesson. It's all bullshit. According to Zola, her mom occasionally worked nights while Zola slept; someone reported it. But Zola felt safe and loved at home; she believed she belonged with her mom. I believed Zola. I took her hands in mine.

"That is . . . I'm so happy. Are you?"

"Yes!" she said, and looked up and around the treetops. "Is this where you *live* now?"

"I wish," I said. "But I get to work here. I'm in a house here on the island."

"Is it good?"

"So far."

"Good." She noticed Sean. "Who's this?" She didn't wait for me to answer. "I'm Zola," she announced, taking her hands from mine and extending one to firmly shake Sean's.

"Sean," he said. "I'm a friend of Muiriel's."

"Oh, okay." Zola nodded. "So am I."

Sean smiled at me, his dark eyes looking *right at me,* and I slyly held the table to steady myself again.

"Well, who do we have *here?*" Natan's voice shattered the moment, and he strode toward us, bun high and tight, and carrying—*oh God, no*—a guitar.

Please, Mother Earth, open a hole to swallow him and that guitar. Please. I beg of you.

Zola watched Natan walking and backed near me as he knelt down before her. I stood behind her and instinctively put my arms around her. "Hello there," he said in a tone most people save for really old people and puppies. "Are you going to hike with us today?"

Zola nodded.

"Fantastic!" he said. "You go, girl!" He held out his closed hand to her in a cringe-inducing attempt at a fist bump.

Zola frowned at Natan's fist, then leaned forward and spoke into it as if it held a microphone. "Is this thing on?"

Natan's smile was frozen and confused.

Sean's bloomed even more bright and beautiful. "Zola," he said, "you might be my new favorite person in the world right now. Maybe ever."

Zola grinned and looked up at me. "Do I get to be with you? In your group?"

"I'll see what I can do."

She hugged me once more and ran back to her class. Natan got busy tuning his guitar and pretending he wasn't just shut down by a tiny girl not about to tolerate his creepiness.

Sean made room for me to sit beside him on the picnic table so we could be away from Natan, who put his feet up on a tree stump. Teva sandals with socks—which he removed. First the Velcro strap sandals came off. Then he peeled colorful wool socks off two long, hairy feet and began exercising his toes. Gross. I stood up, ready to bolt.

"Muiriel," Natan said. "That little girl a friend of yours?"

"Sister," I said, watching Zola race through the grass with the other kids. "Foster sister." Sean turned to look at me.

This is my usual: straight up from the start, unlike the cagey lie I told Kira.

"Ah . . . ," Natan sighed in a dreamy way. "Foster care. Such a gift. Your parents are so generous to give shelter to the less fortunate."

Even more gross.

"No," I said. "I don't have parents. Zola and I were in a foster placement together. Should you be barefoot right now? Aren't we hiking in a minute?"

Sean jumped up from the table, pulled on his pack, and handed me my water bottle. "Let's go ask Jane if you can have Zola in your group," he said.

"Wait," Natan said. "Hold up—you were a foster child?"

"Muiriel, let's go," Sean urged.

"Am," I said. "I am in foster care."

His mouth opened. "Oh!" he said. "Well, then I misspoke—the gratitude is yours! How beautiful."

Oh. My. God.

"Absolutely." I nodded. "I am super grateful for every person who takes pity on me and gives me shelter."

"Jesus Christ, Natan," Sean said, low. "It's none of your business, and for fuck's sake, *gratitude*? The entire fucking point of being born is that someone is supposed to take care of you."

Natan and I stared at him, his words ringing in the stillness.

And what words they were. I was doomed.

Is this what swooning feels like?

Sexy cursing aside, why and how did Sean know to say exactly the right things? Those were some deep "nature of human familial structure" cuts. Were those conclusions he drew from losing his dad? He sounded like me. He sounded like *Joellen*.

Natan shook his head and smiled, forever oily and patronizing, at Sean. "So young," he said. "So hotheaded."

Sean's face was somehow both blank and incredulous. "Dude. You're like five years older than us."

Natan picked up his guitar. "Try twelve, friend. This reminds me of a song I wrote last summer. I call it 'Tender Essence.'..."

Sean placed his hand lightly on my elbow and steered me toward a water spigot near the lodge and away from Natan's noxious cloud of patchouli and tentative G chord strumming.

"Sorry," he said when we were safely out of range, taking his hand from my arm. "Didn't mean to manhandle you."

Manhandle away, sir. I came out of my haze. "Oh no," I said. "We're missing the musical genius that is 'Tender Ess'— Oh Jesus, nope. I can't say it out loud."

"Don't worry," Sean said. "We'll just get it on Tidal."

Oh, we *will, will we?*

He stooped to fill his water bottle at the spigot in the ground. "Have I mentioned yet today how glad I am you're here to avoid him with me?"

"You have now." I liked happy Sean, but pissed Sean was his own kind of delightful. His eyes went to the name tag on my boring, stupid T-shirt.

"Did you make that up?"

"My *name*?"

"The spelling."

"That's what they called me."

"Wow," he said. "I'm kind of a Pinchot guy myself, but I mean—*Muir*. That's cool."

Pinchot. Gifford Pinchot, John Muir's nature nemesis. Sean was the son of a park ranger; where was the Pinchot nonsense coming from? I frowned.

"And what would *that* entail?" I asked. "Being a 'Pinchot guy'?"

"Just that I . . . align with his ethics."

While John Muir was giving his life to fight for *preservation* of delicate, singular natural places, Pinchot was fighting for *conservation*—meaning the forests owned by the federal government should be managed and used for public recreation, logging, mining, scientific studies. So Muir's national parks are often surrounded by Pinchot's national forests. Park Service. Forest Service. Muir saw nature as a transcendental temple humans were obligated to cherish and protect, while Pinchot was in the Bible-minded "humans at the apex" camp and felt nature existed solely to be manipulated for human consumption. In short, Pinchot? Not a fan.

Still. In all my life I had never met another person who knew enough about either, let alone both, of those names to have any kind of opinion about their *ethics*.

"Yeah," I said, sort of into my empty water bottle, and knelt to take my turn at the spigot. "Considering without Muir there would be no Yosemite, no Yellowstone, no Rainier, and also considering the fact that Pinchot is completely full of shit, I guess Muir *is* pretty cool, but I mean, you're totally entitled to your own questionable opinion."

I looked up at him, standing there holding his open, forgotten water bottle.

"Right," he said. "That's . . . you're right."

"But that's a fight for you to lose another day."

"Name the time and place." He just stood there *looking* at me. With—was it admiration?

Muir and Pinchot, and he's seventeen and beautiful and here with me.

Too much.

I filled and capped my bottle. "Let's get these kids worn out and lost." From my day pack I pulled a brass compass and offered it to him. "Want to lead?"

He held the compass, its shine worn from ten years of my anxious hands clutching it. "Heavy for hiking," he said. "Also, I have an innate sense of direction."

"Lucky you." I took it back and rubbed the brass. "*This* is my sense of direction."

"But you could lose it."

"You could lose yours."

"I . . ." He smiled. So much smiling. He was making it hard not to smile back, which kind of hurt; my smile muscles were severely underdeveloped.

The kids lined up. Sean led our group (including the tree climbers and my Zola) into and safely out of the woods, on a path that did not need the help of a compass, except to show the kids what true north looks like; over boulders, across a creek, and I brought the last of the stragglers to where he stood beneath the shade of a giant cedar.

We got the kids hydrated and back on the bus as the late-afternoon sun was still high and hot above the trees—hot for the Pacific Northwest. Seventy-five degrees and we lose our collective minds. Sean walked to the lodge, and I said goodbye to Zola.

"Will you be here if we come again?"

"I think so," I said. "Probably."

"Can I write you emails now because I'm home?"

I shook my head. "*I'm* not."

"When will you be?"

I have no idea.

The buses were ready to go, teachers lining up the kids, and I sent Zola to join them. I waved and walked behind as they pulled slowly away through the trees.

I breathed in the forest air, sunbeams slanting through the evergreen boughs, owls and woodpeckers and black-capped chickadees rustling and singing, unseen. I closed my eyes and exhaled. No sign of Sean, so I collected my pack, said goodbye to Jane, and started down the road to the bus stop.

The whir and click of a bicycle, and there he was beside me.

I smiled into my backpack strap.

"Walking?" he said.

"To the bus stop."

"Join you?"

"Sure."

Good, good, sounds normal, casual, except my breathing is all jacked up—calm the hell down; he's just a person . . . an incredibly handsome person who loves the forest and understands foster care for some reason and seems to like you a lot, no big deal, so keep breathing—no, not like that, not so fast, just breathe like a normal person . . . God!

He got off his bike and walked it. "Where do you live?"

"It's . . . I think at the end of the road the bus turns right—no, left, and then on this one path up a hill past a farm and two more lefts? Then a right down the drive. Toward the water. I think."

He smiled. "You're right, that compass works great."

"I'll know it when I see it," I said.

"Okay."

"I usually walk, but I'm helping with dinner tonight, so . . . bus."

"Too bad. Perfect day for a walk."

" 'I only went out for a walk,' " I said.

He stopped walking. " 'And finally concluded to stay out till sundown, for going out, I found, was really going in. In every walk with nature, one receives far more than he seeks.' "

Jesus. This guy. "That's some good Muir for a Pinchot fan," I managed, so charmed I could have passed out. We continued walking.

"Well. Muir's the better writer—I'll give you that. Also, my dad was a ranger," he said.

"I heard."

"You've been asking about me?"

"Kira *told* me," I said. "Unsolicited."

He smiled. "Okay."

"It's true."

76

"I'm glad you and Kira met. Kira is who you want to know. Toast connection for sure, and also her family is really nice."

"Hey," I said. "Will you not say anything to her? About the foster care? Not a secret, I just haven't—I lied to her. I don't know why."

"Of course not. Not mine to tell."

He meant it. I believed him. We walked.

"But just so you know, Kira wouldn't be . . . Her aunt, we're friends with her, too, she has foster kids sometimes. Little ones. How long have you . . ."

"Whole life."

"Since you were born?"

I nodded. "My *whole* life."

We reached the bus stop, a little wooden shelter beneath the trees. He stood and balanced his bike.

"Well," I said. "See you tomorrow?"

"Sadly for me, no. I'm going on a trip. I'll be gone till school starts."

"Oh." An unfamiliar sinking feeling. "Where?"

"Hiking. Wonderland Trail."

"The whole thing?"

"Ninety-three miles."

Envy. All my life, walking nearly every street in Seattle, I've watched Mount Rainier rise and disappear behind clouds and above the water, and I've wished so badly to be there. Stratovolcano on a ten-year schedule that could erupt any day. John Muir loved Rainier: "Of all the fire-mountains . . . along the Pacific coast, Mount Rainier is the noblest." The Wonderland winds through those fields around Rainier's snowy peak.

"Okay then," I said. Jealous. And stung—gone for *days*? "See you when you get back."

"When I *am* back, would you want to maybe come over to my house and . . . debate the merits of conservation versus preservation? Little Pinchot/Muir rumble?"

"No."

His face fell.

"I'm not 'debating' the inherently superior merits of preservation. Conservation is half-stepping bullshit, and you know it."

"Half stepping how?" But his smile was bright. "We're going into Rainier at the Longmire entrance—you know, the one right at the edge of Pinchot National Forest? 'Conservation means the wise use of the earth and its resources for the lasting good of men.'"

"See, now you're just proving my point. *Pinchot* is proving it! For the good of *men*? Like Earth's sole purpose of existing is to be a usable resource for humans? You can do better than that."

"How do you know?"

"Just— You seem like you could."

"I thought you weren't going to debate this?"

"I'm not."

"Aren't you?"

All that in me for so long, and here was someone who had it in him, too—like finding the only other person in the world who speaks the same dialect of a language I've made up—and now I had someone to talk to about what I love most and he loves it most, too. I was breathing fast and trying *so hard* to not smile.

I failed.

He looked relieved.

"Do you want to go see a movie or something?" he said. "With me? Sometime?"

Go out, not date. "Okay."

Huge smile. "What's your number?"

"I'll ask, I don't remember."

"No, *yours,* your phone."

Here we go. "I don't have one."

"You don't— *How?*"

"I move every few months, and phones are expensive."

He leaned his bike against a tree and stepped nearer to me. "Here," he said, and took my hand in his. He opened a Swiss Army knife, and for a second I thought, *Oh, for crap's sake, this madman is going to carve his number into my skin; have I lost all my human survival instincts because he is so beautiful and can quote Muir and Pinchot—what is wrong with me?* But he pulled a tiny pen from between the knife blades and wrote his number on my palm.

"Okay," he said. "Well. 'The mountains are calling . . .'"

I frowned. "You going to finish that?"

"'. . . and I must go'?"

I waited. "And?"

"And . . . what?"

The bus arrived. "Do *not* reduce my namesake's words to hipster T-shirt, bumper sticker quotes you can't finish. Pinchot lackey."

The bus doors opened, and, still smiling, he watched me climb in and fall into the front seat. Through the window I watched him get back on his bike, no helmet, and ride until we turned a wide corner, through the forested hills back to Francine's house, and the whole way I thought about one thing. *Who is he hiking with?*

* * *

I carry with me an Allen wrench. Because you never know.

All my life I have only ever slept in bunk beds. You know who makes a really sturdy, affordable one? IKEA. They look nice, too, the wooden ones. Give me thirty-eight minutes and an Allen wrench (or hex wrench, as some people call them), and I can have a MYDAL (birch wood, good headboard height for night reading) perfectly assembled, beds made with hospital corners, pillows fluffed. By myself. (I'm really not kidding, parents *love* me.) The NORDDAL is good, too. It has darker wood and people tend to use it more for boys' rooms. But for bottom-bunk headroom, the MYDAL is best. Also that's the name—albeit with a different spelling—of period medicine that stops cramps, so the girls laugh at it, which makes it even more great.

Obviously, I prefer a top bunk. Anyone would. Top bunks establish status in a group, ensure less distractions for a good night's sleep, and offer more privacy. The thing is, even if I started in one, more often than not I would end up in a lower one when a new kid came, or siblings who wanted to be near each other moved in. Because kids coming in were always leaving their actual family, their own house, apartment, car they're living in, whatever, and maybe it was bad there, maybe not so much, but it was *home*, and coming to a strange bunk bed house with strange adults and unknown strange other kids was scary for them. I had no idea what that was like. They needed all the help they could get. So I surrendered the top. Or both, and went to a bottom bunk in another room.

"Muriel," Zola whispered in the dark to me from the top bunk of a MYDAL I had assembled that morning, two weeks into a stay that seemed destined to be permanent for her. She might never go home, and she knew it. "Are you ever scared?"

"Sure," I said.

"Are you going home?"

I reached under the bottom bunk for the tool kit I'd stashed there in case of any loose bolts, stepped on the ladder, and held an Allen wrench up in the moonlight. "Do you know what this is?"

She shook her head.

"What do you think it does?"

"Nothing. It's broken."

"No," I whispered. "This is exactly how it's supposed to be. Little bent piece of metal. This thing is magic. It can make chairs and tables and bookshelves. It made this bed; it's the only thing that could. Would you ever have guessed that?"

She shook her head. We were quiet for a while, listening to the breathing of the three other sleeping kids.

"Different isn't necessarily broken," I whispered. "Sometimes small and bent is the only thing that can make something big and new and safe."

"Don't you *want* to go home?" she said.

I put the Allen wrench in her hand. "I'm okay," I said. "I have lots of homes."

She held on to the Allen wrench and turned to the window, her back to me.

Eight

THE LAST FIRST DAY OF HIGH SCHOOL of my life. A Wednesday, which was weird. I woke before dawn on the sofa, my leg numb where Terry Johnson's head rested all night. I sent him to Francine's room and climbed the steps to the attic room, warm with sunlight, and tried to remember every first day of every grade, every single one at a different school. I'd be at one school in the fall, then I'd leave that house the second semester, at a new school in January with new teachers, new classmates making the same stupid comments about my clothes, new teachers expressing the same concerns about my catching up, and a new house with a bunch of new kids.

I found *The Wilderness World* in the sheets, replaced my bookmark, and took a shower without waiting in line. Got dressed in clothes that were in the same place I'd left them, shoes still beside the door, no bunch of kids moving, taking, misplacing things. Quiet.

Downstairs I collected six pale blue eggs from the hens and found they were good listeners. "Ladies," I said. "I hope you appreciate the luxurious lives you lead here in the yard. No school, no teachers treating you like you're stupid for not instantly understanding how they teach geometry, plus your feathers always look great—especially yours, Karen." Karen was a small, round hen, her black feathers shiny and dotted with tufts of white near her red feet. She was so put together, unique and fancy on the regular.

Terry Johnson and Francine waited for me in the sunny kitchen, the table set with a pot of tea, a glass dish of raspberry jam, and a plate of wheat toast.

"Don't forget your lunch," she said, and put a brown paper sack in my hands. "Call from the office if you need anything. You have enough pencils? Notebooks? Need an extra eraser?"

I unfolded the top of the paper sack; cheese sandwich, cut diagonally. Apple, sliced. Carrots, washed and chopped. Granola bar. An adorable lunch that indicated her foster experience had a median grade level of kindergarten.

"Oh, there's a map in there, too, of the school buildings. I've marked where all your classes are."

My head felt a little spinny. I stared down at the carrot sticks. Was there a box of raisins in there, too?

"Muriel," Francine said. "Would you rather have lunch money?"

"No!" I said. "Thank you." I put the sack into my backpack and grabbed more toast to go. "I love granola bars."

She stood on the porch and held Terry Johnson up to wave with his paw as I walked to the road. "Have a good day!"

I waved back and hurried to the cover of trees to rub my eyes, which were burning and tearing up out of the blue.

This focused attention on me and everything I needed or wanted was exhausting, and also engaging in one-sided dialogue with Karen was not a great sign of my emotional health.

Though I was not lying about granola bars. I do love them.

I walked to Kira's house, which turned out to be less than a mile from Francine's, and waited at the top of her driveway. Her house was pretty. Small and white, shingled, two stories, back from the road and facing the Sound. I wondered if they could see the water.

She came jogging up the steep drive, hair piled on her head, long silver earrings, black jeans, another tank top showing off all her ink. "Hey," she said. "Is that Blackbird toast?"

"Aunt made it, not my fault." I broke off a piece and handed it to her.

She chewed. "Not bad, though."

Again with the lying—Sean said it, and it probably was true: if anyone was going to not give a shit about my lack of parents, it would be this person who obviously wasn't trying to fit in with anyone on this island. If she truly had an aunt who fostered, I wouldn't be an anomaly to her. Honestly, without other kids in Francine's house, I was going to need someone to spend time with. A friend. Kira was an excellent candidate for the position, and she seemed to have an opening. Lying was brand-new to me, the best way to kill a friendship before it began, and Kira wasn't stupid. Did I think I could keep this ruse up for an entire school year?

We walked and talked our way through forests and along the highway, the prettiest walk to school I'd ever had. Inside the building things were familiar, because all high schools are kind of the same. The usual halls crammed with the usual million kids. Doors. Windows. Lockers. I was glad for Kira beside me. Easier not walking in alone.

"You okay?" she shouted above the mayhem.

"Yeah," I shouted back.

She was swallowed and carried away in the sea of faces, nearly all of them white except for hers. In the city, depending on the neighborhood, I was sometimes the only white kid in the house or in the classroom. For all its good intentions, Seattle is not immune to what Joellen described as "a stupid bunch of racist gentrification and discriminatory housing practices."

"Meet me at lunch!" Kira yelled from the crowd. "Find the cafeteria!"

I was used to eating lunch by myself, typically in a corner of the library.

"Okay," I called to her.

Might as well try something new.

"You're so lucky you brought lunch," Kira said, dropping beside me in a chair at a table near a window, harried, hair damp, catching her breath. "This is what the cafeteria calls a salad." She stabbed a plastic fork into a piece of ranch-drowned iceberg lettuce. "I hate having PE right before lunch. I'll always be late."

"Blessing in disguise," Tiana chirped as she and Katrina dawdled past our table. "Less time eating might help you win the cellulite battle."

Jesus. Already?

"Good luck with that." Katrina smiled, and I watched them stroll off into their adoring crowd of girls all dressed alike. Kira was staring into her salad.

"Kira."

"Yeah."

"The hell is up with that?"

She shrugged. "First day. They just need to remind me to stay in my place. They'll get bored sometime in October and move on to someone else."

I took in her small, wiry stature. "But why the fat route? That doesn't even make sense."

"They don't need a *reason* to fat shame anyone, even if I'm not. They're in PE with me; I'm the only one who ever uses the showers. Apparently it freaks them out."

"No one showers?"

"And it's basketball this semester! Plus, we start with a mile run around the damn track. People are sweaty AF and they just spray Axe for girls or whatever all over themselves and then put their *clean clothes* back on. I think they don't want to have to redo their makeup or something? I freely admit I'm a little OCD with handwashing and sweatiness in general, but this is legit full-body cardio sweat; I'm not kidding." She accepted a Francine apple slice and chewed thoughtfully. "I don't know. Not worth trying to figure them out. I'm showering whether they pull a *Carrie* in there or not. It's only one more year." She put her head on the table then and closed her eyes.

"Kira. What's up?"

"I think I may have overdone it," she said, lifting the bottom of her tank top to reveal a pair of nicotine patches near her ribs.

I put my head near hers. "Uh . . . are you supposed to use two of those at once?"

"Probably not," she said, pulling the tank aside to show two *more* patches.

I sat up. "Dude."

"I was nervous!" she whispered. "When I'm nervous I want to smoke. Drastic times!"

"Okay, well, this is more dangerous than drastic. Take three of them off or you're going to get nicotine-high or sick or something." She peeled three of the patches away, I wadded them up and tossed them in the trash, then sat back beside her. "Why is Katiana after you?" I asked.

She sat up and sipped the water I pushed toward her. "Usual crap. Nothing. I dared to come in junior year, they were being awful, I told them to screw off, game on. My parents went to the principal, but their parents are rich—they donate to the school fund, so nothing happened, and who cares?" She picked at her sad salad.

I nodded. Adults love to offer sage advice such as *Stand up for yourself; Tell a teacher;* or my personal favorite: *Try to find common ground, kill them with kindness, and become friends with them!* Being the new kid twice a year, every year, has gotten me ignored at best, shoved into lockers, my backpack tossed into dumpsters, descriptions of my supposed sexual prowess Sharpied on bathroom stalls at worst. There is one answer: Keep your head down, lie low. It'll be over eventually.

"I see the school uniform is the same here as in Seattle," I said.

She looked up from the salad to watch Katiana holding court at the basic-bitches table, all of them dressed in nearly identical variations on a bland theme.

"Uniform?"

"Black leggings. White sneakers. T-shirt, tank top. Lunch in a red-and-white Lululemon shopping bag with black handles. *Tasteless signifiers of mediocrity.*" Joellen taught me that one.

"Oh my God. I can never unsee it now . . . so many Lululemon bags. And you know not one of them has ever seen the inside of a yoga studio."

"Thank God, because they never shower. Their mats would be alive with microbes and infectious diseases."

Her smile returned. She accepted another apple slice.

Behind us, a knocking at the window and there was Sean, back from his hike and beautiful as ever. "Hey!" he said, and jogged to the door.

"He liiiikes you," Kira sang.

"He likes eeeveryone according to youuu," I shushed her.

"Kira!" He smiled, bending to one-arm hug her shoulders. "Muriel, how's your first day?"

"It's all right. How was the Wonderland?"

"Perfect. Some rain, two bears with cubs, a million stars. Every time is more beautiful than the last."

"This is Rainier we're in love with?" Kira asked.

"Yes," Sean and I sighed together.

She smiled.

"*Sean!*" came Katiana's siren screech. "Come sit with us!"

I looked at Kira, resigned and putting the plastic top back on her dumb half-eaten salad. Angry heat flushed my cheeks, familiar from witnessing kids I lived with getting messed with. I stood up and pulled another chair to our table. "Want to sit with us?"

He waved to Katiana and sat beside Kira, pulling out a bag of trail mix. "So listen," he said. "I missed Natan. He play you any sweet guitar riffs while I was gone?"

I smiled brightly at Katiana, sat down, and pulled my chair closer to Sean's.

"Oh Jesus," Kira sighed. "Batter up."

Katiana clutched their Lululemon bags and glared hard at me via perfect cat-eye liquid liner. Sean got busy scrolling through his photos to show us the best shots of the bears.

"Muiriel," Kira sighed. "Please tell me you did not just invite that chaos to come sniffing around the tent flap of your life."

She was right. I was breaking self-imposed rules left and right taunting those girls on Kira's behalf; I was off the rails, but I couldn't seem to stop doing it. I tossed my granola bar to Kira. "They were already *in* the tent," I said. "They're all talk. They're nothing. Screw them."

"Screw who?" Sean asked. "Oh, wait, look, here's one of her eating blueberries! Can you believe how close we got?"

We?

I leaned near him to see the image on his phone: a beautiful, fat black bear nosing her way into a berry bush. "Who do you—did you hike with?" I asked as casually as I could.

"Myself. But halfway I met my mom."

"His *mom*," Kira said, eyeballing me.

"She's a park ranger in the Cascades; she's stationed on Rainier till winter."

I nearly choked. "Your mother is a *park ranger*?"

"She is."

"On Rainier?"

"Yes."

"But wasn't your dad also . . ."

"Yes, he was."

Kira nodded. "Royal family. That'll do."

Yes, it would.

"What the . . . ?" Kira suddenly stood and waved. "My aunt is here. Hey, Francine!"

I followed Kira's eyes, and of course there was only one Francine on the island; there she stood, chatting it up with the principal.

My foster parent. Talking to my school principal.

My heart seized.

The nearly adult, rational part of me understands that not every school administration official is out to get me.

However.

The neural pathways in my brain were carved by a lifelong master class of observing how adults interacted with the kids I lived with, and I learned as a very small child that principals, like police officers, are terrifying. Not as people, necessarily, but more who they *are*. What they do.

Suspicious of children in foster care, ready with blame and itching to "teach us a lesson," they are uniform and business-casual, sport-coat-wearing embodiments of capital *A* authority, hell-bent on muddying the waters of a kid's clean record because they can, and I have avoided interacting with them at all costs.

This is not logical, and obviously not fair. But the lizard brain does not want open and honest dialogue with those we are conditioned to mistrust—it demands only survival.

And so this thirty-minute school lunch was the most eventful and terrifying I'd ever experienced. I felt like crying. I *knew* I wouldn't be able to do this; I could never stay an entire year in one place—already I was on the principal's radar, and not only that, with one lie my potential friendship with Kira was over. Joellen was right; lying punches holes in your boat, and the truth is the ocean, rushing in fast as Francine walked to us. Her face brightened the nearer she came, and Kira went to hug her.

"Hello, my darling." Francine gathered Kira in her arms, and then she saw me. "Muiriel! I was just talking to the principal, and you're all set for Salishwood. Kira, are you two eating lunch to-gether? Hey, Sean!"

Kira was wide-eyed at me. "How have you already met every-one on this island? Francine is my aunt! Friend-aunt."

"I've changed this girl's diapers!" Francine bragged.

"Okay," Kira said "Trying to eat here . . ."

Holy hell.

"Hey, Francine," Sean said.

"Sean's mom is a dear friend," Francine said to my likely ashen face. She turned to Kira. "When did you and Muriel meet?"

"Weeks ago," Kira said. "When did *you* two meet?"

Francine looked to me, and her face changed. She caught up. But too late.

"I'm living with her," I said, back on the brutal-truth-no-reason-for-lying rails. "She's my foster. Person."

Sean watched Kira's face. Then mine.

Francine looked miserable.

I smoothed my paper lunch bag on the table with intense focus, folding it into crisp, perfect squares, smaller and tighter with each crease. Senior year, about to fall over the finish line unattached and self-sufficient, and now what was I doing with all these people? I *cared* that Kira would hate me for lying, that she would now disap-pear from my orbit because I'm in foster care and lied about it. I would never see her again, and I would miss her; it would matter.

Have friends, but don't "life or death" depend on them. Go out but not date; fostered, never adopted.

Emotional energy normally reserved solely for work, school, and gearing up to live on my own would be spent mourning the loss of a friendship I was already liking so much that I was starting flame wars with dumb-ass, run-of-the-mill mean girls? Giving a shit what this Sean guy thinks of me and agreeing to go to a movie with him? Why was I sabotaging my own exit plan?

"Muriel," Kira said. "You know what this means?"

I folded the paper bag into the last, tightest square. "Nope."

She took the paper from my tense hands. "We're like . . . cousins!"

What.

"Francine," Sean said, still looking from me to Kira and back to me—*looking out for me*—"want to see a picture of a marmot trying to steal my granola?"

"For sure." Francine leaped at the chance to defuse the situation and took Sean's phone to get a better look.

What was happening? Who were these people?

"Oh," Francine cooed in her Terry Johnson voice. "Look at that sweet baby. . . . God, I love a nice round marmot."

I slunk down in my plastic cafeteria chair, limp with relief, then tense with anxiety about the relief.

Giving a shit about friendships was exhausting. And it was only September.

"I really am sorry I blew your cover," Francine said for the third time that night at the dinner table. Six o'clock, every night.

"I don't know why I lied to Kira." I passed a few peas to Terry Johnson under the table.

"I do," she sighed. "Kids can be assholes."

I choked on water, and she whacked me on my back until I could breathe enough to laugh. "Are you allowed to say that?"

"Am I wrong?"

"No. But I know Kira wouldn't have been mean."

"You didn't know that. Maybe you lied because you could tell she's worth keeping."

I lined up green beans on my plate.

"Sean's a good kid, too. You meet at school?"

"Salishwood."

"Oh, of course," she said. "You know his mother's a forest ranger."

"I heard. Dad, too?"

"He was. Awful when he died."

I nodded, resisted asking more.

"I would have introduced you to Kira—maybe Sean, too—but I stopped trying to set my kids up with nice island kids years ago."

"Why?"

"Backfired every time. They resented my interfering, which I get. But then they purposely wouldn't be friends with the ones I knew, and missed out on the only kids who would have been good to them. I knew you and Kira would find each other."

I side-eyed her. "Oh, really?"

"Sure. She's smart, like you. And needing a friend."

"I don't need a friend."

She got up and went to the freezer, put an ice cream sandwich in my hand, and unwrapped one for herself. "Okay."

"Okay."

She looked at me. "How was it today?"

I shrugged.

"Did you call Joellen?"

"Yep."

"Think you'll make it?" she asked.

I shrugged.

"You will," she said. We ate the bars and did the dishes together, and I sat at the table to do some already-assigned history reading. The landline wall phone rang.

"Could you get that?" Francine called from the living room. "I got a DOL situation in here."

"A *what*?"

"Dog on lap! Terry Johnson can't be disturbed!"

I picked up the receiver. "Francine's house."

"Muiriel?"

Sean.

"Who is it?" Francine called out.

"It's Sean."

"Oh, good!" she trilled, blatantly delighted.

Oh brother.

"Muiriel," Sean said.

"Yeah. Yes. Hi."

" 'The mountains are calling and I must go, and I will work while I can, studying incessantly.' "

I closed my eyes and smiled.

"Muiriel. You still there?"

"You called to say the mountains are calling?"

"Maybe."

"Did you find that in an actual book or just Google it?"

"What if I Googled to find the source, then checked the book out of the library and read the actual letter because I knew you would ask me that?"

With all this smiling, my face was going to accumulate more lines in a matter of weeks than I've had all my life. Happiness was aging me. "Then I'd say you were right and . . . well done. Muir approves."

"Which one?"

"Both."

For someone not well versed in witty flirting banter, it sure was rolling off my self-deprecating tongue. I could *not* believe that he bothered to find Muir's words, the true circumstance of the quote, and that he wanted me to know.

"First day go okay?" he asked. "How was it after lunch?"

"It was fine. Good."

"Excellent. So . . . I meant it. About the movie. You know there's two movie theaters on this island?"

Seventeen years old and I'd never had a phone call like this. Never had a conversation like this, not once. Ever. My hands were all jingly. I sat on the kitchen stool.

"Can I—let me talk to Francine. I need to. First."

"Oh, right, okay. See you at school. Oh, and Salishwood after?"

"Yes."

"All right. We'll make a movie plan."

"Tomorrow."

"Good night."

"'Night." I sat in the chair and breathed.

"Didn't mean to be nosy," Francine called. "Just doing my job."

"I know," I said.

"He ask you on a date?"

"Not a date. Just out. Movie."

"We need to get you a phone. Remind me."

I groaned.

"Suck it up—I need to keep track of you. And you don't need to ask my permission to go on a date if I know the person."

"Not a date . . ."

"*Whatever.* Sean's a nice boy. You've got a curfew, just tell me when and where. You know that."

I stood up and went to the living room, where she sat Netflixing it up with lap-bound Terry Johnson. "But can I *say* I have to ask you?"

She looked up at me. "Yes," she said. "Of course. That's what I'm here for."

This woman had a habit of saying the right thing, always when I wished she would. It was interesting. And strange.

The mountains are calling, and I must go, and I will work while I can, studying incessantly.

John Muir wrote these words in a letter to his sister in 1873, while feverishly writing his first book and letters to the legislature begging for help to protect Yosemite Valley from irreparable harm.

The mountains were not calling to him to take a nice hike; the mountains were calling to him for help, and Muir was in a constant battle every moment he was awake, compelled to save the wild. Because no one else would.

I gathered my homework and climbed the stairs.

A lifetime in foster care can make a person really hate bunk beds. But there's a lot to be said for always having someone below or above you to ask in the dark, "Are you crying? Are you okay?" Which was always me. Asking.

I had a pillow under my arm, ready to sneak down to the couch, when a hollow scratching came from the stairwell. I shined my key chain flashlight, new batteries blazing, to the bottom of the steps, where two round eyes reflected in the blackness.

I carried Terry Johnson up the stairs, lifted him onto the bed, and he burrowed under the covers.

"Don't get too comfortable, sir," I whispered to him. "I'm only here for a little while."

I turned to lie on my side. Still just a lump under the blanket, he nosed his way into the crook of my bent knees, curled tight into a dog cinnamon roll, and slept there pressed against me all night.

Nine

"I TOLD HIM I'D GO to a movie with him. Just *us*," I whined to Kira after school the next day, my Blackbird seat near the window now firmly established as homework central before Salishwood.

"Well *done*!" She handed me half a scone, untied her apron, and sat across from me for her ten-minute break to eat her half. "I don't know that he's had a girlfriend since I've been here. . . . He was waiting for you."

"Not his *girlfriend*," I whispered desperately.

"Not yet. It'll drive Katiana insane. A date!"

I wrung my hands in my lap. "Just going out; it's not a *date*. I've never had a date; I can't *date* anyone."

"Never? Really? Like, legally you can't?"

"Not *illegal*." I laughed without meaning to. "Just not a great idea."

"Sorry," she said. "Francine's never had someone your age—only, like, fifth grade, younger. Summers here with my grandparents, we'd always play with her kids."

I sat up straight. "You played with Francine's *foster* kids? Where?"

"Uh . . . here? Francine's house. Our house."

Every neighborhood I've ever lived in, we were never allowed in any neighbor's house. Neighborhood kids were not allowed to come to our house to play with us. We were persona non grata to the moms whose kids had come out of their vaginas. They knew our houses, they knew *us,* and they kept their precious angels away.

"Francine told us she wasn't going to take any more kids," Kira said.

"My social worker was desperate. She talks a good line—she's like my agent."

"Good thing for me," she said, through a huge bite of scone. "For Sean, too."

"Okay"—I leaned across the table to her—"listen, I can't *date* a boy because it's a guaranteed way to screw up everything. I'll be out in ten months and on my own; I'm not trying to get knocked up so I have to buy a windowless van to run away in and travel the county busking for change because I'm just *so in love* with some guy who only wants me to help him cook meth and then I'm part of it and I end up in jail with him. Fuck that."

Kira's eyes were wide. "Okay, it's either don't date or . . . cook meth while pregnant in jail?"

"I mean. Basically. Yeah."

She stood and retied her apron. "Listen, man. I don't think Sean's into that kind of thing. Like, any of it."

"You can never tell," I sighed, and rested my head on my forearms on the table. "Until it's too late."

"Oh, my friend," she said. "You are living in an episode of *Jerry Springer* in your mind." She put her hand on my back. "None of that is going to happen."

I smiled into the table and sat up. *My friend.* Almost as dangerous as dating, but I couldn't help liking how it sounded.

"I have seen some shit," I said.

She nodded. "I bet you fucking have. I can't imagine."

My friend.

"Speak of the devil," she whispered.

Bells rang on Blackbird's glass door. And because life is insane, Sean stepped in. "Hey, Kira." He smiled. "Can I get coffee to go? Muriel, you taking the bus to work?"

I looked at my watch. "Yes." I wrapped the rest of the scone in a napkin.

"Good! I'll go with," he said. "You guys hear about the bonfire? Tomorrow night?"

Kira rolled her eyes. As if she or I would have heard about some DL popular-kid bonfire action.

"Tons of people are coming. Some soccer guys. Dale from chem club. Few second chairs from orchestra. I can give you the details—you want to meet me there?"

A bonfire? So, kids on a beach in the dark. No adults. Strangers, probably drinking, potential interactions with cops.

My worst nightmare.

Kira lit up. *"Tell us everything."*

* * *

I carry with me an AA sobriety coin.

I have never not been sober. That I can remember. I entered the foster care system as a newborn, no birth parents or blood relatives to claim or fight over me, all statistically prized and rare characteristics in an adoptable foster child. And yet, for the first year, I was passed from home to home.

Joellen waited until my thirteenth birthday to take me for ice cream and tell me the truth: I had scared away potential parents with a prenatal meth addiction. Which, for me, cleared up a huge mystery and was frankly understandable, but Joellen found it ridiculous.

"Meth is what you *want*," she fumed. "I mean, if you're going to be born exposed to something, alcohol is the absolute worst—opiates are bad, too, of course, but meth you can recover from. Look at you! You're perfect!"

I had some problems with math, but none with words. I needed absolute quiet when I took tests, but otherwise, yes, I had escaped nearly unscathed.

I stirred hot fudge into my two scoops of mint chip and felt bad for my mom, because—God—meth? If it really did what they say it does to your face and brain, she probably hadn't even known she was pregnant. Or had any teeth left. I stirred and stirred until my sundae was soup, all the whipped cream and everything a melted mess, and the pity dissolved and I was angry. The fuck was *wrong* with her? My mother had ruined my chances of anyone wanting me, ever.

And I was furious at Joellen. I wished I didn't know, because now I felt unclean. Ripped off. I pretended to be sick for my next weekly lunch date with Joellen, and she was miserable. She wished she'd told me sooner. Or later. Or not at all. She didn't know what to do, and neither did I. Finally, the third time I tried to ditch our date, she showed up anyway and drove us to the Seattle ferry dock and got me a pretzel, and we sat and watched the ferries come and go and the gulls and the seals playing, and she said she was sorry. She said to open my hand, and she put a shiny thing in it. Brass AA coin.

"Thirteen years sober," she said. "I'm so proud of you."

I understood later that Joellen wasn't just being ironic and funny; she was bitter. Furious on my mother's behalf and mine. Because my mom needed help and never got it. Because people who claimed they "wanted to be parents" were afraid of a baby with an illness I didn't ask for, acting on the understanding I did not *deserve* parents because I wasn't perfect. Punished for something I did not do, had no control over, and was not my fault.

"It's a lucky thing none of them got their hands on you," Joellen said. "You're too good for them. This is your medal for bravery and patience. You will always have me, and I know your true family is out there, still," she said. "They're waiting for you."

She didn't know that by then I had long since found mine; *I* was my own true family. I could never leave. I would always take care of myself. I was all I ever needed. I knew I could never be alone, because I was enough.

Friday after school I did my homework, collected eggs, fed Terry Johnson, had dinner with Francine at exactly six o'clock, and loaded the dishwasher, and then Francine practically shoved me out the door to walk to Kira's house.

"See you in the morning," she said. "Ten o'clock."

"I have Salishwood. I'll drop my stuff off here at eight, walk there, and then be back here by four. Okay?"

"Right," she said, scribbling it all on her wall calendar. "Got it. Eight and four."

"Eight and four."

"Salishwood still okay? Homework's getting done?"

"You've got the password—you can check whenever you want."

Poor Francine. She was not a fan of logging in to the school website to see my grades. I had to help her every time, and then there wasn't anything exciting; everything in on time, as usual. Marks fine, as usual. Reliably unextraordinary.

"I'll take your word for it. Don't you girls stay out too late."

"We won't."

I could not believe I was doing this. That Francine was not only letting me but sort of pushing me to walk to a classmate's house. To spend the night. Then off to a party destined to ruin my life . . . all on purpose. To be with Kira and Sean. For *fun*? I had my toiletry kit, my pajamas, the tangled chain in my pocket, and a burning pit of worry in my stomach.

But beneath the burning pit, I *wanted* to go. Maybe I could do this; I was nearly an adult, I had to stop being ridiculous—an adult could have fun with friends sometimes without losing her ability to exist independently in the world. Right?

The sun was setting as I walked to Kira's house, where she pulled me into the front door and booked it up the stairs until her mom called out, "Kira!"

She was Kira's height, hair up, jeans, sleeveless white blouse. They looked so much alike. Minus the tattoos.

So strange to be in a house that I didn't live in. That I was *invited* into. It was all warm wood and windows, full of pink sunset light and not much else. Some furniture, a couple of rugs, a few paintings on the walls. Like they hadn't finished moving in. But also—like everything that needed to be there was.

I have lived in some cluttered-ass places: messy bedrooms, stacks of boxes of who knows what, way too much furniture—people like to have a lot of *things*. And I mean, no judgment—all God's children and whatev. Francine's house was cozy. Still unnaturally quiet for me, but cozy and not as empty as Kira's, though not cluttered.

Kira's house was magnificent.

On a shelf in the stairwell were three little birds carved from wood and painted with muted, saturated colors. They stood in a row on delicate wire legs.

"Mom, Muir. Muir, Mom. We'll be in my room, okay, thanks!" Kira gestured for me to follow and took the steps two at a time.

"Hello!" I smiled at her mom and followed Kira, unsure of the protocol.

"Muiriel," her mom called to me. "It's so nice to meet you! Can I get you something to eat or drink?" I walked back down the stairs to shake her hand. From the landing above, Kira sighed.

"I'm fine, thanks," I said, feeling Kira's impatient urgency. "Thank you for having me."

"Francine is family, so you are, too. We're so glad you're here."

"Mom," Kira said. "We've got to get ready."

"Kira's dad and brother are in Tacoma tonight for a soccer tournament," her mom told me, "but they'll be so excited to meet you."

"Mom." Kira sighed.

"Francine's been really nice," I said, flushing bright.

"Oh, *good.*"

"Your paintings are beautiful." And they were. Ink and watercolor images washed in clouds of color and texture. Kira sat miserably on the top step.

"Aren't they?" her mom said. "They're Kira's."

"Okay, thanks, Mom—"

"We've been begging her to get back in art class. Maybe you can talk her into it?"

"Oh my God, *Mom*!"

Her mom smiled at me like, *Oh, that Kira.* "You girls have fun tonight; tell me when you go. Back by eleven, right, Kira?"

"Eleven, we got it, bye!"

We passed another really striking canvas on the way to her room, where she shut the door and fell onto her bed. "Sorry," she said. "I get embarrassed."

"She's so proud of you."

"She is. Sometimes she's just . . . a lot. Parents, you know."

I put my bag on a chair.

"Oh Jesus," she said. "I'm an idiot. I'm sorry."

"You're not, and don't be," I said. "I've had, like, twenty *sets* of parents. 'Nice but a lot' is a common variety."

"Muir."

"Kira. Seriously, it's okay."

Her room was under an eve, the roof slanted over it, and it was furnished as minimally as the rest of the house. Big bed, like the one in Francine's attic, shelf of books, dresser, and an easel featuring a canvas primed and painted all shades of pink. Surfboard in the corner.

"Twenty sets?" she asked. "Including yours?"

"Never had any in the first place. So, twenty in eighteen years of foster care isn't so much."

She sat on her bed, deflated. "Seriously. I am so sorry I said that."

"Okay," I said, and sat beside her, "but there's nothing to be sorry for; there's nothing to be sad about, and this is my first party, so you have to convince me that going is a good idea."

She brightened. "It *is* a good idea. We are *going*."

I stood and turned to take in her room. "I love your house. Not a lot of . . . stuff."

105

"Yeah," she said. "I guess having to burn or bury every family heirloom and treasure in a worthless attempt to convince everyone you're a loyal American in the hopes your own government won't drag your family to a concentration camp but it happens anyway and then you live for years on a dirt floor in an empty plywood shack in the desert with nothing and somehow you survive kind of turns your home-decorating aesthetic in a more . . . minimalist direction. For generations."

"Holy crap," I sighed. "I guess that would do it."

"Francine's and ours are both fourth-generation island families. Her grandparents saved my mom's grandparents' house, this house. Pretended to buy it, and they protected it from the government and looting and squatters, held on to the land, made the tax payments, so after the war my family was one of the few who could come home—who wanted to, even with white racist idiots still going after them, telling them to stay away. That's why Francine is family. Human decency is thicker than blood."

I took a pen from my bag and asked for a scrap of paper.

Human decency is thicker than blood. I tucked the paper in my bag. Kira held sweaters up around her shoulders to evaluate tattoo visibility.

"How did you convince your parents to let you get them?" I asked.

She smiled. Kind of sadly. "They had to take me to Vegas and bring their photo IDs and mine and my birth certificate to prove I was their kid and that they were giving me permission. It was a deal we made. Trade."

I sat on her bed and watched her put herself party-together. "Tattoos in exchange . . . for what?"

She pulled a sweater over her head and took her hair down,

went to the mirror at her dresser and put on some bright red lipstick. "It was them giving me something I wanted to try to get me to stop doing stupid shit. Bribery, but they were desperate. I had trouble back home. Los Angeles home. Trouble finding decent friends; like, discerning who was a friend and who was miserable and just wanted someone to be miserable with them. I did a lot of stupid shit. Expensive, professional ink was really the only currency they could offer me."

"Did it work?"

She shrugged. "Sometimes."

"What about when it didn't?"

Another sad smile. "Then we came here to live for good."

I could not fathom the scenario she was painting: parents who loved their kid so much they let her ink her body to try to keep her from something more self-destructive? Who loved their kid so much they uprooted their entire lives to get her somewhere safe?

"Do you miss it?" I asked. "Home?"

She paused her eyeliner swooping and turned to the surfboard in the corner. "I mean, this is home, too. But I miss the ocean. I surfed every day there. Every single day I was in the water."

"You're on an island in the ocean!"

She snorted. "Salish Sea. The Sound has no waves; I have to drive almost three hours for decent surf, through the Olympics and up into vampire territory."

"Do you get to very often?"

"Sometimes. Not as much as I'd like, but . . ." She started pulling dresses from her closet.

"You really made all those paintings in the living room?"

"Yeah. Not the birds—those are my great-grandmother's."

"Artistic lineage."

She went to a shelf in her closet and brought out a battered shoebox, which she put in my lap, then went back to the mirror. The lid was smashed in, a word, maybe a name, written in faded pencil across the top. *Gaman*.

Inside, in wads of white tissue, lay one more carved bird. A thick, flat piece of wood carved in sort of 3-D relief; delicate wire legs; black, white, and gray paint: a black-capped chickadee.

"She made them in prison, at Manzanar. They found a set of Audubon bird identification cards in an old *National Geographic* and carved them from scrap wood. She made paint from plants and berries; the legs are wire from screens over bars on the windows. They're brooches. Something pretty to wear around the detention camp." On the flat back of the bird, a safety pin was glued, still holding on even now.

A *grandma*. Making jewelry in a concentration camp.

The only grandma I had met personally was Zola's. She was slow-moving and soft. Entire families, Kira's family, imprisoned by their own American government for being born not white.

The familiar burn flared in my stomach. I wrapped the bird in its nest of tissue and tucked it safely beneath the lid, replaced the box on the shelf, and sat back on the bed to work the tangled chain in my left hand. The exhaustion of working overtime all your life to prove you are worthy of human dignity, just because the people in charge are ignorant and suspicious of the circumstances of your birth.

Kira held up dresses and blouses and tossed them on the bed beside me.

I pocketed the chain and ran my hand over a black silk slip dress. "Did she make more birds when she came home?"

"No," Kira said. "Nothing. She wasn't an artist before the internment, and not after."

"But . . . they're beautiful. She was so talented."

Kira shrugged. "Survival by art. We never knew she made them; we only found them in that box in the garage last year when her daughter, my grandma, died. My grandma was a baby in the camp; she said her parents never spoke about the war, ever. Their son, Grandma's older brother, died fighting for America in the war while America imprisoned the rest of his family at Manzanar. They brought his purple heart to Great-Grandma in the camp. Gold Star mother."

"Jesus."

"Seriously. Like, *Thanks for the fucking award. Does my dead son prove our loyalty now?* Spoiler, it did not. Poor little birds. They might have been thrown out. I'm saving the chickadee for a shadowbox. It's my favorite."

"Thank God you found them."

"No kidding."

"Hey." I said after a long, quite while. "What does your mom mean, 'getting you back in art class'? You're not taking *art*?"

She tossed some clothes off the bed and flopped down beside me. "First day last year, I go to class and Katiana are in there to easy-A fulfill the grad requirement—they have no actual interest at all in art—and I've got my portfolio from my other school because I have a huge fucking ego, and so the teacher is like, *These are great; I, a teacher, proclaim you are a talented art student,* and Katiana were like, *Fuck that girl, she thinks she's better than us; we are suddenly super interested in being the world's greatest artists who get attention from teachers,* so they started their daily campaign of messing with me, and I didn't enroll this year because why give them prime access to me for ninety minutes three days a week."

I got it. When every day is one battle after another, sometimes it's better to know when to nope out if the alternative is daily misery. "Won't they be there tonight?" I asked.

"Maybe. But it'll be crowded, and they'll be drunk; I can avoid them."

"You sure?"

"I want to go," she said. "I'm sick of avoiding things I want to do because of them. They can have art class, fine, but this is a coveted bonfire invitation, and we are going."

"I bet Sean could get them to stop."

She turned to look right at me. "*No.* I mean it. Please."

"Okay." I studied the pink canvas, barely begun but already beautiful. "It's not fair. *You* should be there, not them."

"Doesn't matter. I can paint better here in my room, away from those assholes. And another good thing is, I'm taking psychology instead and it's *fascinating.* We're studying the Myers-Briggs thing? It's this mother-daughter psychologist team. The mom met the daughter's boyfriend and probably hated him, so she got all compelled to make up these trait and personality categorizations based on Jungian philosophy. I have learned that I put the *J* in INFJ."

She was so smart. Hard to keep up. She obviously wanted to change the subject, so I followed. *"What?"*

"INFJ. Introverted, intuitive, feeling, judging. I judge the *crap* out of people and situations, which I used to think is a bad thing, but, truthfully, human existence essentially consists of going through each day making a series of value judgments. I judge that eating salad is better than scarfing cake. Not getting wasted is better than being a worthless drunk. Katiana are a pair of shallow bitches who lack self-esteem and empathy, so they work hard to make other people feel scared and miserable, which makes them feel better. I judge it, and it is so."

Her candor was so refreshing. "What other kinds are there?" I asked. "Myers-Briggs, what am I?"

She tipped her head at me. "I need to know you better. But I'll figure you out. Francine is an ISFJ: introverted, sensing, feeling, judging. It's a good one. Beyoncé is an ISFJ."

Fascinating. "Is there a JJJJ? Because that's probably me."

She laughed. "We'll make it one. But I have to say, it doesn't seem like you."

"No, it *is*. I'm the worst. I get mad when people decide who I am before they know me, but then I Judge Judy them all day long. I try so hard not to, but *people*. Adults."

"Well," she said, "you've probably earned that." She treaded carefully. "Were they all awful? The foster parents?"

"No," I said. "No, not them, it's just—everyone. The parents, the foster parents, the social workers. They all want to help, but then a lot of them act like it's their job to treat us, treat me, like . . . My Joellen, my social worker, she says they treat us like 'unreliable narrators in our own experience.' Like they know better and we can't possibly understand our own lives as well as they do."

She sat there. Still listening.

"I'm so close to being out. I'm good and obedient and under-standing year after year just so I have some leverage to have the tiniest bit of choice in what happens to me, but all this time is, like, whittling my patience away. It's sort of sharpening a . . . like, a stick of judgment that I use to stab anyone over the age of thirty."

No one at any school had ever been as nice to me as Kira was being right then, listening to all this. I hadn't said so much out loud to someone my own age in . . . possibly ever.

"I mean, metaphorically," I mumbled. "The stabbing part."

"Yeah," she said. "I figured. Is Francine good? Little kids always love her."

"She is. She's nice. Good food."

Kira looked relieved. "Has she made tea yet?"

"Oh my God, the lemon curd."

"The *brûlée*," she whispered. "Hey. *JJJJ* would be a nice tattoo."

"You think?"

"*No!* I'm kidding. Listen to me, words and letters are a gateway drug—tattoos are addictive, don't start. Oooh, want me to make your eyebrows glamorous?"

Lane change. I was grateful. "How are eyebrows glamorous?"

"They set the tone for your whole face." She grabbed a fistful of pencils and brushes. "Yours are great—dark, with excellent arches. I'll just amp them up a little." She sat me in a chair and stood studying my forehead, then went to work. "The key to eyebrows is, you want them to be siblings, not twins."

"Oh jeez," I said. But I thought of Sean. Like Kira's kindness, his attention was also unprecedented. Arguing with him made me feel smart. It made me think about how he'd already seen me wear every piece of clothing I owned. Twice. And that mostly he saw me sweaty, hiking, hair a mess. And then I hated myself for caring what he thought.

But like a new smoker, not yet addicted, I thought, *It's okay to have some of this—a friend, a boy to like. Friend, not "life or death"; go out, not date. Just having some fun for once. What the hell, maybe a couple of months, just for the school year. . . . I can quit anytime.*

She turned my face to the mirror. "See? You're glamorous!"

Who knew eyebrows were so powerful? I liked it. "Thanks."

"My pleasure." She got to work on her eyelashes. "Okay. You ready to go hang with a bunch of drunk, high douchebags and Sean?"

Drunk and high. God, this was a bad idea.

"Just so you know," she said, "I can be a designated driver. And I can keep a secret. If you want to partake. I'm not— I can't. Anymore."

Oh, relief. "I can't," I said. "Not ever. Not till I'm out, anyway."

She nodded. "I wasn't a drunk or anything," she said.

"Not my business."

"Surfing goes well with cutting school."

"Sure."

"And getting high."

"I can imagine." *I couldn't imagine.* "You patched up and ready?"

She revealed a big patch on her hip.

"How many?"

"Just this! God, Mom." But she smiled.

I looked down at my jeans and the gray argyle sweater I'd taken in to fit kind of small, over a long white layering tank. My style can best be described as middle-aged-librarian chic. Forgettable, my freedom linked always to anonymity. "Do you think— Could I borrow something to wear?"

She tossed the mascara onto her desk. "Anything you want!" She went to the pile on the bed, pulling out options best suited for an Italian mobster's widow, and most were entirely too small for me. We settled on some black pencil pants that were big and long on her but fit me fine, and a black cashmere sweater.

"You look like Audrey Hepburn!" she said. "Here, hold still."

She brushed some shadow on my eyelids, liner on my bottom lash line, then whipped my hair up in some sort of a twist-type maneuver and pinned it in place. She moved me to her full-length mirror and stood behind me. "Look at your eyes," she crowed. "All bright and dramatic. My finest work." Her phone buzzed and she read it. "Sean's at the bonfire, waiting for us at the road. Our own personal entrée to the Beach Gatsby. Let's go!"

"I'll be really careful with your sweater," I promised, and looked in the mirror. Bright and dramatic. *Sean.* My hands went all jingly.

"Oh, please," she said. "We're going to a secret bonfire—let's not ruin it by being careful."

Exactly what I was worried about. I pulled the chain from my jeans pocket. I wished I could wear it. It would look nice with this sweater.

"Ooh," Kira said. "Necklace? Put it on!"

I held it up for her to see the nest of tangled knots.

"Oh *no* . . . okay, hold up," she said. She picked up the red lipstick and put a little on my bottom lip. "Smoosh together," she directed. "Lucky you found me, because one of my rare talents is that I am exceptionally good at untangling things: earbuds, thread, Christmas lights—let me do this for you."

I hesitated, held it tight. Ten years, and I couldn't make it right; how was Kira going to fix it? What if she lost it?

"I can do it," she said. "Trust me."

Her smile was so true.

I dropped the tangled chain into her open hand.

Ten

KIRA DROVE HER MOM'S CAR, pointing out her favorite beaches and abandoned water towers, where, according to her, kids hung out to take their parents' blood pressure and glaucoma medications because "they just grab whatever they can and they're too drunk to read the prescription labels."

"Jesus, is it a high school or a rehab facility?"

"I'm serious!" she said. "Not a lot for kids to do on an island of farms, and it's not always easy to take the ferry into the city because everyone's parents have damn Find My Friends and if you turn your phone off . . ."

"Francine wants to get me a phone."

"You should let her! I could text you cat GIFs all day."

"Terry Johnson would never forgive me."

"Fine, dog GIFs, then." She pulled off to a wide shoulder and parked. A light bobbed toward us.

"Hey," Kira called to the light.

"Hey," Sean answered, and aimed a hiking headlamp like a flashlight. "You're here! Hi, Muiriel!"

I heard his smile in the dark. The black pants suddenly felt too small. Was this sweater trying too hard? And the updo-hair nonsense—I was not Audrey Hepburn. I was me, dressed like an administrative assistant on employee-evaluation day.

"Thanks for getting us in," I said.

"No problem, it's a free-for-all."

"Oh, Sean," Kira sighed. "How you can be so completely unaware of your place in the social strata of this school is baffling." She turned to me, aimed her thumb at Sean, and said, "INFP. Light on the *P*."

"Patience?"

"Perception."

He had a knit hat over his dark hair.

Oh my God, why did I let Kira put this makeup on me?

Above the thick stand of evergreen trees between us and the bay, sparks spun and flew. Wood and pot and vape smoke mixed in the sea air, and I followed Kira and Sean along a path into the trees. We walked together, following Sean's headlamp through the dark until the path opened to the wide, fire-lit beach. Dark forms moved, silhouetted against flames reaching into the sky. I closed my eyes and breathed in the woodsmoke, now mixed with sand and seaweed.

"We had bonfires all the time in Huntington Beach," Kira said. "Surf all day, light a fire, drink beer, smoke a bowl, fall asleep, miss school, get suspended. Good times."

Sean put one arm around her.

Her face in the firelight was wistful. "I miss it so much."

I stepped near her. "Well, I'm glad you're here now. And sober you is delightful. For what that's worth."

She bumped her shoulder against my arm.

"Sean!" someone called from the fire, and jogged to us. Tall, whitish-looking guy in a hoodie with a camera—an actual camera with a long lens—on a strap around his neck, trying to see our faces in the dark, and then he brightened with recognition. "Kira!"

"Elliot."

"I've wondered where you are. You not taking art this year?"

"No," she said. "I am . . . not."

"Why?" He turned to me and put his hand up in greeting. "Hey. I'm Elliot."

"Muiriel." His causal friendliness took the edge off how strange it felt being out at night, with other kids. At a *party*. In the dark I was just a regular teenager there to have some dumb fun and then go home after—for all anyone knew, home to a bedroom and a family of my own who knew me well and who in the morning would ask only, "Did you have a good time?"

Tonight I was one of them.

Elliot smiled at the three of us, nodded at Sean. "Ladies' man," he said. Kira and I laughed. Sean was dramatically affronted.

"You don't know! I could be rolling with half a dozen girls; I could be bringing them all here one at a time on my bike handle-bars because that's how much game I have."

Kira patted his arm. "Oh, honey, of course you could. No one's doubting your . . . game."

Elliot watched Kira's every word, clearly charmed. He lifted the camera to his eye. "You guys mind?"

We moved closer together, Sean's hand on my back, and the shutter clicked. No flash.

"Nice firelight," Elliot said. He turned to Kira. "Will you show your ink to Dave and them? They don't believe me."

"Believe you about what?"

"That you drew them . . . that your parents let you."

"Who is 'Dave and them'?" I whispered to Sean.

"Art geeks," he whispered back.

Art geeks? Even I knew that "Dave and them" getting invited to this but not Kira was simply *behold the power of Katiana.*

Kira studied Elliot. "Okay," she said. "Muir, if I lose you in the dark, meet at the fire at ten-thirty?"

And then, above the fire and voices, the already-familiar, distinct cackle of Katiana. Kira exhaled.

"Will you be all right?" I asked her, low. "Stay away from them."

She nodded. "I'll keep the fire between us."

"You *sure?*"

"I'll stab them with the stick of judgment." She raised her voice. "Sean, you keep track of Muir?"

"Yeah, okay! Sure!" he said. We watched her walk to the fire, Elliot beside and towering over her, and over most of the rest of the kids at the fire. Gangly. Artsy. Pretty cute. Kira was smiling up at him.

"Elliot's okay, right?" I asked Sean. "Not a drunk dumb-ass?"

"Oh yeah, no—Elliot's a good guy. We can keep an eye on her from a distance."

We watched the silhouettes in the firelight.

"Hey," Sean said. "She's not taking art?"

"Not anymore."

"Why?"

"Wanted a break, I guess."

"Huh." He frowned. "She doesn't really have a stabbing stick. Right?"

"Little joke," I said. A private joke. Between me and my *friend.* It would have been so easy to tell him Kira needed help with

118

Katiana, ask him to call off the dogs. But I'd promised her—and what was I even thinking, muddying the waters of my imminent life of freedom by caring so much already? I wasn't doing a good job of moderating my response to all this . . . kindness.

Friends, just not "life or death" dependence.

"Want to walk?" Sean asked.

I did.

A little way from the firelight, at the water's edge, we sat on a precarious pile of driftwood logs. Seattle's skyline, lit like Christmas, sparkled on the horizon. Fishing boats bobbed. The ferry cruised past, windows warm with light, sending little waves that lapped the rocky shore.

"What's it like living with Francine?"

"Lots of tea and toast."

"Sounds about right," he said.

"She's nice," I admitted. "It's okay."

"She's been really good to my mom and me. They volunteer for a bunch of random island stuff together; we've known her forever."

"You and everyone else. You've been here your whole life? On the island?"

"Born and raised. You were born in Seattle?"

"California. Seattle when I was a year old and since."

"So now it's just you with Francine?"

"And Terry Johnson. Eleven months and I'm out of foster care and on my own."

"Why?"

"Eighteen. I'll age out."

"Oh," he said. "Right. Then what happens?"

I breathed deep in the clean, cold dark. "Don't know."

"Where will you go?"

I shrugged.

"Really?"

"Really."

Down the beach, laughter and then music. Someone had hooked up speakers.

Sean sighed. "That'll get the cops out." We watched the fire. "Want a beer? Or a lemonade malt beverage *flavored for ladies*?"

I laughed. "I'm good, thanks."

"Then I am, too." He moved nearer to me. Salt air and Ivory soap. Lots of houses use it; I like the scent and the small white cakes with *Ivory* pressed in. Clean.

It was so easy at Salishwood, but here alone with him in the night and the water and the stars and the Ivory . . . my heart thudded.

"I'm . . . sorry about your dad," I said lamely. "Kira told me."

"It's all right," he said. "Kira's whole family, Tiana's mom, Francine—we've got people all over the island who make sure we're okay. It's been almost eight years, so I'm pretty much on the mend."

Tiana's mom. There it was, the obligation Sean was tending. Kira was right; he wasn't friendly with her of his own volition. Aside from that, the idea of a whole island of people watching out for you, up in your business, even in a nice way? Imagining it made me a little claustrophobic, but also kind of fascinated, and sidebar, why did I even bring his dad up at all? I take it from *Where do you live?* to *Let me reopen that wound about your dead dad from eight years ago?* Classy.

"So," he said, "here's the thing: Jason, whose job you have, was kind of a Natan apologist, but I feel like with you, I've got a partner in suffering, so thank you."

A refreshing turn, even if it did involve Man Bun.

"Absolutely," I said. *Partner.*

"And I've got this renewed motivation to . . . get rid of him? Somehow?"

His arm was against mine. I did not move. "Why does Jane keep him around? She's not dumb; she must hear his bullshit like we do. Doesn't she?"

"She must," he said. "I don't get it. And by 'get rid of' I mean, like, fired or something, not like put a hit on him."

"Yeah, I got that." *Get the guy fired?* Bold. I liked it.

"He's got another two years at Salishwood before he graduates, so we need to think of something or we'll be stuck with him. . . . I mean, if we're going to be around that long. If you are."

"Well," I said, pointedly ducking his question, "we can start with how he's terrible with the kids." I tied my shoe, using the opportunity to move my feet right beside his in the sand beneath the driftwood. He did not move.

"*Yes.* Which, by the way, you are a master class in how to be with kids. They listen to you."

My face went warm. "I've just had a lot of practice."

"Right," he said, instantly reticent. "That's . . . That makes sense."

"No, I didn't mean . . . I just like kids. Not just because of foster care. I worked at the library and tutored and all that. . . ."

"Oh, I know, I didn't think—"

I laughed. "Hold up. Let's— I won't be careful if you're not. Compliments just make me itch."

"Okay." He smiled, relieved. "To sum up: my dad's dead, you're in foster care, life is fucked, no walking on eggshells. Done."

If my eyes weren't truly bright before, they were dazzled as hell now. Infinitely more attractive than the *mysterious and sensitive, emotionally scarred boy who lost his father but just can't talk about it* was the *sensitive, emotionally mature boy who lost his father and admits it broke his heart and can freely appreciate how fucked up life can be.*

He was the antidote to my cornball-insincerity allergy.

"Finally," I said. "I know what my first tattoo will be. Will all that fit on my forearm?" I held my arm up and estimated the font size.

"Hey, you know, for someone who says she's never really hiked, your stamina is impressive."

"How do you— Are you *watching* me when you're supposed to be working?"

"Well, I mean, you're right there, I *see* you. . . ."

"You see Natan, too. You hanging out with him a lot by fire-light?"

His was the best, truest laugh I'd heard in forever. I think maybe in my life I've had a laugh deficit.

"Yes," he said. "Every chance I get, so I can learn his Gaia ways. Did you see last week, the beard ponytail? I think he used an orthodontic rubber band. He has to go."

"First of all, how dare you. I am going to hire him to play guitar and sing at all my important social functions. He shall honor me at my birthday with 'Tender Essence.'"

"Gross."

"And at my wedding, he will wear his long, luxurious hair loose and flowing, and he will serenade me as I walk down the aisle, also to 'Tender Essence.'"

"No. Nope. *Not* the wedding. You'll walk through trees, into a clearing with birds singing—that's how that will go."

What?

"Because you love the forest so much," he said quickly. "That's what I would think you would . . ."

I messed with the sweater clinging to my boobs in a way I wasn't used to, trying to even it out. "You're so lucky your mom is a ranger."

He nodded. "My dad always wished she would; she loved the wilderness as much, maybe more than he did. They hiked constantly. I was in a backpack in the mountains five days after I was born."

What a dream childhood. What a horrible loss.

"When he died, Mom took me out of school for a year and we went to California, to the Sierra Nevada. We just walked into the woods and . . . stayed. Till we felt better."

"Oh my God," I said. "Like Roosevelt."

"What's like Roosevelt?"

"*Teddy Roosevelt.* You walked into the woods." He shook his head. "You— Okay, Roosevelt's mother died, then later that same day his wife died—*two days* after giving birth to their only daughter."

"*No.*"

"On *Valentine's* Day."

"Jesus Christ, do not make this shit up."

"I'm *not*!" I said. "You were raised by two forest rangers—how do you not know this?"

"Because! Ranger training is about how to dig people out of avalanches and hand out violations for illegal campfires—I don't know! What happened after everyone died?"

"Well, what do you think happened? He went into woods. Like, went on long walks for days; he would disappear in the trees, away from people and machines and buildings and noise, and he had to ditch his newborn daughter for a while to do it, so that kind of sucked, but the point is—he walked into the wild, and it calmed his freaked-out heart. Being alone in the forest, out by himself, walking in the mountains brought him back to life. It saved him."

Sean looked out at the water. "That is insane."

"Oh, wait, so then years later he's president, and *who* begs Roosevelt to come to Yosemite to convince him to save it from destruction? And *who* in, like, half a day of walks through the valley gets Roosevelt to, of course, completely understand and be all, *I get it. I'm in.* And then ten years later Roosevelt fulfills his promise and makes Yosemite a national park, safe forever, all thanks to *who*?"

Sean turned to me, his face earnest, so beautiful, so close to mine. "Pinchot?"

No sound but the water on the sand and the muted laughter and music from the bonfire.

"Pinchot met Muir in person only *one* time," I said, low.

"I know."

"Talking some shit about letting sheep graze in and destroy protected reserves. Remember what Muir said to him?"

"Maybe."

" 'I don't want any more to do with you.' "

He smiled, his face half in shadow, half in firelight.

"Pinchot knew Muir was right," I said. " 'Earth hath no sorrows . . .' "

" '. . . that earth cannot heal.' Did I mention . . . where we walked after my dad, the Sierra Nevada? It was the John Muir Trail."

Oh Lord. "Two hundred eleven miles."

"Yes, ma'am."

My heart ached.

"Muiriel, who named you?"

"The nurses at the John Muir NICU."

"Do you have a middle name?"

"Medical Center."

He laughed.

Two inches apart.

"Are you ever scared?" he whispered.

"Of what?"

"Being alone?"

"I'm not alone."

Out in the dark water ship bells rang. I couldn't take it anymore. I turned my face to his and kissed him.

He was surprised for maybe half a second, and then he kissed me back.

"Wait," he said. "This doesn't count as a date, does it?"

I opened my eyes. "I mean, there's like thirty other people here, so . . . no?"

"Next Saturday?"

"Next Saturday."

He put his hand in my hair and pulled me to him.

"Muir?"

Kira's voice in the dark shot me up and away from Sean so fast he nearly fell back on the sand.

"Hi," I called. "It's me!"

"Sorry," she said. "I'm sorry, I need— I'm going to take off, but please stay. Sean, can you bring Muir home?"

Sean stood on the driftwood. "What's up? You okay?"

"Yes, I spilled beer all down my front. I'm going home to take a shower."

I climbed over the logs and seagrass to her. "I'm coming with."

Sean was right behind me.

"Muir, no, we just got here." Kira's voice was strained, and when I stood beside her, I could see she was near tears.

"Kira, stay," Sean said. "You can wear my hoodie, come on!"

She stepped back. "Thanks, but seriously, I smell like a brewery. I think I'm done for the night. Muir, you stay. Please."

I turned to Sean. "Listen. We have a packed schedule of braiding each other's hair and having tickle fights in our negligees to get to."

"Well, sure," he said. "That goes without saying."

"Muir," Kira groaned. "Stay . . ."

"Sean," I said. "Walk us out?"

"Of course." He put his hand on Kira's elbow. "What happened?"

She shook her head.

As we maneuvered around the bonfire to the road, Tiana's screech rose above the music, and I could see her shadow jumping from the crowd, waving frantically. "Bye, Kira, have a great night!" Then laughter.

Kira did not spill beer on herself.

Sean stood with his headlamp beside the road, and as Kira got in the car, he pulled me quickly to him. "She's not okay," he whispered.

"I'll find out."

"See you in the morning?"

"See you in the morning."

He kissed me again, fast, and opened the passenger door for me, and waved as we pulled away for the quiet, beer-drenched drive back to her house.

"How'd she do it?" I asked.

Nothing.

"Kira. Did she pretend it was an accident?"

She nodded.

"What did you say?"

Silence.

"Kira. *Why?* You are a badass; you could shut her up for good in two seconds!"

"You didn't say anything to Sean?"

"*No.* I didn't and I won't. But, Kira—"

She held the wheel tight. "Nine more months," she said, tears spilling. "After graduation real life will start, and I'll never have to see either one of them again. Just let me do it the way I need to, okay? Please?"

Already I was hatching a secret, elaborate plan to get Tiana expelled.

Friend, not "life or death" dependence. You'll be gone after graduation, too.

"You're right," I said. "You're right. I'll leave it alone. I will."

I will try.

Eleven

"MY HAIR STILLS SMELLS like smoke," Kira groaned. It was morning, the sun was barely up, not yet seven. "Now I have to wash my pillow."

"At least you don't smell like Natty Light anymore." I yawned from my sleeping bag on the floor.

"Oh, please," she said. "I'm sure it was European or a local microbrew. They've got their parents' money and highbrow taste in what they prefer to throw up."

We'd somehow gotten back to her house, clothes into the washer and Kira into the shower, without a parental run-in.

"Stay for breakfast? My mom would love to make you eat a thousand pancakes. She's as bad as Francine with the food pushing."

"I wish I could," I said honestly. "I'm off to Salishwood."

"Oh, that's *right*." She smiled. "Work: the walk-of-shame edition."

"We *talked*."

"Tell that to Katiana," she sighed. "You're on their radar, you know. They're jealous."

"They're toothless. If you told Sean—"

"No," she said.

"Okay."

"I'm serious."

"I know you are."

"Just be careful," she said.

I rolled my eyes. *"They* better be. Dime a dozen peaking in high school cookie mannequins."

"Accurate."

"But now, *Elliot* . . ."

She put her face in her smoky pillow.

"He seems *nice,"* I said. "And like he should be a forward on a basketball team."

She turned over and smiled wide. "He is one of those mythical sensitive, smart, straight boys."

"Sasquatch of the XY pool."

"And *talented.* He uses real film and takes actual photographs and makes these collages. . . ." Her smile was gone. "That was fun, last night. Hanging out with those guys. Art class people. Three of them want me to draw their tattoos."

"Kira. *You* should be in that class. Not those bitches."

Stay in your lane.

She picked up her phone. "Ugh. Someone called in sick. Work in an hour. No pancakes for anyone. Want a ride to Francine's?"

"Kira."

"If you want a ride we're going in twenty. Shower's down the hall."

"I'll shower at Francine's."

"Okay, then wait for me here. If you go downstairs, Mom will shove food down your gullet till you beg for mercy." She stumbled, still tired, to the door.

"Kira."

She turned.

"I need . . ." I could not believe I was saying it. "I need new clothes. I need to wear something different sometimes."

"Of course, look in the closet, you can borrow anything!"

"No, not just today. I mean, like, everything. New."

"Oh."

"I told Sean I'd go out with him on Saturday."

Her smile was back. "Okay."

"That's all."

"Okay. We can go shopping tomorrow."

"I don't need you to *Pretty Woman* me, I just . . ." Why was my throat getting tight? "I don't have anything . . . nice."

She stepped back in and grabbed my toes through the sleeping bag. "You will tomorrow. I promise."

"Okay."

"Sean working today, too?"

"Yes."

"Leave the eyeliner on."

I arrived, as always, twenty minutes early at Francine's, who smiled a lot and made sure I took a banana for breakfast. She did not comment on the eyeliner. Then I rode the bus to Salishwood, where Natan creepily did.

Kira and the Myers-Briggs had set my guilt free. Yes, I silently derided Natan nonstop, but my instinct was not "judgment"—it was, in reality, more of an objective evaluation of abundant evidence. And all evidence pointed to his creepiness. Which I was *not* obligated to put up with.

"Well, well, *well*," he sang. "Look who's a painted goddess this morning."

I rest my case. Who says three *well*s like that?

And what kind of jerk feels the need to comment, unbidden, on a woman's physical appearance *every single time* he sees her?

I filled my water bottle and wished Sean would show up. My habit of arriving everywhere early was great for my foster care punctuality reputation, but not great for avoiding Natan, who seemed to never not be at Salishwood.

"Muiriel, you are a natural beauty," he said. "There's no need to conform to society's patriarchal norms for the world to see you. Because we already do. We see you—the *true* you."

I turned and walked to the lodge to get the day's lessons lowdown from Jane and put some space between me and Mr. Anti-Sephora. The schedule was posted on the corkboard near the office. *Leave No Trace Ethics 10:00 a.m. Natan*

"Oh, dear God, no," Sean said behind me.

I turned. "You need to tell me when you're getting here from now on," I said. "I can't deal with him alone; he is horrifying."

"Done," he said. "From now on we'll walk together."

"In the interest of Natan avoidance."

"Yes."

Then we stood and smiled dopily at each other so that I had the actual thought, *Who the crap* am *I?* Eyeliner aside, those girls—all of them, any of them—were so beautiful. Delicate, glossy hair, makeup always pretty. What could he possibly see in me? And what was I doing worrying about it? Disregarding a lifetime of careful avoidance of just this sort of distraction from my goal of aging out independent and unencumbered? Where was my backbone of unwavering self-esteem?

Alone in the lodge Sean kissed me, two days in a row kissing a guy, praying I was doing it right and thinking, *Seriously, who the hell am I?* His strong hands, that dark, shorn hair, those dark eyes—to be fair I could have resisted all that. Beautiful boys have always adorned the halls of Seattle's high schools. But his beauty combined with his wilderness prowess and his admiration and respect for the forest and for my encyclopedic knowledge of the wild and Muir's place in it, which everyone else my age I've met thinks is ridiculous but he thinks is enviable and somehow means I'm really smart, which then only seems to make him like me more?

That's where my backbone went.

We hiked with a wily group of fifth graders, and then everyone gathered on the lawn around Natan, who was sitting like a benevolent overlord on a tree stump and soaking in the attention of all the eleven- and twelve-year-olds required to listen to him. "So," he said, rubbing his long bony hands together, "Leave No Trace Ethics. Who knows what we should leave behind in the forest when we hike or camp?"

The kids were excited. "Footprints!" they shouted.

Natan closed his eyes. "Hands, please, one at a time."

"Natan, give them a break," Sean sighed. "They're excited."

Thank you.

"Everything we bring in, we pack out"—Natan barreled forward—"and how do we pack out all the things we bring in? Let's start with feces."

Oh, we definitely started with feces. Rolling it in cat litter, bagging it, tucking it into the backpack. His was a unique talent for making each detail as sordid as possible.

The kids tried for a while to not laugh, and then they gave in.

"Children," Natan barked. "This is imperative. Especially young ladies, you need to understand that when the time comes for your moon blood—"

The boys howled. The girls were suddenly miserable.

"Whoa," I shouted from my place in the back of the group, and I stood. "Natan, stop. Now."

He gave me his sympathetic *You poor, uneducated girl* look. "Muriel, I understand the male-dominated world has led you to believe that your monthly blood is not an appropriate topic, but please understand—"

"No, *you* understand. Stop saying 'monthly blood'! The male-dominated world is *you*, co-opting a normal thing and turning it into your gross 'moon blood' Mother Earth crap. Just say 'period'! Just say 'menstruation'! Use actual words! All of you boys, shut it right now."

They did. Eyes wide.

"Listen," I said. "There is nothing gross about having a period; it's why every one of you was born, so get over it. This is wilderness ethics, we're not going into the entire process of the thickening of uterine lining and how it is expelled, but I'd suggest you all go read a few pages of a biology book or ask your parents to give you the lowdown. And boys, figure out your squeamish little insecurities before you come back to this class. That goes for you especially, Natan."

He shook his head at me from his tree stump altar. "Muriel," he clucked. "Let's try some harmony. We are all brothers and sisters here."

"Natan," Sean said. "We *get* it. We wrap and pack out sanitary products just like any other tissue or trash. Move on dot org."

Thank you, I mouthed to him.

And he winked at me and then I died.

"Young ladies," Natan said. "If I may speak frankly, you might take a more selfless tack. I suggest you refrain from exploring the wilderness altogether during your special time. Blood attracts predators such as bears and mountain lions. No need to put the rest of us in danger."

My head whipped around to Sean, who was already on his feet.

In thirty seconds Sean had Natan's arm in a firm hold, leading him to Jane's office, and I had vehemently debunked the bears-and-blood bullshit for the kids, who seemed to understand and be properly creeped out by Natan in the first place, which helped.

"What about sharks?" a small girl asked. "Can I swim in the ocean if there's blood?"

"Yes," I said. "Of *course* you can. Bears and sharks are not out to get you; don't ever be afraid to explore the world. People, please listen: If any adult ever tells you that you can't do something because you're a girl, or because you're a boy, or because you're having a normal bodily function—always be suspicious. Because they are *lying.* Trust yourself. Find the truth. And remember to pack your poop out of the forest."

They laughed. They were smart. They got it.

When the kids had packed up and the buses were gone, I joined Sean in Jane's office, Natan nowhere to be seen.

"I'm sick of running interference with him," I said to her. "He lies to the kids, and he's inappropriate in all kinds of ways. . . ."

"Document it," she sighed. "Write everything down. I've spoken to him; he's promised to try harder. Okay?"

"But—"

"I appreciate your concern, Muir, I do, and I'm handling it. Okay?"

Not angry, she seemed more . . . resigned?

Like Kira.

"Okay," I said. I walked with Sean to a granite boulder tucked into the trees, and we sat together to drink water, eat trail mix, and spy.

"Something is up," Sean said. "Jane is too smart for his shit."

"It's like he has something . . ." And then there he was. Natan walked from the parking lot straight to Jane's office. "Over her?"

"Come on," Sean whispered, took my hand, and we ran, crouching low, to hide beneath the open office window.

Even in the spy excitement I was preoccupied with his hand holding mine.

Get yourself together! Come on!

Jane's voice was hushed, but aggravated. "These are *children*. There are specific ways to interact with them. Boundaries, Natan. I need you to run everything by me before your next class, and do *not* go off script."

"But—"

"If schools stop sending kids for classes, we can't stay open."

"I didn't say anything wrong! Who said I did?"

"Natan," she hissed. Sean's eyebrows shot up. We'd never heard that tone from Jane. "No more. Please don't pretend this is the first complaint I've gotten; I can't keep defending you. I love my brother, I love you, but I'm not willing to lose my job because my nephew refuses to interact appropriately with little kids who just want to learn about nature."

"But a woman's menses *is* nature—"

"Natan!" Full voice. She sounded exhausted. "Go home. Please."

A silent pause.

"Honey," Jane said, her tone softened. "Natan, please don't cry."

Oh my God, I mouthed. Sean shook his head in disbelief.

"I don't feel safe right now," Natan sniffed. "I feel like you're threatening me. This isn't how family treats each other."

Safe? A-plus manipulation. Yikes.

"Oh, sweetie," Jane said. "Of course we're family, you matter more than anything. I promised your dad I'd help you graduate, and I will. I *am*. But I need you to help yourself; I need you to try. Okay? Please."

"I *am* trying!" he wailed. "I am exploring my options for true happiness in life, and I'm real sorry it's taking too long and inconveniencing everyone so much."

"Honey, I know he's hard on you, and I understand you're still . . . exploring. But don't you want to have a job one day? Move out of your dad's house, have your own place, live an independent life?"

"Dude is like thirty-two years old," Sean whispered near my ear.

"Sure," Natan practically spit. "As soon as *you* get an *independent life* and stop borrowing money from my dad."

A chair scraped the floor. We bolted and watched from the trees until Natan was safely gone, and then Sean walked me all the way to Francine's.

"I mean . . . ," he began. "I feel dirty."

"Me too." I sighed. "And I think we're stuck with him."

"Family," Sean said. Then he took my hand again and pulled me to him, hugged me right there on the side of the road. "Not all of them are," he said, "but that's a super fucked-up one."

"Oh, I don't know," I said. "I feel like I can say, with some authority as an observer, that this one is of a pretty common variety."

"That's depressing. And you do have the authority."

"What would your dad have said about that whole . . . situation?" I asked.

"Plenty. None of it real considerate of Natan's delicate sensibilities."

"What about your mom?"

He smiled. "She'd be pissed at the brother. And Jane. She'd say they made him who he is and now they don't get to be pissed he's a grown man living at home 'searching for his happiness.' My parents would give me a tent and send me to forage in the woods alone rather than have me in Natan's situation."

"Learned helplessness," I sighed. We walked until we reached Francine's road. "Your mom sounds like my kind of person."

"You're definitely hers." He looked down the road to Francine's house.

"Want to come in?" I saw her car was gone. "Except wait, she's not home."

"Shouldn't I?"

"Not a good idea," I said.

He kissed me. "We'll figure out Natan. Okay?"

"Okay."

"See you Monday?"

"Monday."

Sunday afternoon at the Island Thrift Shop was the happening place—for moms and bored, tantruming kids after church.

"You sure you don't want to go to a regular store?" Kira asked, pushing aside hangers on the "Ladies' Blouses" rack with more force than necessary. "Don't get me wrong, I love a good thrift shop find, but if we're revamping your whole wardrobe, I gotta tell you: this island has a big retired people population and they do a lot of the donating. . . . It's going to be mostly 'active adult senior' style."

"Not everything."

She held up a coral-hued turtleneck shirt.

"Okay, not a winner, but keep looking. There will be gems in here, I'm telling you."

"Lot of jewel tones, for sure," she sighed, and pulled out a deep royal-blue silk blouse with an attached neck bow. "Come on, man."

"Okay," I said, "but it's three bucks! And see, I take off the sleeves and the bow and hem it, and it'll look—"

"Like a weird thing an assistant principal would wear. Muir. You're perpetually annoyed at old people but then you're determined to dress like one. Please let me show you the ways of bargain hunting for stuff that was made in this century."

It was too humiliating to explain that a bargain for her would be two weeks' worth of allowance for me. Never had I wanted clothes that might draw, if not attention, then at least appreciation for not being the same thing I'd worn the day before. And the day before that.

I would never say it out loud, not to Kira, not to Francine or even to Joellen, but I wanted to feel like Kira did every day; the way pretty girls feel and take for granted. Wanting that embarrassed me. I shouldn't need it. That kind of external validation is not what an independent person requires. But I wanted it.

My plastic wallet featured a picture of Disney's Bambi. He and I, just two orphans looking to figure shit out. It was full of some cash I was willing to part with. But it had to stretch far.

"You just need some stuff to mix in with the clothes you already have. Like, okay, jeans but then not the sweater-vest. T-shirts but maybe with a skirt. Get kicky. You're seventeen. We'll never look this good in our lives again, ever."

I sighed. "Okay. One regular store, but if it's too much we're coming back here."

She tossed the blue blouse on the rack and pulled me out the door to run three blocks to the shops on Main Street.

"Here," she said, pushing past tourists to a rack shoved in the corner of a tiny boutique. She held a beautiful pale pink sweater under my chin. "Try this. And this." Skirts, jeans, three tops, and the sweater.

"Did you even look at the tags?" I whispered.

"*Yes!* I know what I'm doing, get in there."

In the dressing room I read the tags and felt like crying. Everything was as expensive as it looked. *Jesus, Kira.* My eyes predictably welled up.

"Do your math," she called through the door of the room next to mine. "Seventy-five percent off. Nothing will fit, but you can fix that, right?"

I sniffled. "Seventy-five?"

"Yes! They're last season's, returns, but it's all new and cute. There may be a stain or a small hole, but they'll give us a bigger discount for it, and it's all workable."

Hope crept back in. "You are magic," I said.

"Not magic, it's that I'm not made of money, either," she said, yawning. "I've been at Blackbird since five this morning."

I stepped out of the dressing room and knocked on her door.

She opened it, wearing a black tank dress that was hanging off her, and I put my arms around her small shoulders and hugged her.

"Oh, Muir," she said. "It's just clothes."

"I love this sweater."

I'm going to miss you when I go.

Back at Francine's I washed everything and carried Terry Johnson up the stairs to the big room, where he lay on the bed to watch me pin and hem and sew.

My suitcase was open on the floor. None of this new stuff would fit in there. I would have to get rid of a lot of things.

The blackbird-collection pillowcase took up prime real estate. I pulled it out. Held it. Wished I had the tangled chain to work on.

If I got rid of my clothes and kept only the new ones, I'd be back in the same stupid situation, three or four outfits on rotation, day after day. If I kept what I had, like Kira said, and mixed things in, I'd have an entire extra week of combinations.

I looked at the dresser. Wide, empty drawers waiting to be filled. *Unpack! Move in, get comfortable. I'm all yours.*

The pillowcase went back in its hiding spot beneath the socks.

I folded everything new as it was altered. A nice, neat stack *on top* of the dresser. Not in.

* * *

I carry with me a sewing thimble. There is an urban legend that Albert Einstein, in an effort to save his brainpower for only crucial science and math thoughts, eliminated the daily decision-making of what to wear by buying a whole bunch of the same outfit: ten white shirts, black coats, pants, socks. A life uniform. This has been proven total nonsense. Plenty of photographs show the guy in swanky vests and sweaters, even sandals in later life. It's just a made-up story, like the one about him telling Marilyn Monroe he wouldn't have a baby with her in case it got his looks and her brains (a bullshit, sexist story; Marilyn supposedly had a super-high IQ but unfortunate taste in men).

Anyway.

I like that idea, not having to think about what to wear every day. I like eliminating being sad or mad if I lose something, when someone takes my stuff, steals my shirt, my shoes, I lose my socks in a new house's washing machine or in a rushed move. So I took some saved allowance and work money to the mall and bought myself an Einsteinish wardrobe: three blue and three gray scoop-neck T-shirts, three pairs of jeans, one pair of black pants. One pair of shorts. Indoor shoes. Outdoor shoes. Done. All replaceable. Any of it can be worn with anything else, and most of all, it is a wardrobe that, like my entire existence, stays safely beneath the radar: utilitarian, muted, inoffensive, breaks no rules, draws no attention.

Clothes one loves and chooses because they fit and look good are the luxury of a free person, a person who depends solely on herself, who can decide where they live and with whom, and can screw up and break rules and get in trouble, with only herself to answer to. A wardrobe a person really loves is for someone who has somewhere to keep it—a closet, in a place where she can stay as long as she wants.

A mom I lived with when I was twelve had a sewing room. An entire room dedicated to fabric and a sewing machine, and she let me play with a needle and thread and scraps of cloth. She didn't exactly show me how to do it, but I figured out that if I found something to wear at a thrift store that would work for the Einstein wardrobe but that maybe was too small or too long, I could fix it. Make it fit. She gave me all the thread and needles I needed.

But what I really wanted was her brass thimble. I loved how it kept her fingers safe from needle pricks, how shiny the brass started and how warm the patina after she used it for a while. She had a ton of them, like a person with a bunch of reading glasses lying around the house. She was nice. She never yelled at the kids; she always had many types of bread for toast. I liked to sit and listen to the hum of the sewing machine when she worked on patterns for dresses for herself or the little girls. I began to like living there with her.

So I called Joellen, who came to take me to a new house, where, she confirmed, no one knew how to sew.

As I carried my suitcase out to the curb, there in the dust near the baseboard in the hallway was a lone thimble. I picked it up and took it. Protection from hurt.

Twelve

THE FOLLOWING SATURDAY, after a week of successfully avoiding Natan at Salishwood and unsuccessfully sneaking in any decent time with Sean there or at school, I raced off to the bus to get to Francine's so I could spend the next four hours obsessing over *Oh my God, we are going on a date.*

Terry Johnson trotted out to watch me hose the mud off my walking shoes and place them neatly on the porch. He followed me to the kitchen, where Francine stood peeling potatoes at the sink. "Look what I found!" she said. On the table was a phone.

"You *found* this? Where?"

"At the phone store!" She wiped her hands on her apron and sat with me to unbox and figure it out. "So this is what they call Android, and I don't know what that means, but you can text and call and there's maps, too. And I like to take pictures with mine. You can press this thing and take a picture of yourself!" She leaned near to me, held the phone up, and took a picture of her smiling, me trying not to laugh.

"Francine," I said. "I know how phones work; I just don't want one."

"Too bad. Look, I put my number in, Kira's number, her parents' number, Sean's mom's number—"

"I haven't even met her!"

"You will; you'll love her. Now, look, this is what's called an app. . . ."

"Francine." She put the phone down. "Have I been bad at contacting you? Have I been late?"

"Of course not," she sighed. "This is for *me*. And you. I get a stipend from the state every month, you know that. It's for your care and necessities, and I'm deeming a phone a necessity. I need to know where you are. I need to be able to get to you if you need help, and Joellen does, too."

"Yes, but—"

"And don't you want to talk to your friends?" She slid the phone to me.

"I can't have a monthly bill and a permanent number. I'll get all that someday, but being with you is temporary. I'm nearly out—I need to save the money I've got. Please."

"The stipend is *your* money. Your allowance comes from it. All of it belongs to you. Your job is going to school, the state of Washington can pay for the phone."

"Yes, for now, then in a few months I age out and I'm stuck with a bill before I have a job that can afford it; I'll miss the payments and ruin my credit."

She looked at me so sadly. "Listen," she said. "Listen to me now. This thing is in my name. I won't let your credit be touched."

She knew better than that. Kids in care get our credit stolen and screwed with all the time. Birth parents, random CPS workers—they have our Social Security numbers, everything. I check mine twice a year on free websites at the library. Thankfully, still nothing.

"I don't know."

"Muriel. Somewhere along the line your mother needed help. But instead of getting help, she was trapped into an impossible situation and made the only decision she knew to make. Now, if the government that we all pay taxes to had deemed helping your mother a priority, things may have turned out differently."

God, she gets it. She knows.

"Okay. So that means I have to have a phone?"

"It means they're pitifully reimbursing you on the back end. This money is the government saying, *Sorry we didn't help your mom take care of you in the first place, but here's some money so someone else can do it, and part of being taken care of means you having a phone, so here you go.* You kids get screwed around every which way, and a little money for a phone to keep you safe and let you text an emoji to your friends once in a while is a small consolation, but it's all they're ever going to offer, so I say take it."

She was as angry as Joellen. Mad. Maybe as mad as me.

I could not stop the warm rush of affection that surged into my chest.

Still, the idea of the constant connection, this obligation, made me nervous.

"But everyone will have my number, and when I leave I'll have to get a new one. That's just confusing."

"And *that* is you being ridiculous. Quit grasping at straws—it's a phone, not a tracking device."

"It kind of is. I've heard about Find My Friends."

She got up and brought me a bowl of tomato soup and buttered toast.

"People can learn new numbers. I won't make anything worse for you. I promise."

Normally that word makes me preemptively furious. *Promise.*

It didn't sound so bad when Kira said it.

Sounded okay from Francine, too.

In the bedroom I unlocked the phone and opened the photos.

Francine and me at the table. Then twenty-three close-ups of Terry Johnson napping.

The movie theater was small and old, near the water and walking distance from Francine's, so we did. Sean and I. To go out. *Not a date.* He came to pick me up wearing jeans and a gray sweater. I was nervous in my new pink one, black leggings, and a skirt. Hair up. Eye makeup from Kira. Francine hugged him, asked how his mom was doing (*Great, thanks*), and put Terry Johnson in his arms.

"What time is the movie over?" Francine asked.

"Ten-thirty."

"Okay, so home by eleven."

"Yes," I said. "Home by eleven."

"Call if you're going to be even a minute late."

"Okay."

"Ooh, or you could text!" she said, her eyes lit with excitement.

"It'll be a surprise."

"Wait, you have a phone?" Sean perked up.

Francine rushed to give him the number, and then the phone buzzed in my pocket. "You kids stand there, let me take a picture."

"Francine," I whined. "Come on!"

"For Joellen!"

"No way."

"Fine." She took Terry from Sean to give to me. "Say goodbye to Terry Johnson at least."

I held his face to mine and kissed his snout. "Wait for me," I whispered. "I'll tell you all about it when I get back."

"Oh," Francine said. "Got it! I'll send it to Kira; she'll love it. Look!" She held her phone to Sean.

"Awwww," he said. "You two are in love!"

I put Terry on the sofa and pushed Sean to the door. "We're going now. See you at eleven."

Off the porch and safely at the road, he said, "Check your texts."

you look beautiful in pink

Beautiful? I nearly passed out. "You . . . look beautiful in gray." I struggled to get myself together.

"I've been told I'm an autumn."

"By who?" We crossed the road and onto the path to the theater.

"Took a quiz in a *Cosmo* at the dentist."

My phone buzzed again. Kira.

OMG YOU HAVE A PHONE HAVE FUN TONIGHT

I held the text up for Sean. "What is this?"

"That is . . . time to turn off your phone."

The path opened to hug the shoreline, Sean leading the way, no room to walk beside him until we reached the sidewalk near the theater, and then he took my hand.

"Does your mom not like it when you're out on a school night?"

He thought for a minute. "I'm not in the habit of going out a lot. With people."

Does people *mean girls?* "You mean, besides bonfire parties?"

"I mean, just with one person."

"Oh." *Why?*

"Also my mom isn't around a lot until December. She mostly lives at Rainier in the ranger cabins, but she's back for winter soon."

I stopped walking. "Wait—not around a lot, like she's not *home*?"

"Yeah."

"How much is 'a lot'?"

"Well. She's home from December until the first of April, then she's on the mountain."

My hands hung limp at my sides in disbelief. *"What?"*

"What what?"

"You live *alone*."

"No, she's just working."

"Three hours away, on a volcano!"

"She comes home some weekends, at least once a month, and she's home all of winter and some of spring. . . ."

I caught up with him, almost to the theater.

"Do you live in a house?" I asked as we walked. "Do you have raging parties all the time? Do you cook? You do your own laundry?"

"Yes. No. Yes. Yes."

"Huh," I said. "Wow."

What if CPS comes and finds you underage, living by yourself in a house?

"It's a ranger's dream assignment," he said. "Kind of a miracle to get a job so close to home, and everyone wants Rainier. She had my grandparents stay with me while she worked in Utah and

Montana and Wisconsin for a while, mostly being a guide in boring historic houses when what she really wanted was to be on a mountain. When she got Rainier a few years ago, it was winning the lottery. She came home after the first season and said, *I'll be here till I die.* My aunt stayed with me for Rainier, when I was younger, but now I hold down the fort."

I had stared for hours at library book pictures of Rainier's grassy snow-dappled fields, evergreens and alpine wildflowers, hillside creek beds of crystal water splashing over rocks and tumbling down sheer cliffs in roaring falls and the gorgeous snow-capped peak, rising above a veil of mist I could see as I walked Seattle's streets. It hurt, knowing how close it was and what it looked like, and I ached, wishing I could be there.

"I don't blame her," I said.

"Me, either. That's why I want to go to UW for environmental science, and if Natan gets the hell gone, I can apply for their master's program with Salishwood. Because then I might have a better chance for a mountain position near home, maybe even Rainier. What are you smiling about?"

"You in a ranger uniform on a mountaintop. I like it."

He smiled back. "Hopefully. Where are you applying?"

"Applying?"

"College."

"Oh," I said. "I'm not."

"You're not?"

"Look!" I said. "No line." The sidewalk in front of the box office was empty, a hopeful sign we'd have good seats. Except the movie had started twenty minutes earlier.

"We walked too slow," I said. "I distracted us with my demands for your in-person AMA. I'm so sorry."

"I'm not."

In the frozen yogurt place beside the theater, the only other thing open after 5:00 p.m., Sean demonstrated a sophisticated layering technique of yogurt, then gummy bears, more yogurt, Oreos, and so on. Recipe of an eight-year-old. Or a seventeen-year-old living without a parent around. I filled my cup with vanilla and strawberries and mint cookies and we walked to sit in the near dark on rocks at the water's edge, but this time in the light of the setting sun, watching ferries cruise to and from Seattle.

"I have to say, I thought living on an island would feel—smaller? Trapped? But the open water, the forest, so many stars. Feels big."

"*Yes,*" he said. "Everyone I grew up with can't wait to leave, and they give me shit for this, but I don't want to. I would miss it. I mean, I want to travel and explore, but this is *home.* My mom's got the perfect life: mountain in the summer and fall, home on the island for winter and spring."

"Nothing wrong with that," I said. "You're rooted."

"I am."

A pang of something rang in me. An ache.

Jealousy?

"Was your dad on the same ranger schedule?"

"He worked different mountains and parks every season. He must have been gone a lot, but I mostly remember him home, the three of us backpacking."

"You got the nature/nurture combo," I said. "What if you'd been like, *Screw you guys and this wilderness crap. I'm going to be a tax attorney and there's nothing you can do about it?*"

He laughed, sending nearby gulls flying. "I'd like to say they would have said, *Whatever makes you happy, have fun!* But honestly, they would have been totally disappointed and had a—what's the drug-addiction thing where they get you in a room and tough-love-style tell you you're fucked up?"

"An intervention?"

"Yes! *We love you too much to watch you destroy your life learning tax codes; here's some CLIF Bars and a pup tent—you're going into the woods for six weeks to get clean!*"

"I'm so sorry he's gone," I said.

"Thank you."

"They sound like dream parents. You're so lucky."

"Do you know anything about yours?"

"No."

"No names, nothing?"

"Hospital found me in a lobby."

He moved closer to me.

"Do you ever think about doing the 'spit in the tube and mail it in' DNA deal?"

I shrugged. "No."

"Not even to see . . . like, what ethnicity you are and what cancer you'll die from or, oh, what if your ancestors are from Ireland and then you can go to Celtic fairs and do a maypole without culturally appropriating?"

His straightforward lack of sentimental bullshit was delicious. The main thing Joellen worries about is my being "allergic to sentimentality," which I see more as an allergy to cornball fake sincerity. Creepy words give me hives. When people's voices get all breathy and quiet and they say stuff like *I see you* in reference to emotions, or describe feelings as *tender,* I get the major icks. I never lasted more than a day in a therapist's office, and Joellen eventually believed me when I explained that, yes, I like people, I can love them, I just don't want to talk about it. People say all kinds of shit they don't mean. Creeptastic words don't indicate emotional health. Case in point: Natan. Sean seemed an unlikely candidate to call emotions *wounds* or insist that we *dialogue* about something.

"Maypoles are German," I said.

"Okay. But don't you want your genetic code to reveal the mystery of why you hate cilantro?"

"Are we doing *my* AMA now?"

"Maybe."

His straight, dark eyebrows; those near-black eyes in that handsome, kind face; his lean, strong, mountain-climbing . . . *self.* Then he's smart and funny, too? Being so near him was making it difficult to keep up with the conversation.

"I *do* hate cilantro," I said, "and it's because it tastes like dishwater probably does. I'm pretty sure I'm generically white, and also I don't want to get accidentally hooked up with any blood relatives, distant or otherwise. I'm respecting my mother's privacy, and also there was a meth problem, in that there was some. In me."

"Oh God," he said. "Really?"

"Could've been worse," I said. "My social worker, Joellen, always says if you have to be born addicted to something, meth is what you want."

"For fuck's sake! She says that to you out loud?"

"Because it's got the best recovery outcome." I laughed. He was *interested,* not curious. "Obviously meth is gross; Joellen was just trying to make me feel better. Alcohol is way worse."

"Joellen engages in some tough love."

"She thinks I need to cry more is all. The meth isn't the reason I'm not interested. It's not that I don't care. It's more just . . . I've lived with so many families. I've seen what blood relatives can do to their own kids. I've seen foster parents, social workers, even babysitters be kinder and take better care of kids they've only just met. And then there's the opposite—wonderful birth parents who just need some help; social services who act like kids are criminals. It's all subjective. Maybe I want to know and I'm suppressing it. Maybe I care and wish I didn't. I have no idea anymore. I only know worrying about who I'm related to makes me tired, so I leave it alone and just wish people would stop being assholes to each other.

Human decency is thicker than blood.

" 'We're made of star stuff,' " he said.

"Yes!" Carl Sagan. Muir would have loved him. "So, for mountains in the summer, which would you rather: Olympics or Cascades?"

He stole a cookie from my cup and chewed it. "Okay. *That's* the reason I've never gone out much until now."

"What is?"

"Olympics versus Cascades. I've never known anyone, let alone a beautiful girl who goes around quoting John Muir all day, who would ever think to ask that question."

"Oh. *Well.*"

"So I guess I was waiting."

Not a date. Not a date.

Fuck that. I want this to be a date.

"Did you live with a family that camped a lot?" he asked. "Backpack?"

"No. Not once."

"But . . . you love it so much. You *know* so much."

"I read a lot."

"You're a natural. Should we go sometime? Backpacking? The sky is so black in the wilderness, so many stars that it's like dust."

153

"I don't know if I'm allowed. I could ask Francine."

"We'll take her with us."

"Then Terry Johnson has to come, too," I said.

"As long as he packs his own bed and food."

"I'll carry him," I said. "He is a delicate creature." Sean took my paper yogurt cup from me and set it beside his on the sand at our feet. We watched the water in the bay turn pink, the moon rise above the trees, and lights blink on in the houses and cabins on the water.

"Like a necklace, all the lights in a row," he said.

"It'd be prettier without them."

"People need to live somewhere."

"I just mean trees are prettier than houses," I said.

He smiled. "Spoken like a Muir."

"Are you *baiting* me?"

"Just stating facts."

"Oh," I said. "Okay. We're doing this now? This is where we get this over with?" I moved over to my own space on the rocks and faced him.

"Yeah," he said. "Let's go."

I took a deep breath of salty sea air. "John Muir saved your *life.* You said so yourself."

"Wait, what? He did not, when did I say that?"

"*His trail.* You hiked his trail; he saved you. And you can put a pin in this for another day, but he saved me, too, and above all else, you were raised by two national park rangers! So I would like you to explain to me how Pinchot gets *any* play in this at all."

"Reality," he said, loving this entire situation. "Pinchot understood people have to use natural resources—"

"*Destroy* them."

"It's *management*!"

Nothing like getting worked up about nature preservation with a boy I liked *so much,* and on a moonlit night, but, God, it was exhilarating! I felt like I'd been waiting to have this fight all my life.

I moved in for the kill.

"Hetch Hetchy," I nearly growled.

Sean's shoulders dropped.

In California, the Hetch Hetchy valley's beauty—photographs and Muir's words demonstrate—was rivaled only by Yosemite. A magnificent place of natural wonder, Muir nearly gave his life fighting to save it. But Pinchot fought for and eventually won the construction of a dam that would flood the valley to feed the water needs of nearby San Francisco. There were alternative water sources, but Pinchot, being the dick that he was, would not yield. The valley, its unfathomable Yosemite-worthy glory, was flooded and washed away. Destroyed forever.

Any fool can destroy trees. They cannot run away; and if they could, they would still be destroyed—chased and hunted down as long as fun or a dollar could be got out of their bark hides.

"Okay," Sean said quietly. "I may need to rethink some things."

I checked the time on my phone. "I have two hours and fifteen minutes. Take your time."

He smiled at the sand.

"What would happen if you were late?" he asked. "With Francine. Versus other people."

"Don't know. Never been."

"*Never?* Your whole life?"

"Not being perfect is for people who have families; you can screw up and they still keep you."

He moved so his shoulder was touching mine beside him on the rocks, warm and strong. "Perfect how?"

"Just—I am never late. I have never been rude or disrespectful to a parent out loud, never been drunk, no bad grades. Like that."

"Your whole life?"

I drew circles in the sand with my toes. "Soon as I figured it out, yeah."

"Did you want . . . I mean, were you being perfect for them so they would want you?"

"No. It was for *me*. Muir couldn't stop moving. He tried so hard to want to stay and be a guy living in a house tending a farm and be married and raising kids, but he just kept . . . leaving. He missed being in the world. I had to keep leaving houses because sometimes they wanted me to stay."

He moved my hair out of my eyes. "*You* left?" he asked.

"I did."

"How many?"

"In my life?"

"Yes."

"Don't get freaked out."

"I won't."

"And this is counting, like, five in the first year because hospitals and such."

"How many."

"Francine is twenty."

He moved my hair onto one shoulder, fingertips along my neck. I was getting dizzy. "Can you stay here?" he said. "For the year at least?"

"I'm trying," I said.

"Try hard."

Skinny-legged plovers ran through the wet sand to a nook in the rocks and grass. The moon was rising fast in the darkening sky.

He pressed the back of my hand into the cool sand and traced the lines of my palm. "Have you ever *wanted* to stay?"

I wished I hadn't given the gold chain to Kira. I wished I had it now. "Sometimes," I whispered without thinking. I barely admitted that to myself; what was I doing saying it out loud to this person? To *this* person? Tears blurred my vision. "Sometimes."

He held my hand.

"You must be exhausted," he said.

Oh, my heart.

I rested my head on his shoulder until I turned to kiss him.

The moon on the water was bright white and high when we moved to sit in the seagrass and he kissed me back, safe from the night wind, time flying.

"I was half a minute from calling Joellen. *Thirty seconds.*" Francine stood in the blazing kitchen, every light on, so wrong at nearly midnight.

"Francine," Sean said, breathless from our sprint through the dark back to her house. "It was my fault, I told her to turn her phone off, I forgot mine was off, too. I didn't set an alarm; we missed the movie; we were just at the beach—"

"Okay, Sean. Go home now," she said.

"It wasn't Muriel's fault, we were only talking, please don't—"

"Now."

He put his hand on my shoulder as he walked out the door. Terry Johnson barked. Once.

I'll be homeless or dead in a year.

Francine dropped heavily into a kitchen chair, head in her hands. "Muriel."

"I know."

"I called and called. This is *why* I got the phone in the first place, to avoid this exact moment we are currently in."

"I turned it off and forgot. Kira sent me an eggplant!" My voice was unnaturally high.

"She sent you what?"

"Joellen can pick me up tomorrow if you want—just, please, Francine, don't tell her why; she'll have to put it in my record. *Please.*" It had been years since I cried this hard. Seriously. *Years.*

"Muiriel," she said, loud. *"Stop."*

I turned and ran upstairs to the lonely bed in the attic room and couldn't stop crying, so I did not notice when she sat on the bed.

"Why won't you tell me what kind of shampoo to buy?" she said.

I tried to breathe. *"What?"*

"None of your stuff is in the bathroom. Where do you keep your soap?"

I pointed to my suitcase, as always packed and neatly closed, on the floor.

The scratching came from the stairwell, Francine got up and brought Terry Johnson to the bed. "He's worried about you," she said. He climbed on me, found my face beneath my hair, and went to town licking my salty, tearstained cheeks.

"Listen to me. I would have only called Joellen, not the police. And you know Joellen never would do anything to hurt you. We wouldn't do that to you. I swear."

I held tight to Terry Johnson.

"You're not leaving," she said. "This is not a tragedy."

Being homeless is a tragedy.

"I've known Sean his whole life. I trust him, and I know I can trust you; I've just never had a kid age out. I'm figuring it out as I go, trying not to confine you so much you do something stupid, but you're not like other kids I've had—you're so rigid about behavior and rules, the first thing I thought when you missed curfew was *Well, she's dead. I lost one.* I'm not angry at you. Do you understand?"

"No," I said. "I don't."

"I was *worried,* not mad."

Interesting.

"Well. Kind of mad, but only *because* you made me worry. Scared me to death for a minute there. What does an eggplant mean?"

I sniffled and turned to face her. "I think probably a penis."

"Oh, *Kira,*" she sighed. "Listen to me. You're so close. I'm here with you. Joellen is, too. You can do this. Use the phone." She stood and went to the stairs.

"Francine?"

"Yes."

"Terry Johnson sleeps with me. Sometimes."

"I know."

"You do?"

"I'm just glad you're not sleeping on the sofa anymore. Terrible for your back."

Terry Johnson burrowed under my knees and curled up tight.

"Muiriel, unpack. Stay. Let me help you."

It was the thought that it *would* be so nice to have help—*her* help—that made me cry harder. Because very soon, the second I aged out, I would have no help from anyone at all. Relying on her kindness now would make my life a million times harder than when I had only me.

I pulled Terry Johnson up and let him rest his head beside me on the pillow. I could have stayed awake and called Joellen to get on a ferry and come pick me up, like I'd done every time, with every placement, year after year after year.

But now I'd slipped. And Francine was *not mad.*

Worried, but not mad.

I was so tired.

The phone lit up.

Are you okay? I'm so sorry.

I didn't respond. Terry Johnson snored me to sleep.

* * *

I carry with me a brass key to a door I will never open.

For a room to be legally used as a bedroom for foster placements, it must have a window and a closet. I lived once, when I was eleven, with two other girls in a bedroom that had a closet door, but it was locked. All the time. Because even though the mom pretended it was for us during inspections from CPS, really it was a Christmas closet. I knew this because one early morning I was the only kid awake, still in bed reading, and she came in, put her finger to her lips, and unlocked the door to toss in some rolls of wrapping paper. Inside was a life-sized light-up Santa, huge plastic bins of garland and greenery, and a fully assembled fake tree.

We kept our clothes in our suitcases and in a small dresser, one drawer for each of us. Our shoes stayed beside the front door in wooden apple crates.

The man and woman whose house it was seemed really wealthy; they had two grown children away attending colleges with one-word names, and we could never tell if they were fostering kids now because they were lonely for their own kids or bored or wanted attention or what. The dad was barely around, and when he was, he only ever said some variation of *Hey, I know! How about you kids show some gratitude once in a while, see how that works out for you.* He and the mom loved rhetorical sarcasm, and they both seemed to confuse foster care with juvenile detention. "Well," the mom often said to the kids with a smile, "that kind of attitude isn't going to get you back home with your parents anytime soon, now, is it?" But the house was very clean and fancy, warm on cold nights, with nice blankets on the beds. They had really good food delivered from delis and restaurants all over the city, and, best of all, they paid for school lunch accounts, as much as we wanted. I got two cartons of chocolate milk every day, just because I could.

The two other girls in the house were only a little younger than me, not related, both on weekly visitation schedules with parents, and neither situation was going well. One was visiting her mom in county jail; the other had both parents at home. Every time either one returned from a visit, she would be angry or crying or exhausted, or all three. I felt horrible for them and wanted badly to know them, comfort and protect them, which I knew would be dangerous for my own psyche—so I learned to stay after school and take my long, long walks on days *Bio Visit* was written on the wall calendar in the kitchen.

I had no idea what these visits entailed, but watching how it wrecked them made me—again and still—glad I did not have parents; from what I could see, having parents meant nothing but soul-crushing court-ordered visits and getting dragged in and out of foster care year after year. No, thanks. And all the while these girls got yanked around, no one who was in any position to help them seemed to be able to, and the girls' response to this bullshit was bullshit of their own: fighting, and screaming tantrums, and things thrown—shoes and lamps, sometimes food. When I got back from my walks, I just picked up the wreckage of our shared room and helped the foster parents clean up any damage done to the living room or kitchen, and by then the girls were usually asleep, so I could go lie down, too.

The foster mom got the wrong idea. She loved my housekeeping prowess, my good grades that kept her out of meetings with teachers and social workers, my squirreling away allowance money so I never asked for field trip money or bus fare. She misinterpreted my well-honed survival techniques as affection for her. I was home sick from school one day, alone in the bedroom, and she came in to sit on the edge of the bed and smile. She handed me a tiny gift-wrapped box.

A brass key.

"To the closet," she said. "You could use it for your *clothes*! This whole room would be yours, just for you." I knew what was coming. I thanked this woman very much, expressed my gratitude for all she and the man had done for me over the past four months, and politely refused her offer of adoption.

She was still crying when the man came home that afternoon. His voice, loud enough to make sure I heard him, echoed from the beautifully tiled kitchen. "That kid just passed up the best offer she'll ever get in her life. She doesn't know how good she's got it. She doesn't know how to be grateful."

My face burned, stomach swam.

He isn't right. I am my own best offer. I am all I need.

When Joellen picked me up the next morning, I said goodbye to the girls, slipped the forgotten key into my pocket, and sent a prayer to the universe that the woman would never again be able to get back into that fucking Christmas closet.

Thirteen

"THIRTY MINUTES?" KIRA SAID at lunch on Monday. "That's it?"

"Thirty-*two*. I've never been thirty *seconds* late in any placement, with anyone, ever. God, I think I'm getting an ulcer." I held the right side of my abdomen, feeling a tight and sharp pain that had been there since Sunday morning.

"Have you talked to Sean?"

"Texted him yesterday. Told him I needed to cool it for a while for Francine's sake. He said he understood."

"*Cool it?* Okay, grandma. Did Francine say you couldn't go out with him anymore?"

"No."

"So this is a self-imposed 'cooling'?"

"Yes."

"Do you *want* to stop seeing him?"

"Of course not!" I wailed pitifully. "I want to see him! I want to go out with him! I want to do all the stuff with him!"

"All right, okay, I don't need *all* the details. . . ."

"You know what I mean."

"Muiriel," she sighed. "What the *hell*?"

"I can't throw my life away for a boy."

"Who's throwing anything away? Just don't be late anymore, problem solved."

"It's . . ." She had no way of ever understanding the gravity of my need for perfection in all things recorded in *the file*. "I got careless," I said. "I like him so much. I've never let myself down, ever, until this, which means I like him *too* much. I need to finish foster care the way I started."

She sat back in her chair, blew her hair off her face, and looked half-stern, half-sad.

"Okay, so that means, what, having no friends? No boyfriends? Giving yourself an ulcer over being a few minutes late, for getting caught up with *talking* to a boy and enjoying some nice, refreshing damn froyo?"

"Thirty-two minutes," I said into my sandwich.

She sat forward and leaned on her elbows toward me. "You know what we talked about in psych today?"

"Um, about how it's not art class and you shouldn't be there?"

She almost smiled. "I'm telling you *your* life now—you can tell me mine later. Shut up and listen."

I laid my head on my arms. "Fine."

"You need to separate the nobility of your cause from the misguided means of pursuing it."

"*What.*"

"You're buying into the sunk-cost fallacy!"

"Nope. Get back in art class."

"Okay, look. You *think* you're making a rational decision, based on the potential future value of something—the perceived value of your perfect, pristine, ulcer-producing, solitary life."

"Oh. Okay." My eyes rolled up into my head.

"Yes! You think your lifetime of perfection will protect you and, like, secure your future when you age out. You believe it's going to keep you off the pipe and off the pole. It's going to guarantee your safety and a viable income, right? But *really* what's happening is, your decisions are tainted by the emotional investments you accumulate—the more you invest, the harder it becomes to abandon it."

"Seriously, you don't miss watercolor paints? Pottery?"

"Muir. It isn't worth it. Don't you feel that? You're punishing yourself for nothing. Your brain is like, *Well, we've done this for seventeen years, can't stop now, my entire life of self-deprivation will have been for nothing if we stop now,* but it isn't true! You can let yourself live a little! Let Francine take care of you. You can make a mistake now and then and *it won't destroy your life.* Don't let Sean go. He is a really good guy, and he is in love with you. It's so obvious."

I wished she was right. She didn't understand how aging out works—that Francine couldn't help me. Joellen couldn't help me. In a matter of months I would have no one but me. No matter how nice Francine was.

Unpack. Stay.

Kira suddenly looked past me and smiled. I followed her gaze and there was tall, hoodied Elliot.

"Oh my," I said. "Let's discuss *this* turn of events, then, shall we?"

She whipped her hair up into a ponytail. "He's coming over

here—oh no—tell me when he's here; I can't look." She pulled a book from her backpack and pretended to read, and I watched Elliot smile, walk toward our table—and then Katiana were there beside him, talking and laughing, holding his arms, looking right at me. Daring me to do something. Daring me to stop them.

"Need some help in the pottery studio!" Tiana said. They steered Elliot away and out of the cafeteria. Elliot looked back over his shoulder.

And I just sat there.

"Is he coming?" Kira whispered into her book.

"Uh . . . no," I said. "Some guys came over and got him for something. They're gone."

She looked up. "Oh," she said, sad. "Just as well. I look crappy today."

"You look beautiful, as always, and you know it."

Now she rolled *her* eyes.

"If you were in art class," I said, "you'd see him almost every day."

She put her book back in her backpack. "Yeah, yeah. We are failing with our potential romantic entanglement interactions today," she sighed.

"One thing I'll say for psychology," I said, "it's making your vocabulary jam-packed with lots of syllables."

"Indeed." She nodded. "They take the place of an active dating life in a surprisingly satisfying way."

Salishwood on Saturday morning after the date night was an exercise in self-control. Even before Sean got there, because of course fucking Natan was there, right where I'd been assigned to pull out some blackberry roots, strumming and tuning his stupid guitar, and he started in on "Ring of Fire," which made me wish I could personally apologize to June Carter Cash. Everything we'd heard through the window, all we knew about Natan's life and Jane's, the nepotism that kept him ruining every otherwise-perfect day spent in the trees, made me even less inclined to make eye contact with him.

"You like this song?" he said, humming flat and sharp and just—wrong.

I pretended not to hear.

"You know, the title of this tune is one we naturalists think of in a completely different way than Johnny intended. You see—"

"Hi, guys." Sean's beautiful, beautiful voice saved me.

"Good morning, sir," Natan sang. Gah.

Sean smiled at me but did not hug me, as per the promise he'd made. Which, when he walked toward us, so lean and strong and *perfect,* I regretted asking for. He was right there, and I already missed him. He caught my eye, tipped his head toward Natan, and made a *Well, this is awkward* face. I nodded.

Sunk-cost fallacy.

Maybe Kira was right. My head pounded.

Summer was finally cooling into autumn. The whole island was slowly turning red and gold against the Pacific Northwest clouds and a few remaining bright blue skies. Kids spilled from the buses, including Zola, whose familiar face made me secretly so happy I could barely keep it in. She ran to me, and I let my arm hug her shoulders for a moment. "How's things, kid?" I asked.

Her arms were little and strong as ever around me. "Okay," she said, definitely not meaning it.

"Hey," I said, and knelt beside her in the grass. "What's up? Your mom doing okay?"

She shook her head. "I'm at my grandma's house, but she's really old. They think she's too slow to take care of me."

"Too slow?"

"Tired. She can't walk a lot. She doesn't live by my school, but I take the city bus. I don't know."

Goddamn it.

I let her hold on to me until Jane came out and called for the kids to line up.

"Hey," I said, holding Zola back. "You doing okay in school?"

"I guess."

"Make sure. Keep your grades good."

"We don't get grades yet."

"Okay, well, just—show up. Always on time. Pay attention, do all the worksheets and stuff. Make sure you're learning. Got it?"

She nodded.

"Zola. Okay?"

"Okay," she said. I zipped her sweater all the way up and watched her run to join her class.

"Is Zola all right?" Sean asked, suddenly beside me.

"I don't know."

"Well," he said, "could— I mean, could Francine do anything to help?"

My brain was not fast enough to stop my arms from wrapping around him. His huge, selfless heart. The blue-gray knit hat on his dark hair. I hugged him so hard he stumbled a little but righted himself and hugged me.

"Are *you* okay?" he asked.

I collected my wits and pulled back. "Sorry," I said. "You're just . . . you are so kind."

"Muir."

"Francine can't help her. But it's so nice of you to even think of it."

He squeezed my hand.

We took the kids, Zola beside me the whole time, tromping through the forest to find late-summer birds' nests and moss gardens, and I waved to her as the buses pulled away. I brought my lunch to the picnic table to sit if not beside, at least near, Sean.

"Muiriel," Natan said, eyeing my container of roasted carrots Francine made that morning. "You know women need essential fats in their diet, especially at childbearing age."

I swallowed wrong and choked until Sean whacked me on my back.

"Jesus Christ, Natan." I coughed. "What is *wrong* with you?"

"See, again, this is what's wrong with our patriarchal society. Men can't even talk about a woman's cycle—"

"Not *men,* just you," I said. "Especially when you're offering an unsolicited bad opinion, but if a man who was, say, my *doctor* wanted to lecture me about my diet, I'd be okay with that."

"Oh, a *doctor.*" Natan smiled, nodding in his oily, slow-motion way. "Western medicine strikes again. Those doctors just want to cover up illness and cause more with their pills. Food is the only medicine we need, sister." He opened a jackknife, cut a huge hunk off a log of salami, and dropped it into his bearded head hole. "Paleo is the way to go, Muiriel. The way our original ancestors ate."

"Yes, because Neanderthals thrived on carcinogenic nitrates in their lunch meat made of domesticated pigs," Sean said. Natan shook his head and turned to wipe the knife on his pants.

My cheeks flushed. I moved nearer to Sean despite myself.

"How was Zola when she left?" he asked me, low.

"She was quiet," I said. "Not good."

"Well," Natan said from eavesdropping central, "never can tell what a kid like that is up to."

It was a day of failing to control my impulses. "A kid like *what*?" I said.

"Relax, sister, I'm not talking about you. A kid like Zola."

"I am not your sister. Like *what*, Natan?"

"You know. Adopted."

"Adopted is a past-tense verb, not an adjective, and Zola has not *been* adopted; she and I are *in* foster care."

"Right . . . ," Natan said. "Well, see, that's what I'm saying—whatever *you* did to get yourself put in the system, you've obviously worked hard to overcome your poor choices. Look at you! Holding down a job, going to school, staying out of trouble. You are the exception to the rule. Little Zola will choose to improve herself, or keep making mistakes—but it is *her* choice. Don't get wrapped up in it."

I stood.

"Muriel," Sean said, "I forgot to show you . . . a thing. Come on." He grabbed my carrots, and I let him lead me to a boulder in the trees, away from Natan and his jackknife and the potential murder scene.

"Breathe," Sean said, and we sat and ate in peace. "Maybe we should talk to Jane. Tell her we know why he's here, say maybe she could figure out a way to get rid of him and not ruin her already-bizarre family dynamic. I hate that we know all that crap."

"I hate Natan," I said.

"I'm going to get us T-shirts made that say *Jesus Christ, Natan*, so we don't have to talk to him anymore. He can just read our stock response to every single thing he says."

"I was the one who got him going. Talking that shit about Zola, I swear to God . . ."

"You really worried about her?"

"I don't know. Every day can be different; it's hard to tell what's going on."

I finished my carrots. He offered me half his CLIF Bar.

"Adopted *is not an adjective,*" he said.

"Joellen says that. It's an event that happens, not who you are. As an adjective it implies inherent bullshit about a person that isn't true. A *person* is not 'adopted.' They *were* adopted. Words matter."

"They do."

"Sean. Why are you being so nice to me?"

"*Nice?*" He pulled off his hat and ran his hands through his hair, a thing I gladly would have done for him—*I'm a mess.* "I've never had anyone to talk with like we do. I've never known anyone, ever, like you. I'm not being nice; I'm trying to change your mind."

He moved nearer; I stayed still, and he leaned in to kiss me. I gave in, closed my eyes.

Then the guitar was there. And so was Natan's braying laugh.

"Ooooh, dipping your pen in the company ink, little guy? Listen, you like this song? I was telling Muriel earlier, you know the title is a little goof for us naturalists, it's the name of—"

I stood and yanked the guitar from his hands.

"The Ring of Fire is a horseshoe-shaped series of trenches and volcanic belts in the Pacific Ocean where a shit ton of earthquakes and volcanic activity happen all the goddamned time, and it includes the volcanoes in the Pacific Ring of Fire, the star of which is our very own Mount Rainier, more correctly known by its Salish name, Tahoma, and many volcanologists and seismologists think maybe Seattle is due for intense plate movement, causing an earthquake that would send the entire Pacific Northwest into the Puget Sound, killing us all, which, when I'm at work lately, makes me hope it happens sooner rather than later, but really cool story, bro." I stalked off to gather my stuff, dropped the stupid guitar on Jane's desk, and walked, fast, down the winding forest road to the bus stop.

"Muir," Sean called, running to catch up. "Wait." We walked together, not talking for a while.

"You are so smart I can't stand it," he finally said.

He stopped in the middle of the road. "Francine talked to my mom," he said. "It wouldn't happen again; we would never be late."

"Sean."

"*Muir*. I'm here. Kira's here, Francine is here."

"Yes," I said. "Right now, you are."

"Where do you think we're going?"

"I don't know."

"Or are you going? Are you leaving the second you graduate?"

"I don't *know*."

"Well, then what? What can I do to convince you?"

"Convince me of what? I've known you and Kira and Francine for five weeks."

"I mean. More like six."

"Stop it," I half laughed. "Don't be funny."

"I'm trying to *convince* you to let us be with you. Let me."

"But you can't be with me forever."

"How do you know?"

"Sean! When you turn eighteen, is your mom kicking you out alone with nothing and telling you to never come back or ever speak to her again?"

He looked right at me. "No."

"Well, my parent is the state of Washington. And when I'm eighteen, Washington is kicking me out."

"What about Francine?"

"What about her? She is paid to let me live with her. When they stop paying her, I have to leave. That's how foster care works."

"What if she adopted you?"

I walked. He followed.

"Muir. I'm sorry, I shouldn't have . . . is adoption bad?" he said, trying to keep up with my anxiety-fueled pace.

"No, adoption isn't bad. It isn't anything. It isn't true."

"What?"

His confusion made my heart hurt. Also made me furious. How could he not understand that I did not choose this life? I was forced to be alone; I couldn't have best friends or a boyfriend or any normal shit other kids get to do in high school because I did not want to die, and love was a land mine of attachment.

"I'm sorry," he said. "I wish you would let me help."

"I wish you could."

"I *can.*"

We walked and walked until Francine's road, and I could not help it, I hugged him and he held on tight. I wanted so badly to kiss him, but why salt the wound?

"I'll see you at school on Monday," he said. "Because I go there, too, and I . . . am your friend." He turned and walked across the road and into the trees, on the path to his house. His mom's house. Where he would always be welcome. Always home.

He can't help me. I can't help Zola. Land mines everywhere.

Terry Johnson came tip-tapping to me, and I scooped him up.

All through dinner Francine watched me being gloomy but didn't say anything until I turned down the oatmeal cookies she offered for dessert.

"Dessert is the most important food group," she reminded me.

"I know." I tried to smile.

"I talked to Sean's mom," she said.

"I heard."

"You can both read a clock. No more penis emojis."

"Francine."

"Muiriel. He's a nice boy."

"I know." I cleared the table, Francine rinsed the dishes, and I loaded the dishwasher. I wrapped the cookies in foil and excused myself for bed.

"You want to take Terry Johnson up with you now?" she asked. "He's going to end up there later anyway."

Terry Johnson's ears lifted at the sound of his name.

"You sure?" I asked. "Doesn't he want to watch *The Bachelor*?"

"He probably does. But you look like you could use some extra warmth tonight."

I picked him up, started to the stairs, and stopped to bury my face in his soft neck. "Or we could watch with you," I said. "So he doesn't fall behind and get confused."

He curled between us on the sofa, and we all shared Francine's blanket. It was a terrible, terrible show.

But the nicest night in a house I'd had in so long I couldn't remember.

In the bed in my room upstairs, I scratched Terry Johnson's ears with one hand, held my phone in the other.

"Joellen," I said when she answered. "Are you allowed to check in on a kid who isn't yours?"

174

* * *

I carry with me a library card for a county I no longer live in.

Not only are libraries the greatest invention ever for a person to get her hands on every single book she ever feels like she might want to read without having to buy and carry the heavy things along with her every six to ten months when she moves to a new house—they are also a peaceful and clean and cheerful place to get some quiet alone time. Living with a bunch of kids is chaotic and exhausting, and so there were many Saturdays in my life when my morning and a good part of the afternoon were spent curled up in the toddler picture-book area of whichever library was near the house I lived in at the time. The adults there, the librarians, were so kind. They spoke in modulated low tones that made the top of my head tingly, and they brought new books to my attention that they thought I might like, and they forgave my late fees. My favorite days were rainy ones, especially in the Seattle Central. That whole building is practically made of glass; the wind blows the rain at the windows, and there are warm drinks for sale in the lobby. Heaven.

My favorite books when I was little were a series of seven that I now understand are actually a romanticized celebration of white people barging into the homelands of indigenous people, participating in their genocide, and stealing the land for themselves, but which, as a little white kid with no parents, I knew only as cozy stories about an adventurous pioneer home life—Laura Ingalls Wilder's Little House on the Prairie.

Here was a loving family that moved every year or so, again and again, just like me. Except they were searching for better luck, not with people but with new places. They were searching for a home. I liked the intricate descriptions of domestic life, the floor sweeping and water fetching and window cleaning and bed making written so deliciously I wished I had a twig-bough broom to use on a dirt floor, and a straw-tick mattress to fill with sweet, sun-warmed hay, and goose-feather pillows to plump. I read all the books in order, then reread them, and then I read only the disaster chapters (locusts, long winter storm, chimney fire) or only the new-house chapters (dugout, brand-new wood house, log cabin) or—my favorite—the food chapters (hog slaughter—ugh; oyster crackers at the surveyor's house; pancakes from wheat in Almanzo's walls; Pa survives a blizzard by eating a pound of candy).

But my very favorite food chapter of all was the one about a social supper. I like this one, first, because it's a potluck—the whole town meets in the church and every lady brings her best dish—and, second, because it's the only time Laura's mother, Ma, is ever pissed about the patriarchal bullshit that keeps her and Laura in the kitchen all night while the men lounge and eat and drink, waited on like princes while the women wash and dry the hundreds of dishes and only then are allowed to pick the scraps off the leftover pig and chicken carcasses.

But this chapter also gave me the willies because at the potluck, Laura is a teenager and she's got a teenager friend from school, Ida Brown. Ida is the minister's daughter, and so of course she's in the church kitchen, working her ass off all night, and when at last Laura thinks they are free to eat, another huge load of dirty dishes comes into the kitchen and Ida rolls up her sleeves.

"Aren't you going to eat now?" Laura asks her, and Ida is super cheerful and says she can't, because even after eight hours of cooking and cleaning, she doesn't deserve food yet.

"I'm only an adopted child, you see," Ida tells Laura. "I must be obedient and grateful to my parents. I'll eat tomorrow," or some such horseshit. I remember thinking maybe she was adopted, like, a month ago and still buying into that crap, but no. The minister and his wife had adopted poor Ida at birth, and then spent the next sixteen years making sure she knew she wasn't really an actual person, "only an adopted child" and not worthy of respect or dinner at a reasonable hour, not until the manual labor was all done. Ida was, it seemed, less of a daughter and more of a beaten-down indentured servant.

Laura's equally creepy response to Ida's chirpy declaration that she was "lucky to be taken in by the dear Reverend and Mrs. Brown" was not the horror and a hearty *Bitch, let's saddle up some Morgan horses and get you the hell out of Dodge* that I yearned for. Instead, the titular character was charmed by Ida's "dear and cheerful heart."

Oh, girl, I thought. *You're not lucky. You're trapped.*

Fourteen

SALISHWOOD IN OCTOBER was more gorgeous every day, a romantic Abercrombie & Fitch backdrop against which Sean's nonstop sweetness made resisting the "we're alone, so let's make out real quick" opportunities even more agonizing. With my phone I sent him links to PBS and Netflix documentaries about kids aging out of foster care, and he watched them and asked questions, which I appreciated and hated because it made me like him more.

"You're so gloomy without him," Kira said on a Monday afternoon over the noise of Blackbird's espresso machine. "Just—you don't have to marry the guy. Can't you go out with him and *not* let it ruin your life?"

I ignored my homework to watch her pipe perfect frosting wings on sugar cookie bats and didn't say that being friends with her was also dicey AF. The more I depended on her kindness and company, the more anxious I felt. But I held on, maybe because I'd left friends behind never to see them again, and maybe I could do it again with Kira and still be okay.

Except none of them had been as smart and funny and understanding as Kira was. No one had ever been so nice to me. And I hadn't ever liked any friend nearly so much.

I dipped my toast in the raspberry jam. "I'll survive without the company of a boy. Or, hey, how about if you take art next semester or have an actual conversation with Elliot, I'll go out with Sean again."

She flipped me off and stole a piece of toast crust from my plate.

"Oh, speaking of . . ."

The bells rang and Elliot materialized as if summoned. I liked that he deviated from the other kids' standard-issue boy uniform of knee socks and basketball shorts (no matter if they played or not, no matter the weather). Elliot, like Sean, wore actual pants that went all the way down to his shoes. Kira put down her piping bag and ducked behind the counter, smiling and straightening her apron, and then the bells rang again.

"Oh, hey, Kira?" Tiana's saccharine upspeak gave me the creeps. Everything was a question. "I didn't know you worked here?" She put her hand on Elliot's arm.

"Yes, you did," I said. "Everyone does."

Kira exhaled audibly. Tiana glared.

"Hi, Kira," Elliot said, smiling shyly. "How's it going?"

Kira's voice was quiet but determined. "Great, good, thanks. Thank you. I'm— Can I get you something?"

"Yeah," Tiana said. "We're just getting some cookies and muffins to go? The art showcase is next week, so we're working on setting up the studio? For the displays?"

"Why didn't you enter something?" Elliot said to Kira as a line of customers formed behind him. "You don't have to be enrolled in class. Are you painting lately? Tiana, have you seen Kira's acrylics? They're amazing."

Oh, boys. They can be so clueless. Tiana laughed and shoved through the line to examine croissants in the case.

"I'm really busy this semester," Kira said, running the register and pouring coffee. "Lots of psychology homework."

"Kira," Tiana said, "we're going to need a dozen cookies, ten scones, and we'll take the rest of these cupcakes? Sound good, Elliot? Artists get hungry, amirite?" She laughed and googly-eyed him.

This was an after-school special with a shitty actor trying to be a mean-girl bully. She was so mediocre. She wasn't even good at being a bitch. She was just—*nothing*. And Kira, who was happy to see me every day, who was herself the reason I never felt nervous or had to eat alone at school, who was nice to everyone—she put her head down and filled boxes with the pastries Tiana pointed to, impatient and entitled and wallowing in Kira's humility.

I wanted to push Tiana off a cliff.

"Kira, see you at school?" Elliot called as Tiana dragged him out the door, balancing boxes of pastries.

Kira got through the line of other customers, untied her apron, and sat miserably beside me.

"Don't listen to me about anything," she said. "Ever."

I gave her my last piece of jam-drenched toast. "I will listen to you about everything. Always."

She bit the toast and chewed sadly. "Till you leave."

"Well," I said. "Yeah. But always till then."

"The Irish story of Halloween says there was once a dickhead named Jack who played a trick on the devil, so when Jack died and was turned away from heaven, the devil was still mad about being tricked and wouldn't have Jack in hell, either. Instead, the devil banished Jack to wander earth in darkness forever, with only a burning bit of coal in a carved-out turnip to light his way. And that's why we make jack-o'-lanterns!"

Twenty little kids sat on a carpet of red and gold leaves in the Salishwood field and looked up at Sean, eyes wide, hands full of seeds and stringy innards from the pumpkins they were carving.

Zola wasn't there. She would have loved this. Joellen couldn't legally tell me anything about Zola's life beyond the fact that she was safe where she was. Try as I might, Joellen would not talk to me about Zola, the state of her happiness or lack of it. I hoped she had a pumpkin to carve. I hoped she was with her grandma. Or, better yet, home with her mom.

A small girl raised her hand. "Isn't *dickhead* a bad word?"

"It sure is," I said. "Grown-ups shouldn't even say it, *right,* Sean?"

"*That,*" Sean said, "was a test, and you passed! Everyone keep going, we've got half an hour till the bus comes, and I want to see some scary faces carved into those gourds."

The leafy trees among the pines and cedars blazed crimson like fire; I'd never seen such an autumn. Seattle's parks and streets are full of and lined with trees, of course, but this was another world, lit and glowing orange. I sat with (not *next to*) Sean at the picnic table.

The kids flung gourd guts at each other. We let them.

"So. What are you doing tomorrow night?" he asked.

"Sleeping through the whole thing."

"Hold up. You don't like *Halloween*?"

"I love it."

"Explain."

"No kids in Francine's house. It's kind of making me sad."

"I'm sorry," he said.

"Just different. You know?"

"This island is in love with Halloween."

"Yeah," I sighed. "I can tell." Main Street had been lined with carved jack-o'-lanterns for weeks. Kira was giving herself carpal tunnel trying to keep up with the demand for her exquisite cookies, more bats and pumpkins with fondant vines and especially the vampires, each one featuring a different expression on its white frosting face, glittery red sugar blood dripping from every fang.

"Main Street is a block party. There'll be a million kids there running loose."

"Not mine. Not ones I can take trick-or-treating."

"Okay, but there's a parade, and, listen, Salishwood has a booth. I ran it last year, and I told Jane I'd ask you to come with this time."

"Sean."

"Please," he said. "Come with me. It would be so fun. *Not* a date."

Nearly impossible to say no to that smile, but I summoned all the resistance I had left.

"Sorry," I said. "I'll be eating KitKats in bed with Terry Johnson."

He sighed. "That dog needs a new name."

The next evening, said dog and I were settled in with our KitKats for Halloween, not in bed but on the sofa, waiting to answer the door to trick-or-treaters, and I was working hard to convince Francine I honestly did want to stay home by myself.

"Oh, come *on*," she called from the bathroom, where face painting was happening. "It's such a fun night, and won't Kira be there?"

"She's working."

"Blackbird closes early; she'll be done by seven!"

"I'm good. Thanks, though."

The doorbell rang.

"Muir?"

"Got it." Terry Johnson huffed when I moved him off my lap to open the door to Sean leaning on a carved wooden walking stick, wearing a floppy hat and a long white beard.

Terry Johnson barked his head off. He hates hats.

"The mountains are calling," he said. With his free hand, he offered me sheep ears on a headband. "I'm John Muir," he said, smiling behind the beard. "Herding sheep. In Yosemite. Get it?"

"Oh, I get it," I said, trying to play it cool and hide my swooning. *When will he figure out I am not worth all this effort?*

"Please be my lamb," he said. "If you don't, no one will know who I am."

Unfair the way he always, *always* made me laugh.

"Ohhh . . . ," Francine sighed dreamily, leaning out from the hall bathroom door. "Muriel. How can you possibly say no to *that*?"

"Hi, Francine!" Sean called.

She came to the door and smiled the way she did when the hens give an egg with two yolks (*Look at that! It's magic!*), and then we all stood there together, Francine looking from Sean to me, hands on her hips in her gardening overalls.

Just a party. Not a date.

"I should be Muir," I said at last. "It's *my* name."

Sean yanked off the beard. "Here, put this on!"

"I don't want to."

Francine clucked at me.

"Oh jeez, fine, just hold on," I said, and took the stairs two at a time.

"Where are you going?" Francine called.

"I have to put on a bra if I'm being forced to leave the house."

"Take some vampires!" Kira shouted over the madness of people in Blackbird. She tossed me a paper bag full of them, and even in my balance-throwing lamb ears, I caught it.

"Come find me after!" I yelled back.

"Text me!"

I held my phone aloft.

At the women's shelter booth, Francine and her pals were giving out candy and letting kids pet Terry Johnson, who was wearing devil horns and not looking real pleased about it.

"Sorry, buddy," I whispered to him.

"Francine," one of the pals sang, "is this your new girl?"

Francine smiled up at me apologetically. "This is my foster daughter Muiriel, yes."

The pal took my hand. "Well, Miss Muiriel, you are a very lucky girl. I hope you appreciate that," she said, and winked. Or got something caught in her eye. Couldn't tell.

Francine blanched. "Muiriel isn't lucky, Eileen, she's entitled. To at least one good parent. *I'm* lucky this wonderful creature agreed to come stay with me. Look, ladies, Sean is John Muir!"

A melty, tingly warmth poured over me, and the ladies nodded and smiled in a way that told me they were used to being schooled by Francine.

She smiled up at me, flowers painted all over her face, poor Terry Johnson squirming on her lap.

"Here," I said, and handed her a vampire cookie. "From Kira, frosted today."

"Thank you, sweetheart. You two go have fun now," she said. "Midnight, okay?"

"Midnight," I croaked through my swollen throat.

Sweetheart. Easy. Like it was what she always called me.

And I did not mind.

Sean took my hand. "Don't want to lose you in the crowd is all," he said. "Safety first." I gave in and held his fingers tight in mine.

He was not wrong about the island's deal with Halloween. A million little kids raced around blocked-off Main Street, and it made me feel better. Familiar. I yelled at them to slow down their running, tie their shoes, pick up that wrapper they dropped.

The Salishwood booth was all about Sean and me showing taxidermied owls and mice to the kids who came by, and I sat on a stool applying temporary tattoos to little arms and faces.

"Glad you came?" he asked.

I nodded and reached into the bag to put a shortbread vampire in his mouth. "So good, right?"

He nodded, chewing and grinning at me in the dumb beard, which I reached out to straighten.

"Young love," came a voice from the crowd, and then Natan emerged, leering in a vape cloud, the stupid pipe jammed in the corner of his mouth like he wished he were a nineteenth-century

British detective. Bun stringy and high on his head, his usual Teva sandal situation on his feet but wearing a wool sweater and a batik wrap skirt, which, good for him smashing patriarchal clothing norms but then negating that with his vape-free arm wrapped tight around a pasty, waifish girl, lank blond hair to her waist. She took a hit off the vape pipe and gazed, glassy-eyed, up at Natan.

"Hey there, my wee protégé. How's the Halloween lovefest going? You two sneaking in a make-out sesh?"

I felt Sean's entire body tense beside me.

"Hello," I said, extending my hand to the waif. "I'm Muiriel."

"HarmonyOceanJustice," she said.

Of course.

"Having a good Halloween?"

Natan smiled and lifted Harmony's hair from her shoulders and answered for her. "We're just riding the autumnal high of Gaia's beauty," he said. "Hook us up with some sweet ink?" He picked up the temporary tattoos, sat on the stool beside me, and pulled his sweater off his bare shoulder. "Right about *here,* I think, Muiriel."

Sean hopped over the table, slapped a tattoo on Natan's shoulder, and whacked him on his back. "All set, man. See you at work!"

Natan smiled at me, stood and put his arms around Harmony, and steered her into the crowd to infect it with his patchouli stench.

"I'm sorry, you guys *know* him?" Kira shout-asked, still watching Natan's retreating height as she made her way to us through the crowd, her arms full of bags of broken but still delicious ghost and jack-o'-lantern cookies.

"Salishwood," I sighed.

"Someone needs to tell that girl to never go with a hippie to a second location."

Sean shivered. "I feel like I need a shower."

"Thanks for taking the bullet for me," I said.

"Of course. He's so gross. I'm sorry I didn't . . . I don't know, punch him in his vape hole?"

"We can't resort to violence," I said. "Sadly. Jane would side with him, and we'd get fired. But I appreciate the sentiment, and I would happily join you in the endeavor."

"Me too," Kira said, and took over tattoo duty, drawing on the kids with markers—*This is art!*—and I sat beside Sean, wishing so badly I could hold his hand under the table.

When the moon was high and the candy-hyper kids were gone, the three of us walked home on the waterfront along the docks, sailboats bobbing in the harbor.

"Elliot said he was going to come by," Kira sighed. "Guess he was busy with Tiana. Or Katrina. Or both."

"I'm so sorry," I said. "That's stupid. He's stupid if he's with her."

"He's not dating either one of them," Sean said.

Kira and I stopped walking.

"He's not?" Kira's voice lit with hope.

Sean shrugged. "Don't think so. People tend to tell me gossip like that. I would have remembered. Why don't you ask him out? You could be artsy together."

Kira hugged Sean impulsively, and we kept walking.

The moon followed us along the water and into the trees to light the path before us. We dropped Kira at her house, then Sean walked with me to Francine's porch. I handed him the sheep ears.

"Keep them," he said. "They're adorable."

"This was a really good Halloween. You were right."

"I know I say this a lot, but you are magic with little kids. I'm so glad you came."

My cheeks went warm.

"I have something for you," he said. "I've been carrying it around all night, should have left it here to begin with." He pulled a flat, butcher-paper-wrapped package from his coat pocket. Tied with string.

"Sean."

"It's just a thing! It's not romantic, I swear."

A paperback book. *Lost Woods: The Discovered Writing of Rachel Carson.*

"I thought maybe we could dispense with all the Muir/Pinchot dick swinging and get with a woman who could have taught them both a shit ton about the ocean they never knew but should have."

Honest to God, I could barely breathe.

"Thank you," I whispered.

He held out his hiking watch. "Look at that. . . . Fifteen minutes before curfew and I'm not even going to try to kiss you."

"Sean."

That beautiful smile. "I just wanted you to have fun tonight. Look, here's all the space. . . ." He backed down the stairs and to the road. "I understand. But I'm also not giving up hope." He waved the hat, walked into the trees, and was gone.

I stood for a while, watching the bats swoop and flit in the moonlight.

"Good Halloween?" Francine asked from the sofa when I got in the house. I sat beside her, and Terry Johnson yawned, stretched, and cinnamon-rolled right into my lap.

"Not bad," I said.

On the TV a woman on *Antiques Roadshow* described the origins of an old clock to a man who broke down in tears when she told him it would fetch, at auction, at least fifty thousand dollars.

"I had no idea," the man sobbed. "It's been in my carport getting rained on all this time; we thought it was worthless. I would have taken better care of it if I'd known it was so valuable!"

"If you'd been more careful with it," the woman scolded, "it would have been worth twice as much."

"People are ridiculous," Francine said. "Priceless treasures right there in the house with them their whole lives and they never bother to notice."

"*You're* a treasure," I told Terry Johnson, smooshing my face into his neck. "We notice you!" He growled at me and curled up again.

I lay awake that night for hours, the moon refusing to let me sleep, until I gave in, pulled my blackbird treasure bag from my suitcase, and took out *Bread and Jam for Frances* and *The Wilderness World of John Muir*, and I put them together, beside my new clothes, on top of the dresser with the Rachel Carson book. A neat row of three.

I could hear Joellen's voice. *Two is a pair; three is a collection.*

* * *

I carry with me a paper Dixie cup.

My third-grade teacher let us eat candy in class and watch *Mary Poppins* for Halloween. She was super into it. In the morning she had us make hats from construction paper. Girls made flat boaters and decorated them with red tissue paper poppies; the boys made top hats, like in the bank scene. I was psyched, movies in school always felt so special, and I had never seen this one.

As far as I could tell, this movie was about parents who had two cute children they were determined to spend as little time with as possible. And so they hire a woman who constantly gaslights the kids and makes them doubt their own sanity; she takes them on fantastical trips, then says they never happened. She gives them the powers of flight and time travel, encourages them to surrender to the magic and enjoy themselves, then acts all affronted and accuses them of lying when they mention how fun the adventure was. The whole movie seemed to be introducing the concept of what a nanny was and, at the same time, arguing against ever employing one. The parents are so desperate to get away from their children that they pay this stranger to pretend to love the children, and Mary does—so well, in fact, that the children fall in love with her, the only adult (aside from a rando chimney sweep who takes a turn babysitting the children one afternoon when literally no one else will step up) who actually seems to want to be with them. The children are confused and manipulated, desperate for Mary's love, which she doles out sparingly, just enough to keep them wanting more—and then she leaves them. Without warning, without saying goodbye, back in the care of two buffoons whose idea of parenting is to pass their children off to any paid stranger who walks through the door.

When the movie was over I found myself in trouble, terrified and sobbing and waiting outside the principal's office for ripping up a bunch of the paper hats, and for screaming that *I hated that stupid movie* and also noting that *Mary is a lying liar.* I had never been in trouble in school, never even met the principal. Now look what I'd done. I was sure I'd end up in jail.

The office door opened, and the secretary stepped into the hall. She was old like a grandma and wore a pumpkin-colored sweater. She gave me a paper Dixie cup of water and sat in the kid-sized chair beside me.

"I heard what happened," she said. "Don't tell anyone, but I hate that movie, too."

I drank the water and stopped crying. "Here," she said, and uncapped a black Sharpie. "I'm going to write your name on your cup; you can have as much water as you want. Okay?"

The cup was white, and it had blue dots in the swirly shapes of flowers all over it. I asked her if she would write on the bottom instead. She smiled. "It *is* a pretty cup," she said, and wrote my name, spelled the right way, on the cup's flat bottom.

My punishment was staying in the office with this secretary for lunch and recess all week, drinking from my cup and drawing with highlighter pens on her various notepads. It was the best week I'd ever spent in school.

Fifteen

EVERY TREE ON THE ISLAND was bare by the first Wednesday of November, and Kira and I were wasting our early-release day in the library. School was out at noon, but instead of a stroll on the beach or in the woods, I was inside, trying to help her not freak out about her unstellar SAT scores and the related panic over applying to colleges that would wonder why she hadn't enrolled in classes in the discipline she planned to major in, studio art, during this, her senior year.

"One hour, and then I'm walking to Salishwood early," I whispered, and spread out some homework of my own.

"Ooh, look," Kira whispered back, "it's your husband."

There he was, being all respectful, giving me the stupid "space" I had requested, all while being heart-stopping handsome. He dropped his backpack onto a table and pulled out some homework, completely missing us in a corner study nook.

"Look at your face," Kira whispered. "Stop punishing yourself. Stop punishing *him*."

"I'm not punishing anyone; I'm trying to use my brain and not my nether regions to make decisions."

She put her hands on the table and got all *Law & Order* Olivia-Benson-in-the-interrogation-room on me. "Listen," she whispered. "Look. Listen *and* look. This is not some dumb crush; you aren't twelve years old, and you're not being guided by your hoo-ha. You two never shut up, you yak nonstop with each other when you're together about stuff no one else in the world understands or gives a shit about—do you know who had even half a clue what you guys were dressed as on Halloween?" She didn't wait for an answer. "No one! Only you two! I've known him forever, and I know I only just met you, but I feel like you and I . . ."

"Yeah," I said. "Me too."

She smiled. "Okay, I get you, you get me. Great. So, then I can say, you know goddamned as well as I do that you aren't messing around letting your hormones take you down a life-ruining path by being with him. And *he's* definitely not. Put yourself and him out of his misery. Put me out of *mine.* Trust yourself. He's *waiting* for you. Go get him."

"I need a book," I whispered, and ran to hide in the stacks to watch him like a freaking stalker instead of just walking up and saying hello like a normal person because I could not be more spineless. Or more lonely for him, even though I saw him nearly every day. *I am a mess.* I stood in the biographies section and watched his lean, strong arms move as he turned pages, and wrote notes, and put his hand on the close-cropped dark hair on the back of his head, and, wait—*who is that?*

He smiled up at a long-haired girl, her back to me; he stood, and they talked.

She was at least three inches taller than him.

Katrina.

Kira was instantly beside me, peering through the shelves at

Sean chatting with the other half of our euphoniously conjoined nemesis. *"What the shit is she talking to him about?"* she whispered. "He is so— Can't he ever be mean to *any*one?"

He gathered his stuff, pulled his backpack on his shoulders, and they left the library together.

"Wait," I said. "I'll be back."

Down the hall, to the parking lot, she was laughing; he didn't talk much. They got in her car and drove away.

My stomach swam.

Back in the library, Kira pounced. "What is he doing?"

"Don't know."

"You didn't *ask* him?"

"No."

"Just call him and ask, say, *Hey, I saw you, what's up?*"

"It's not my business. Doesn't matter."

She dropped back in her chair. "Why are you giving up so easily?"

I sat beside her. "I'm *jealous.*"

"Okay."

"Jealous, while I'm stringing him along."

"You are not."

"I *am.* I'm too scared to be his girlfriend, but then I decide he doesn't get to be with anyone else? He can't have a conversation or get in a car with any girl who isn't me? That's not fair. *And* I'm not doing my homework. Jealousy is the most dangerous trap of all, now I'll never know if I want him because I do or if I just don't want him to be with anyone else."

Kira shook her head. "You are *killing me.* I could barely follow that line of . . . nonlogic, twisting yourself in knots. He isn't 'with' anyone else."

"And now I feel guilty because you have your own life, you shouldn't have to hear about all this garbage. I need to remember why I'm here. None of this matters."

She looked a little stricken. "It matters to me."

"*Why?*"

"Because," she said. "Sean was my only friend at this school, on the entire island. Until you came. And sometimes, when you talk about leaving so soon, I wish . . . I like you two together. I like you having reasons to stay."

The ache, the tug I'd been feeling sometimes, pulled again.

"You *do* want him for him, and there's nothing wrong with that. He is in. Love. With. You. Screw Katrina. Screw Tiana. Screw them both." And then her eyes lit up. She looked down at the pile of SAT prep before her and said, "You know what? You're right."

"About what?"

She started gathering her stuff, shoving it into her pack. "About everything. Except Sean. Let's go."

I gathered my books and ran to catch up to her, charging, with purpose, down halls and up stairwells.

"Kira," I panted. "Where are we going?"

"Art room," she said, walking faster. "I am entering that goddamn art fair. I have really good pieces I made and left in class last year, they're sitting on a shelf collecting dust, and they're better than anything anyone else has made this year, which I know because you are not the only one who can obsess and spy, my friend, oh, no, you are not." She stopped abruptly and turned back to me. "I should be in that class."

"Yes," I said, excitement replacing the misery of just moments before.

"*Me,*" she said. "Not them."

195

"Yes!"

She put all her small but determined weight against the art room door and pushed it open.

Kind of anticlimactic. Enya playing from a laptop, wall of windows and natural light, a few kids milling around working on stuff. They looked up, nodded at Kira, and went back to painting and gluing feathers on a papier-mâché bird. "Look," she said, beaming, and pointed.

On a high shelf were a couple of small canvases, a wire mobile, and a sculpture. "That's my favorite," she said. "*You* will especially love it."

I could not wait to see.

"You guys, is Mr. Taxera here?" she asked the room. Everyone shook their heads. "I'm going to get a ladder." She went searching in an adjacent supply room.

"Muiriel!" Elliot backed in through the classroom door carrying a box of a dozen seedling plants, camera strapped to him as always, and right behind him (*Why, Elliot, why?*) was Jerky McUp-Speak.

"Hey, Elliot." I smiled, ignoring Tiana ignoring me. "Kira's looking for a ladder, do you know—"

"Kira?" He dropped the box of baby plants on a shelf near the window. "Where?"

"Uh, back there?"

He ran to the supply-room door.

Tiana was pretending hard not to care about the whole exchange. But she saw me looking up and followed my gaze to the shelf.

"What do you need?" she asked.

"Not a thing," I said brightly, and moved away to look out the windows and wait. I could hear Elliot and Kira chatting it up in the supply room, laughing about who knows what—private jokes about tempera paint and stippling. It made me happy to hear her happy.

Then a sickening crash.

"Oh my gosh," Tiana said blandly. "Oh no."

The sculpture from the shelf was a pile of dust and shards of pottery clay. Tiana stood over the mess with a metal pole in her hand, the kind janitors use to open and close tall window blinds.

"Tiana!" I screamed.

Kira, Elliot on her heels, ran from the storage room before I could get to her sculpture, shattered into nothing.

"Oh," Kira said, and I could hear the tears in her voice. "Oh." She picked up one round, curved piece. "What happened?"

"I was trying to get it down for you," Tiana sighed. "You shouldn't leave things in here if you're not enrolled; this isn't your personal storage unit." She leaned the pole back in the corner where she'd found it, strolled over to the teacher's desk, and sat down to stare at her phone.

"Tiana," Elliot said. "What is *wrong* with you?"

Elliot and I knelt to help Kira pick up the pieces.

Tiana didn't look up from her phone. "I was helping," she drawled. "It was an accident. Jesus, calm down. I'm sure Michel-angelo can whip up another dog tomorrow."

"It was a dog?" I asked.

"Terry Johnson," she whispered.

I stood so fast I knocked a chair over.

Everyone in the room looked silently from Kira to me to Tiana and back. Tiana didn't seem to mind; she just sat and texted, laughing softly and probably scrolling through selfies.

I stepped toward her.

"Muir, don't," Kira begged. "It's done, please, let's just go."

The other kids just kept creepily watching the show.

"Did any of you see Tiana smash Kira's sculpture?" I asked. They all mumbled a group *no*.

Tiana smirked.

"Well, thanks," I said. "You've all been super helpful." And I stood at the teacher's desk, inches from Tiana's fake, smiling face, glaring down at her while Elliot helped Kira scoop the remains of the Terry Johnson sculpture in a plastic bag.

"Muir," Kira said. "Come on." She and Elliot had their stuff and stood waiting for me by the classroom door. Tiana looked up from her phone.

"Better go with your friends." She smiled.

On the front steps of the school I put my arms around Kira—backpack, bag of sculpture pieces, and all. "Why?" I begged. "Why can't we go after her? We'll tell Mr. Taxera, and she'll be kicked out tomorrow."

"No one saw her do it," she said. "Not even you. He'll never believe me."

"I'm so sorry," Elliot said miserably. "If a guy pulled that shit, I could punch him, but with a girl, I mean . . . what do you do with that?"

"The age-old question, my friend," I said. "You did the right thing."

"I didn't do anything!"

"Yeah, you *didn't* punch a girl in the face. You're on the right side of history. Come on, you guys, *one* of those kids had to have seen her do it."

Kira shook her head. "I'm tired. I just want to go h—"

"I'll take you," Elliot said.

"—ome," Kira finished, smiling weakly.

"Muir, can I give you a ride, too?"

I inhaled the fall air, saw the street buried in autumn leaves. "Thanks," I said. "I think I'll walk. Take care of this one." I hugged Kira once more, watched Elliot open the car door for her, and waved as they passed. One happy thing for the day.

I walked to Salishwood, turning the Sean-and-Katrina mess over and over. Kira's talent and confidence were so boldly on display at home, at Blackbird, everywhere but school, where Katiana were free to make her feel small. I directed some fury at the teachers and the school administration, grown-ass adults who let those yoga-pants-wearing, Lululemon-bag-carrying dumb-ass girls destroy Kira's spirit again and again, right out in the open, with no consequences. I understood why Kira wouldn't go to them for help; they never offered any.

* * *

I was told I carry with me a primal wound.

The house when I was twelve years old was a remodeled Victorian in the Madrona neighborhood, a few streets away from the house where Kurt Cobain died. Five bedrooms and six kids. I was set to have a top bunk with one other girl in a room with a window facing the water and looking toward Medina, at Bill Gates's house. Madrona is beautiful, tons of trees and walking distance to school. Cozy library right near a cupcake shop.

The couple was a man and a woman, and the house was full of shelves and shelves of books. Which was exciting until I tipped my head sideways to read the titles and they turned out to be mostly nonfiction: psychology/meditation/*how did my life turn out this way?*/parenting/adult coloring mandala/self-help books. Every wall in the house featured art from a different country in Africa, every corner was full of drums and carved wooden masks, though the man and woman were white, the neighborhood was white, they invited their "dearest friends" to a party the night I arrived, and all those people were white. They wore sandals and batik clothing and served lentils and pita bread, and the other kids in the house were okay—bunch of hyper boys, but the girl sharing my room seemed good. I fell asleep after my traditional Joellen first-night phone call. "It's going to be okay. I'm all right. I'll call you next week."

The next afternoon I walked back from school, and the man and woman called me into the living room and invited me to sit on the sofa, while they knelt on the shag area rug before me.

"Orlando and I want you to know," the woman said in a cloying, floaty voice, "that we've read your file, and we understand with open hearts that you are wounded, and we will honor and respect that."

"I'm— You may have someone else's paperwork," I said. "I'm totally healthy."

She smiled the way a person might smile at a dog wearing an uncomfortable Halloween costume. "Oh, dear one," she said. "*Wounded. In here.*" And she reached up, a million jangly bracelets sliding down to her elbow, to put her hand over my heart. I put my own hand on her wrist and gave her hand back to her.

"Sorry," I said. "What is this, now?"

She put one of the books on my lap, a dog-eared paperback

with a giant glossy author photo. White lady smiling. Not a scientist. Not a doctor. Lady with a bad haircut and some kind of "spiritual theory."

"You're suffering from what is known as a primal wound."

"I am?"

"Yes," Orlando said, also very softly, which made my skin crawl. "This means you are not, nor will you ever be, a whole, complete person. The trauma of being separated, ripped from your mother, has altered your molecular structure and left a void in you that can never be filled, but we can show you how to honor and nurture that void."

I sat and blinked stupidly. "I don't understand. This is in my file?"

"It's not like you can't have some kind of a fulfilling life someday," the woman said. "Just that your relationships will suffer; you won't be able to develop healthy attachments to those you may love. You will always be wounded. *Primal*—the wound is in the very fabric of your being, and will never heal. Due to the trauma."

"Wait, so which trauma is this?"

"Of the separation. From your mother."

"Oh," I said, relieved. "No, there was no separation, I never met her. I was never with her—in my file, didn't you see? She left me at the hospital; I didn't know her."

"You knew her," the woman said, her eyes closed, head nodding. "You *knew* her for nine months; you bonded; you were together—one soul, one heart—and now that part of your soul is missing. Muriel, I am so sorry to have to tell you this, but we want you to know we care for you—" And she broke down, sobbing on the floor.

The man rubbed the woman's back through her patterned tunic top.

"What about the dad?" I asked. "Do I have a wound from him, too?"

The man put his hands together in prayer position and touched them to his forehead.

"Not relevant," he said. "Your mother, your *real* mother, is gone. No one else can ever take her place, and that's why Daphne and I will never adopt. We are not in the business of stealing other mothers' babies. So if you were hoping—I'm afraid you aren't going to find that false solution here with us."

"Okay."

"What we *can* offer," Daphne sniffed, "is the opportunity to help you nurture the vivid memories you have from living in your mother's womb, to try and recover the time when you had a real family, and together we can try to revive your heart." Her face was pink, shiny with tears and sympathy.

The house was dark, eleven-thirty and everyone was asleep when I snuck down to the kitchen to use the cordless phone they kept there.

Joellen answered on the second ring.

"Come get me, please," I said. "Now."

* * *

"Well, blessed afternoon to you, too, Happy!" Natan said when I walked at last, still confused and frustrated, through the lodge and into the field to my respite, my Salishwood. This day had been crap, and I was not here for Natan making it worse; I made a bee-line away from him. Glad to be early, I filled my water bottle and went to the quiet of the trees to get a minute of calm. A quick recon walk, as Sean called it, to the trail slated for the day's classes.

Perfect time to find new birds' nests to point out to the kids later, check for trail debris. And get away from Natan.

The birds were noisy in the late-afternoon chill, maybe already sick of the cold, too, and complaining about it. I love seeing nests, hidden the rest of the year among the leaves, now exposed but safely tucked in the crooks of the bare branches. Trees are baby-bird nurseries.

"Muiriel." Natan came loping up the trail, bun bobbing, shattering my calm. "I keep forgetting to ask you something."

If there's one thing living in a city had instilled in me, it was iron-clad personal-space boundaries and an acute and trusting ear for my own inner voice. That voice screamed that I did not want to be alone in the woods with Natan.

I stood, feet firmly planted in a wide stance, arms crossed and not even a half-assed attempt to hide my annoyance. "What *is* it, Natan?"

He bent forward and caught his breath. For a self-professed "explorer of our home, Mother Earth," he was in pretty crappy shape. Skinny and pale and always dragging behind, even after the kids. "Your name," he said. "You know it's spelled an unusual way."

I stared at him.

"It's not the way you normally spell *Muriel*," he explained.

"Natan," I said, "I am aware. It's *my* fucking *name*."

He smiled his lesson-giving smile. "Yes, of course, but let me share with you the gift of your name that you *don't* know. There was a man, a lover of nature, in fact, whose surname is spelled the way your given name is."

"Nope." I moved to pass him and walk back to the field, but he widened his own stance, and trees and boulders on the trail edge trapped me.

"Two words: John. Muir."

I was going to need surgery to get my eyes unlodged from the back of my head.

Joellen's job involves driving to places she's never been on almost a daily basis, so she loves the GPS navigation thing on her dashboard. But sometimes she'll accidentally turn it on when she's leaving her house to drive to her office, a route she's driven for twenty years, and the GPS lady starts directing her how to leave her parking spot and drive down the driveway to the street she's lived on forever, and she can't turn it off and she just starts yelling at it, things like, "Oh my God, yes, turn right at the stop sign; I am going to kill this thing. Shut up shut up shut up!"

Natan was a GPS navigation system with a patchy goatee telling me how to get out of my parking space, and I wanted to kill *him*. Blood thundered in my ears, I moved to step around him, a good ten inches taller than me and he would not budge. My heart raced. I scanned the ground around me.

Something to use, a heavy thing I can hold.

"I can tell you all about the man whose name you share, anytime. I notice you're not with Sean the way you once were," he said, performing concern, his voice a husky whisper. "I'm so sorry to see your bond has lost strength. Tell me, was your relationship with him one of a sexual nature?"

I was panting, shallow, like riding out an asthma attack. Maybe I was. My racing brain paused for a moment to consider.

All that city night-walking, all those years riding public transportation, foster houses galore, but it has to happen in the forest, the place where I'm safest and that I love best?

Not today.

Fallen branch. I stared at it, gnarled and big, partly buried in dead leaves and moss, I could get it with both hands—

Stupid to take my eyes off him.

"Muriel." So close I felt his hot breath, and I screamed, my body twisted, my bent knee moved straight up, strong, hard.

Contact.

He howled, curled over himself but still standing on the trail in my way. I leaped to the branch and pulled it loose, bigger and heavier than I anticipated, and I brought it down, hard, against his knees. Now *he* screamed. The crack may have been the branch or his bone—either way, he dropped to the dirt. I flung the branch and ran, furious tears making my vision sharper, to the lodge where Jane ran out to meet me.

She took me to the kitchen and sent a grad student and an office clerk to bring Natan from the trail while I washed my hands and face, then sank down in a chair.

"But he didn't *touch* you?" she asked again and again.

"No," I said. "Because I got to him first. He was too close, I didn't like it, and he is always awful. He is inappropriate and terrible with kids, and I don't care if he . . ." I nearly called her on the family mess. But I loved this job. I wanted so badly to stay. Jane wasn't a bad person. She was just one more adult who could not figure her shit out.

She nodded. "Do you want to call the police?"

"No." Louder than I intended.

Never. Never police. He'll say I attacked him; they'll arrest me. I am so close to freedom—NO.

"No police," I said again. "But I'm not coming back if he's still here tomorrow," I said. "Or ever."

"Okay," she said, relieved. "All right."

There was shouting outside.

"Oh no . . ." Jane went to the window. "Oh, *Sean.*" She went to the door.

I stood and grabbed my bag. "I'm going out the back," I said. "Okay?"

"Muiriel—"

"Please, just no police, okay? Tell Sean I went home; make sure he's okay? Please?"

She nodded and stepped out the door. "It's not Sean I'm worried about," she sighed.

I rode the bus home, my head bouncing against the window. Two texts from Sean. Three, four. I responded, *I'm fine just went home sorry talk later,* and then I texted Kira.

Are you okay?

In a while she wrote back.

Yes, I think so. I'm sorry.

FOR WHAT?

I'm embarrassed.

NO. You have nothing to be embarrassed about. We will figure this out they are not in charge of your life and by the way how was Elliot

You know you can just say BTW for by the way

Whatever. You sure you're okay

I am. Thank you. Elliot is . . . I can't type it but he is good.
See you tomorrow.

You know you can just type tmrw.

I half smiled and turned off the phone.

At Francine's I walked up the porch steps, and she called from the henhouse in the backyard, "You're home early—how was Salishwood?"

"Good."

"You okay?"

"Tired."

"Dinner at six."

I took a shower, long and hot, I washed my hair twice and used up all my soap. I needed to go shopping soon anyway. I was almost out of floss.

I walked into the kitchen and there was dinner: a green salad, macaroni and cheese, and baked potatoes with all kinds of stuff to put on them. I looked at the table, at my plate with the potato still wrapped in foil to keep it hot, and I sat down and cried.

"Muiriel." Francine came rushing from the sink where she was filling a water pitcher with ice and lemon slices. "What's the matter?" She pulled her chair close to mine and sat beside me, her hand on my back. I wiped my eyes with my sleeve and tried to breathe. I took a sip of water.

"I love baked potatoes," I said. "I love macaroni. I love salad in my macaroni because it's a nice crunch in there."

"Well, sure," she said. "Especially if it's a nice firm romaine with no *E. coli*."

That made me cry more. She *understood*. Lettuce in pasta is nice.

She full-on put her arms around me. "Are you not feeling well? Is school okay? Whatever it is, you can tell me."

In that moment, more than any other I could remember, I wished I could. None of it would matter soon anyway, no reason to risk screwing everything up so close to the end. But still, I wished.

This dinner, though. It was the next-best thing. Like she knew I needed comforting. I dried my eyes again.

"It was a really long day," I said. *True.* "But this dinner is turning the whole thing around. Thank you. So much."

She put her hand, cool and soft, on my cheek. "Sweetheart, of course. It's just dinner. You're welcome." She moved her chair back to her place and put her napkin on her lap. "Now, give Terry Johnson a little bite of a noodle. He's worried about you."

There he was, brow furrowed, peering up at me from beneath my chair. He took the bite delicately from my fingers and ran back to the sofa.

Dinner was, as I suspected, delicious.

"I'm so sorry," I said. "I meant to ask you how was your day?"

She smiled and passed me more sour cream for my potato. "It was very productive, thank you."

We washed and dried the dishes, and then without asking this time, I followed her to the sofa, where she handed me a bag of

Newman's Own chocolate chip cookies, part of the blanket, and the remote.

"What do you want?" I asked.

"You've got the plinger."

I laughed. "The *what*?"

"The thing. The clicker."

I scrolled and searched and finally found the perfect, happy, neutral thing.

Hi, I'm Ina Garten, the Barefoot Contessa. And I don't know about you, but nothing says comfort to me better than brioche French toast with hash browns and peppers, cheesy grits, and homemade hot chocolate with whipped cream.

"She's going to make *real* whipped cream," I whispered.

"Of course she is."

I pulled Terry Johnson's ears straight up and rubbed them, instead of what I felt like doing, which was reaching over to hug Francine.

Suddenly she turned to me, took the clicker, and paused Ina.

"Muriel," she said. "I don't honestly know that I've ever met a more grateful person than you."

"Oh." I'd heard that a lot in my life.

"Let me ask you something. Don't you ever get angry?"

I scratched behind Terry Johnson's ears so vigorously he hid them with his paws. "Yeah," I said. "I do. A lot."

She sat back. "Oh, thank God. Don't ever not get angry. You've got every right. No reason to hold on to it forever of course, just always give anger its due. Let it show sometimes. Respect it."

I'd never heard *that* ever in my life.

"Understand?" she asked.

"I do."

She unpaused Ina, and we watched the woman pour an entire carton of heavy cream into a mixing bowl. Looked like Elmer's white school glue.

I moved closer to Francine on the sofa, to give Terry Johnson room to stretch. And after some discussion and a minor debate over the merits of cinnamon and whether the hens were laying enough eggs to spare, we decided to make brioche French toast in the morning.

Because Ina was right. There is no comfort better than toast.

At school the next day I searched every class and hall, the cafeteria, but no Sean. Which left me disappointed and relieved at once. Kira found me in the library during break before third period.

"How are you?" I asked. "You see the hydra today?"

"Just Katrina in passing. She *smiled* at me. I flipped her off. You look awful."

"Didn't sleep. Terry Johnson says he's ready to model anytime for a new artistic rendering of his magnificence."

She sat beside me on the study sofa and put her legs over mine. "Thank you," she said sadly. "Go home, you really don't look well."

"Thanks."

"I mean it, are you getting a cold? Just leave."

"I can't."

"Yes, you can!"

"No, I mean I have never ditched or been late. Not ever."

"You're not ditching, you're sick. Haven't you ever been sick? Go to the office, get a pass, go home. I'll come with you; it's easy."

She was so concerned. So nice to me. Something, just then,

shifted. An imperceptible movement somewhere in me, and I told her all of it. Natan's grossness, not calling the police and why. Not telling Francine. She listened and listened, and I knew she understood and would keep it all safely to herself. The third-period bell rang. We were late. I was late.

"I don't want to go home," I said. "I want to go to class, but now I don't know how to come in late."

"Being late is fun," she said, and stood and pulled me up.

"No," I whined.

"Suck it up," she said, and marched me to class. "Tell Mr. Murchison you were busy smashing the patriarchy. And a dude's balls."

It felt so good to laugh.

I texted Sean twice and got no response. After an early dinner I took a shower, sat in bed to do homework, texted him again and at last a response:

I'm okay just sleeping

Enough.

I got up and dressed, went downstairs to stand beside Francine and Terry Johnson on the sofa, and took a deep breath.

"I know it's late," I said, "and a school night. But I wondered, could I go to Sean's house for just a little while to say hi, because he stayed home sick today, and I don't know if his mom is around, so I thought I'd just make sure he's okay."

She put Terry Johnson on the floor. "Do you want me to drive you?"

"Yes," I said, startled. "Thank you."

—

She stopped in front of his house.

I pulled out my phone.

You home?

Yes

Mom awake?

Where are you

Outside, Francine drove me.

The front door opened three seconds later and he stood there, in boxer shorts and a T-shirt. Gorgeous.

"Looks okay to me," Francine said. "Healthy, I mean."

I nodded.

"Well. Tell him to put on some pants, and I'll pick you up or have him drive you home," Francine said. "No later than eleven."

"Eleven. Okay."

"Be careful," she said. "And give him my love." She waved to Sean as she pulled away, Terry watching out the passenger window.

I stood on the bottom porch step.

"I've been sick to my stomach worried about you," he said, "but I didn't want to freak you out and show up or keep texting or calling. . . . Will you please just tell me you're okay and what I can do?"

"What's going on with Katrina?"

It began to rain.

"*What?* Come up here—I can't hear you; I don't have shoes."

"Katrina. You left with her after school. What's going on with that?"

He looked so confused. "Her parents asked me to tutor her for the SAT retake because I'd helped Tiana. They're obsessed with college. The parents, I mean. I don't think either of the girls is— they could give a shit about the SATs, and it shows. But the parents are all, like, university legacy families or something, and they keep paying me kind of a lot, and, honestly, I need the money."

"Oh." Well. What do you know—tone-deaf high-pressure parents guilt-tripping their kids, who then turn around and bully nicer kids into submission with no consequences. Well done, Mom and Dad.

"I understand if you don't want to talk about it, but can you just tell me, are you okay? Did he— What did Natan do?"

"Nothing. The usual creepy. I just got to him first."

"You really did. I'm so sorry, but shouldn't we have called the police?"

"I can't."

"Yes, we—"

"No, *I* can't. Please."

"But—"

"*Sean.* I don't want to think about him anymore. I thrashed the hell out of him, and it's over. I'm begging you."

The rain fell harder.

"Please, come up here; it's starting to pour."

"I can't."

"Why? Wait, you saw me with Katrina at school?"

"Yes."

"So why didn't you say hello?"

213

I looked down at the porch step. It needed paint.

"Muir?"

"Please don't tell Kira you know this. Katrina is awful to Kira. So is Tiana."

"They . . . oh, man. Awful how?"

Seriously—boys. So clueless. Wasn't I betraying Kira telling him this? But I wanted them away from her so badly, off her back for good.

"They're mean any way they can be, and Kira does *not* want you to know. But I want to help her. And I didn't say hello when I saw you and Katrina because it wasn't my business; I told you I needed space and all that. . . ." My hands were actually shaking. "But then I saw you and I was jealous and that isn't fair and now I'm humiliated."

"Please don't be. I'm sorry, I would have told you about the tutoring, but the space . . ."

Fucking space.

"Katrina's mom called me the night before I met with her, and that was the first—and last—time I tutor her."

"No, you don't have to stop because I'm . . ."

"I won't say anything to Kira. I swear. But she's practically my sister. I believe you. Katrina can screw off."

"Tiana, too?"

"Tiana even more."

I felt better. Still embarrassed, but saying it all out loud was . . . freeing.

"You didn't answer my texts," I said. "Before."

"I was asleep, I took a bunch of Advil."

"Why?"

He held up his right hand, bandaged and iced.

"Oh God. Is it broken?"

"Just sprained. But only because they pulled me off him too soon."

"Sean."

"Also it was the first time I'd ever punched a guy, and I'm pretty sure I did it wrong. I swear I'm not violent, but he said your name. . . ."

A rush of warmth spread from my chest; for his hurt hand, for the thought of his defending me.

"Muir."

"Yeah?"

"Do you want to come in?"

I tried to see past him into the house. "Your mom awake?"

"She's on the mountain still."

The rain was cold and insistent.

"Come inside," he said.

"Do you have a car?"

"Yes."

"Can you take me home by eleven?"

He looked at his watch and stepped toward me. "We have an hour and fifty minutes. I'll get you home early. I promise." Their porch had no cover, he kissed me and the rain soaked my hair, and we went inside.

I was back at Francine's by ten fifty-five. Promise kept.

Sixteen

SCHOOL LET OUT the day before Thanksgiving, and I spent the afternoon in the kitchen with Francine, peeling eight thousand potatoes, russet and sweet, for the next day's dinner at Kira's house. Francine used handwritten recipe cards stored in a little metal file box. Rain beat the windows, and Francine was blasting a James Taylor CD. I felt sixty years old, like Francine and I were two old ladies living in our Golden Girls retirement home for active adults. I loved it.

Pies baked and cooled on racks, apple and pumpkin. She had cider in a pot on the stove. We ate salad for lunch, in readiness for the eating marathon.

"I love Thanksgiving," I said, trimming the crust off yet another pie.

"This is the quietest one I've had in years. Yours, too, I bet."

I nodded.

We cooked and baked all day.

In the evening I took a shower and lay in the big bed doing

homework the best I could manage with Terry Johnson sprawled across my open history book when my phone lit up. Kira.

Can you come to Blackbird

Nine-thirty. Blackbird had closed at noon. I put on a sweater and my raincoat and asked Francine if I could go.

"Home by eleven," she said.

"Eleven," I repeated.

The rain had stopped but the sky was pitch black. I used Francine's headlamp and walked fast to town, where Blackbird's windows were lit up warm and bright, chairs on the tables. I knocked on the glass door and stepped in. Kira, up on a six-foot ladder, turned to me as the bells rang.

"I am a paid artist."

The huge, long chalkboard behind the register was covered, not with a menu but with a mural of the Puget Sound. My mouth hung open.

It was intricate and beautiful, all color and life and birds and water, ferry boats and whales and, in the center, Mount Rainier's snowy peak.

"I don't even know what to— When did you do this?"

"Today. I called my boss yesterday and asked if I could, and I came in after we closed and showed her my portfolio and she said do it and I started and couldn't stop. I've had four cups of coffee. *Four!*"

I stared and stared. "Kira," I said. "You're going to be an artist. You *are,* I mean—for real. For your *life.*"

She was exhausted, which may have explained the tears streaking her rainbow chalk–dusted face, still smiling like a tanked-up caffeine junkie.

"Hold up. How many patches are you wearing?"

"None! I've been thinking," she said. "Since you beat the shit out of that guy. Sean sent me all the movies you told him to watch."

"What movies?"

"The ones about aging out?"

My stomach twisted with embarrassment. "You didn't need those. I just wanted him to understand—"

"*I* didn't understand. I watched them all, and I think I wasn't truly listening to you. I am now, I will always, and you have to know you aren't alone," she said. "I mean, you don't have to be. I wish you liked it here; I wish you would stay."

"And live where? Do what? Also, aren't you leaving for college?"

"Like my parents could afford housing! I'm ferrying in and living at home, no matter who accepts me. Community college, whatever. But I mean, besides my wishing you'd stay for my selfish reasons, you could have us all around. You know? Like, if you went to school . . ."

"I can't. But with a clean record I can work at lots of places. Starbucks. Grocery stores, that's good money. I can get temp jobs. I'll live."

"Okay, but is that what you want to do?"

"Kira. I'm aging out. I don't get to do what I *want*."

"All right, wait, wait, wait—we did this in psych; this is an Oprah thing, hold on. . . . Silence your inner voice, shut off your brain, and then say out loud: 'If I could do anything and get paid, what would it be?' "

"It doesn't matter, I don't even—"

"No! Don't think! Just say, 'I want to be paid to spend all day . . .'"

"Walking in the woods."

"Good!" she said. "Yes! What else?"

"That's it."

"Okay, so you're a park ranger, you and Sean."

I shook my head.

"Why not?"

"You *just* said you watched the movies!"

She climbed down from her ladder and sat on the counter. "Muir. I haven't painted or touched clay since last year. I feel like a failure and I'm embarrassed; I feel so *sorry* for myself, being dragged from the only home and friends I knew, and Katiana is my punishment for that self-pity. I gave up the thing I loved most so easily. I'm scared to death of them, I still am—and then you came here. And talked to me and let me be your friend when I didn't have anyone. I didn't have myself. You've made yourself into this person who can live anywhere; you've raised yourself to be a person who can't stand not making things right, and I think you do believe, deep down secretly, that you deserve to be happy, or else you wouldn't have bothered defending yourself from that—I can't even say his name—*chad*. I imagined you doing that, saving yourself from him, and I thought, *I am done dicking around. I am an artist.* And here I am."

"Kira," I said. "It's not—"

"You are worth having a life with people who love you; you have just as much a right to happiness as anyone. If you want to stay here, if you want to go to school, then do it. There are ways—I watched those movies, and they scared the absolute *shit* out of me.

I get why you're so careful. And I understand you're scared of being trapped, but I *know* about the ways to stay, the ways to do things like school. We're here. We've got you."

I blinked fast, unable to say what I was thinking: that no friend had ever said anything so nice to me, ever. That I did believe her; I knew she meant every word, how much I wished it could all be true. And how truthfully scared I was to try to live alone.

Then the coffeemaker clicked on and started brewing another pot. I walked behind the counter and unplugged it. "I'm cutting you off. You and your ways."

"Whatever. I'm done anyhow."

I stood beside her sitting on the counter, and we admired her manic, glorious creation, the ink on her arms spattered in dust of every color.

"I'm going surfing next weekend at La Push," she said. "I haven't surfed in months. I miss it so much I ache. I'm done punishing myself."

"Oh, Kira." I wished I could see her in the ocean, brave and daring in the wild, freezing waves. Maybe one day she would invite me. But I understood this was *hers.*

"And Elliot is coming here tomorrow to take pictures of this for me," she said. We gazed up at her masterpiece.

"What exactly are that young man's intentions?" I asked. "He being good to you?"

"*Very* good." She sighed dreamily. "He's growing these field grasses in little boxes in class and making a photo-movie of their lives, all the way until they go to seed."

"What the hell is a photo-movie?"

"I have no idea. He's a genius."

220

She seemed happier than in all the months I'd known her. She hugged me, full of joy and relief.

"Want some toast?" she asked.

Best. Friend. Ever.

*　*　*

I carry with me a dollhouse's dollhouse.

Thanksgiving is a rough holiday when you live in a city named for Chief Seattle—hard to ignore the murderous reason the day is celebrated at all. For a white kid in public school, even in Seattle, reflections on genocide were eclipsed by construction-paper Pilgrim hats and handprint turkeys. As with the Little House books, I was oblivious. I took my joy anywhere I could get it. And Thanksgiving gave me a *lot* of joy.

I love every bit of consistency I can get, and every house I lived in celebrated Thanksgiving, every house had traditions for the meal—potatoes the way Nana So-and-So made them or it *just wasn't Thanksgiving*. People got agro over these things, and it made me happy. I have had a seat at thirteen tables, that I can remember, for people's very favorite versions of this, the very best meal of the year, recipes so complicated and full of fat and sugar they are made only this one day.

It was almost always noisy and fun; the kids' table was *the place*, and some nice auntie or grandma always let me help in the kitchen. I have made mashed potatoes with so much sour cream and butter it would stop your heart, but you keep eating them because they are *so good*. I helped create a pumpkin pie from an actual pumpkin and found I like frozen Sara Lee pies better, but it was fun to make a real one, fun to roll the crust and crimp the edges and brush it with butter, fun to whip actual cream and sugar instead of using a spray can, and magic to stew actual tart and sweet jewel-colored cranberry sauce.

Only one year was Thanksgiving not so great. Seven years old, second grade, my last before I stopped eating animals. The foster parents had kids of their actual own, and they were going away to Oregon to be with the grandparents for the holiday. The other foster kids were going for home visits, but they had to find respite care for me.

Respite care is basically a babysitter who's got foster security clearance. I was sad about the prospect of a halfway Thanksgiving by myself. Then, two days before the day, a new kid came. His first time in care, he was near my age and already terrified, and to make it worse, he was denied a visit home for Thanksgiving. Oddly enough, he was not super comforted that at least I, a stranger, would be with him.

The respite lady lived alone in a mobile-home park in Tacoma. She was nice, but there was no Thanksgiving dinner. She did heat frozen turkey dinners for us, in the oven instead of the microwave, so they were good—but nothing like the Thanksgivings I loved. And even though he didn't talk to me the entire time, I could tell this was definitely different from what the new kid was used to. We ate on trays in front of the TV.

The respite lady sat and crocheted. The boy looked at the *National Geographic* magazines the lady kept in a stack on the floor. I wandered around the mobile-home park and found wildflowers growing near a chain-link fence. I picked them and asked the lady for some string. She gave me a piece of dental floss, and it worked fine to wrap the flowers into a bouquet, which I put on my TV tray. Frances the badger put a tiny vase of violets on her desk at school for lunch, and I agreed it made things cheerful.

After dinner the lady dragged out a basket of toys for us. Most of them were for toddlers, lots of bath toys and old Playskool stuff. But she also brought out a dollhouse. It was wooden and had rabbit dolls instead of people. The girl rabbit wore a wedding dress and a veil. I dressed and undressed her, adding a kicky pink top, fluffing the veil and smoothing it, and then, in the rabbit's upstairs bedroom, I saw it: the *dollhouse.* It was plastic, blue, with white shingles and a red front door. I held it in both my hands and could not believe something so mind-boggling could even exist. I *stared* into the rooms, each one tiny as a marble, where even tinier furniture was glued in place. In all the world there was never anything so perfect.

The new boy was rooted on the sofa with the *Nat Geo*s. I brought him snacks. "It's not usually like this," I told him. "Thanksgiving is usually fun." He took a lot of naps, and while he slept the long weekend away, I sat outside in the autumn sunshine examining that tiny meta house. I looked up sometimes and he was awake, sitting by the window. He waved, and I waved back, and he picked up another magazine.

I was nearly asleep Sunday night, safely back in my bottom bunk in the foster house, when the bedroom door opened a little and the light from the hall spilled in.

"Muriel?"

The boy stepped in, put the dollhouse in my hand, and left, closing the door behind him.

* * *

Thanksgiving morning Francine was up before dawn, which is not such an accomplishment in the Pacific Northwest, where the winter sun peeks over the horizon at the crack of 9:00 a.m., but she was up in the dark. Chickens fed, eggs collected, Terry Johnson walked and napping on the sofa, half-watching the Macy's parade.

"There's nothing left for me to do." I yawned, scratching Terry's ears until he growled.

"You wish," Francine said. "We need to be at the Aoyamas' by two o'clock; here's three pounds of carrots and onions for you to chop."

I ate my toast and tea, tied on an apron, and happily got to work.

"I've spent every Thanksgiving I can remember with the Aoyamas," Francine said. "With Kira's grandparents, and her mom, until she left for school and married, but they always brought Kira, then Ryo, every year from California. I watched that girl and her brother grow up. I'm so glad they're all here now."

"Was she a cute baby?"

"Kira? Oh Lord, yes, much cuter than her poor brother."

"Francine."

"He's a great kid and I love him, but that doesn't change the fact that he had an awkward phase that lasted from age two till, like, sixth grade. He's fine now."

"Nice."

She shrugged. "Ask anyone. Ask his *parents.* But Kira—sweetest girl, wild hair, little-bird voice—she made us all place card holders for the table every year, turkeys out of pinecones and feathers and glitter. I have all of mine somewhere. She still want to study art in college?"

"She does."

The kitchen was warm, and the Macy's parade was a *lot,* but it was nice background noise against our chopping and whisking.

"You sure you don't want to apply anywhere? School?" she said.

"Francine. Come on."

"Come on *what*? Free tuition's not nothing. If you want to go, there are ways; nothing is impossible. I mean, look at your grades, and all your volunteering. Muiriel, I've been giving this a lot of thought, and I think we should talk to Joellen about—"

At the front door someone knocked loudly, twice, and Terry Johnson barked. Once.

"Hold on," Francine yelled above the suddenly loud parade, a Broadway show tune being performed by nearly naked guys wearing hot pants in subzero temperatures in New York. I kept chopping, and when she didn't come back right away, I leaned back to look down the hall to see Francine standing in the doorway, talking to Sean.

I whipped off the apron, washed my hands, filled them with water, and kind of tossed it on my hair, aiming for what effect I couldn't say.

"Hi," he said, and walked, smiling, into the kitchen. "Happy Thanksgiving."

"Look what Sean brought us," Francine said, hefting a colorful, foil-wrapped chocolate turkey that I recognized from the window display of the candy shop next to the Blackbird.

"Wow," I said. "That is . . . a big turkey."

"Yeah," he said. "It's solid."

"It is?"

"Not hollow."

"Right."

Why was it so weird being together with Francine in the room?

"Okay," he said. "Well, I'm off to meet Mom and fifty of our extended family at the ferry. Oh, and, Muir? My mom wants to meet you. Soon."

"Tell her it's mutual!"

"Give your mom my love," Francine told him. "Tell her I have a ton of eggs for her."

"I will."

"I'll walk you out," I said.

On the porch I kissed him as long as would not be suspicious, and then Terry Johnson came out to bark that it was time to wrap it up.

"I brought you these," he said. "Is that stupid? If it's stupid, use them for a centerpiece or something. . . ." A bouquet of wildflowers, in November, on a national holiday, when all the flower shops were closed.

"Where did you find them?" I inhaled. Alpine. Mount Rainer meadow flowers.

"Mom is friends with a nursery owner midisland. Please don't worry, Mom's really nice, and meeting her doesn't mean we have to get married."

I smiled and sighed with relief. *God, he gets it.*

"I mean. Unless you want to."

"All right, pal," I said. "Take that show on the road to the ferry."

"Happy Thanksgiving." One more kiss and he drove away, and I waved, Terry Johnson watching with bland disapproval.

"You're just jealous," I said, and carried him into the house and up to my room, where I put the flowers in a jam jar of water on the dresser beside my books.

Later, at Kira's house, I met her dad, who was as kind and welcoming as her mom, and her brother, Ryo, whose face scarcely left his Nintendo screen and was not at all awkward-looking, so I had no idea what Francine was talking about. Her parents did the whole

Go around the table and say what you're thankful for routine, and I realized that I had so many things to catalog I could not believe it. Kira being my friend. Francine's kindness, her warm home with the bedroom that felt less lonely every day. Salishwood. When my turn came, I feared I would cry on my green beans and was so afraid to say some of the things I really meant, so I said only:

"Thank you for inviting me today. I've never had a . . . Kira. Or a Francine. Or known a family like yours. It's . . . these are the best mashed potatoes I've eaten in my life."

No one spoke for a moment. Everyone raised their glasses. I did, too. Francine wiped her eyes with her napkin. Kira used her sleeve. Her mom straight up went to the bathroom for tissues, pulled out a bunch for herself, and handed me some, too.

"This is a depressing Thanksgiving," Ryo snarked.

Everyone laughed, and Terry Johnson, a guest on a pillow under the table, barked for us to shut up, bothered by our loudness.

Kira's mom stood up. "We are, as always, so very thankful for the gift of Francine and her family. And especially this year, because she has brought us Muiriel."

What?

"We are so grateful for your friendship to Kira, because we made her leave the ocean and we moved her at a time in school when it is not easy finding new friends, especially really true friends, but it seems she has found one in you. She's not so mad at us anymore, and for that we are *beyond* grateful."

"Oh, I'm still pissed," Kira assured them.

Kira's dad raised his glass. Everyone did.

I smiled all the way to my toes.

Later, in my attic bed trying to find room around Terry Johnson sprawled in the middle, when Joellen called and asked, as she did every Thanksgiving, "How was it?" I tried to not let the dread of *I cannot get attached to this; I have to leave it and be alone soon* overtake my happiness, at least just for this one night. My throat burned and I said, "It was okay. Pretty good."

"That all?" she asked.

"Do you know where Zola is?"

"I do."

"Is she okay? Is she happy?"

"That's all I can tell you."

"Is she still home? If she is, don't say anything."

Silence.

"Thanks," I said. Home for Thanksgiving—thank goodness.

"But today, you really had a good time? Francine said it was good."

I listened to her smile through the phone.

"Well," I said. "I helped make pies. They were excellent."

Seventeen

BEGINNING AT MIDNIGHT on December 1, Francine's house was decorated like she was entering a Most Festive House on the Planet contest, and the TV was never turned on because she played Christmas music from the moment I got up for school all the way until bedtime. But I was mostly out of the house, at school or Salishwood or at Blackbird or at Kira's house or with Sean—and so I got just enough of the music to love it instead of being driven nuts by it. A lot of Dean Martin. Nat King Cole. "Old guys who know how to do 'Jingle Bells' right," she said. I did homework to it, fell asleep to it, woke up to it, and to hot cider and cinnamon rolls and apple strudel and a hundred dozen sugar cookies for the women's shelter.

Her volunteering there was a big deal in her everyday life. Normally I could not care less about what the foster parents did. Besides fostering. But Francine—what had her life been before now?

I was determined to not ask. To stop wondering. Wouldn't matter soon, anyway.

She said to me one morning as she set a plate of Swedish

pancakes with warm lingonberry jam before me, "Listen. If I ever get diagnosed with a terminal illness, like with a time limit, months to live? It is Christmas. Get out the decorations and keep them up until the end. I will die at Christmastime. You got that?"

As if I'd always be there with her to make those decisions together. To unpack the tinsel and string the lights the way she had, around every single window in the house, including the bedrooms.

I just nodded, my mouth overfull of pancakes and jam.

Maybe even more festive than Francine's house were Kira's brightened spirits—she was back in art class.

"Mr. Taxera says I can make up quizzes and as much studio work as I can over winter break so I'll be ready for next semester," she had whisper-squealed during the breakfast rush at Blackbird. "But the very, very best part is, he came in last week and saw the mural and *he's letting me paint a mural on the classroom wall!*"

"Oh, *Kira.*" The long line of tourists at the counter had to deal with some major jumping-around excitement. "You are the Pacific Northwest's Diego Rivera!"

She made a face. "That guy was a dick. I'll be Marion Greenwood."

"No. You'll be Kira Aoyama, better than any of them."

It was true. Her classroom mural, with some directed help from Elliot, who also documented the daily progress in photographs, was a wonder to see come to life. At some point, every student in the school stopped by the class to watch her paint, especially Sean and Elliot and me, who ate lunch watching her each day until it was finished. It was another gorgeous wave of water and sky and light, lit by the art classroom's wall of windows. She was so proud.

Her smile was infectious. Especially when Elliot was around.

He was sweet with her, tall and protective. He posed for her oil paint and pastel portraits, she for his million photographs.

I was caught off guard by how happy her happiness made me.

And how it incensed Katiana. They skulked in the art room when Kira worked on the mural, and they stalked around the cafeteria like unfixed cats, marking their territory and glaring at anyone who did not fall in line, including and especially the four of us—Elliot, Kira, Sean, and me—eating together in the lunchroom once the mural was complete.

"Aren't they exhausted, monitoring your every movement like that?" I asked. "Is it bonkers with them in art class?"

"We're getting better at ignoring them," Elliot said.

"They spend a lot of time in the corner talking about how paint is a worthless medium and making these sculpted wire things, kind of like a nest all tangled and strung with colored glass, suspended from the ceiling? Which, I mean . . . they're really beautiful, to be honest." She stole a few chips from Elliot's plate and sat there chewing while we all stared at her. She looked up. "What?"

"Teach me your ways," sighed Sean, who had stopped tutoring or even speaking to Katiana the moment I told him they'd been torturing Kira. He never asked me for evidentiary details, just wholly believed my word and was now actively pissed off at them on Kira's behalf.

It was things like that—my joy in Kira's happiness, her and Sean's constant unquestioning belief that I was always telling the truth—that made me wish, for brief moments, that I was not aging out. That I could somehow stay, even just a little while longer. Time was flying.

"I mean," Elliot said, "you're not wrong about the wire things.

But it's hard for me to appreciate the beauty in anything even remotely related to Katiana when they're such . . ."

"Soulless monsters?" Kira said. "Oh, for sure. In perpetuity."

There's my girl.

She smiled. "I think I'm just too busy—and dare I say, happy—to give a shit."

"Cheers to that," I said.

Happiness. Aside from my baseline anxiety about being on my own alone in mere months, and my nagging concern for Zola's safety and whereabouts, I had allowed myself, with these people, on this island, to dip my toe in the pool of happiness more than ever before.

Salishwood, since Jane's promised Natan exodus, was heaven on earth for me and Sean. She kept her interactions with me professional and brief, just the way I liked them, and she hired a woman to replace Natan, a thing she should have done a year ago, but all's well, as Francine liked to say. Sean rested his hand on my knee, my head on his shoulder, me with friends and this boy I liked so much—at our *regular lunch table.* Holy cats, happiness is a hell of a drug. Dangerous.

I should have guessed it would not last.

Just days before winter break I sat in algebra, holding my head in my palm and concentrating hard, when a kid interrupted class to pass out bouquets of white daisies, a fund-raising thing that, in every school I've attended, I'd always considered cornball and stupid. Until I held a bouquet of white daisies with *my name* on the card written above the words *Happy Solstice. XO Sean.*

So maybe not *that* cornball. It's nice to raise money for the SPCA.

I waited at our lunch table for Kira, Sean, and Elliot at second lunch that day, the flowers on my backpack like a snowball of happiness. I smiled to myself and at my fruit cocktail, liking the whole situation a little too much, but it was so hard not to. I watched the door and texted her *Where you at?* Katiana made their entrance, looked right to me, and strolled over. I pulled out my Rachel Carson book, but they stood beside me, weirdly close and smiling.

I smiled back. "What?"

"Dining alone?" Tiana said.

I opened Rachel and tried to read.

"Nice flowers," she said.

"Thanks. You going to tell me it'd be a shame if something happened to them?"

Tiana frowned. *"What?"*

I nodded. "Exactly."

"Oh," Katrina said, "Muiriel, I've wanted to let you know my SAT sessions with Sean went really, really well?"

Not to vocal shame, but their shared upspeak was truly grating.

"Uh. Okay?" It was catching.

"Yes," she said breathlessly, "I learned *so* much?" They laughed.

"I'll bet," I said. "He's really smart."

"Yeah, he helped me. A *lot*?"

Of all the ringleaders I've met, these two had to be the least skilled. Their repertoire was either inelegant and bumbling (destroying Kira's artwork) or Hallmark-movie cheesy (*I boned your boyfriend!*). If the teachers or administrators would ever confront this kind of garbage, just once—it would be a miracle.

"Wait," I said, "hold up, I get it—do you mean, like, 'learning' is a euphemism for 'Sean was teaching you exciting sex maneuvers'? Because of all the sex you two were having when you were supposed to be studying on that one day he tutored you? Sounds great, don't forget to invite me to the wedding." I went back to my book.

They changed course.

"All righty then," Katrina said. "Say hi to Kira for us when you see her? If you see her? An artist's work is never done."

Tiana shushed her and smacked her arm.

"Ow," Katrina whined, and let Tiana pull her to the "leggings" table.

"Bye, girls! Great to see you!" I called.

I marked my book page, looked again for Kira's text, and heard Tiana laugh.

An artist's work is never done.

I ran.

The mural was erased.

No violent defacement; it was just *gone.* The wall was blank, two fresh coats of flat interior white paint, maybe a layer of kill beneath them. No trace of the hours and days of intricate color and lines and beauty. Kira sat on the floor, staring at it. I sat beside her.

"They must have come so early," she said. "What time do the janitors open the building? Five? They worked fast."

I pressed my finger into the white. Tacky. But nearly dry.

"What did Mr. Taxera say?"

She shrugged. "He assumed I did it."

"Why?"

"Because it's so deliberate. Look how careful they were. They put painter's tape on the baseboards."

"No, why would he think *you* did this?"

"Because . . . to demonstrate how beauty is fleeting, art is alive and fluid, it was a painting version of a sand mandala, time to blow it away, some Artist's Way transcendental shit. I don't know. He applauded my 'bold statement.'"

"But what did he say when you told him you didn't?"

She shook her head.

"*Kira,*" I moaned. "You didn't tell him?"

"I have no proof! There is no proof. I don't want to start it all again; I want to stay in class."

I stared at the wall, white-hot as my rage. I had a *bold statement* for that teacher. Kira had worked so hard, it was so beautiful—was he really so blind to Katiana's cruelty, or was he just exhausted and willfully ignoring what was happening before his eyes so he didn't have to spend his teaching time parenting a bunch of asshole teenagers whose actual parents couldn't be bothered?

So very many reasons to contemplate. All of them garbage.

I stood up. "You are staying in this class. *They* are leaving."

"No."

"Kira."

"*No.*"

Months ago I would have left this alone. Probably even left the room.

Now I crouched down beside Kira. "Since I've lived here, which is approximately five months, I have witnessed those girls destroy your artwork *three times.* That's not good math."

"Not three."

"The ferry cookies were art. She literally threw your art in the garbage, and you didn't say a word."

She put her forehead on her knees. "This is my penance," she said. "I am not being dramatic, I'm not self-flagellating; this is what I deserve."

"For what?"

She closed her eyes tight. "For being *them*. In California. I was the top of the food chain. I watched people get ignored and made fun of and I didn't give a shit. I cared about what I wanted, which was cutting class to get high and surf with my cool, fucking drunk and high friends. That was it. I was an asshole to kids like you, and I got away with it because, even cutting class, I still pulled grades, so no one said no to me."

"So you deserve this? Katiana is your real-time karma?"

"Yes."

"Okay, well, first of all, full disclosure, I know basically nothing about karma, but wouldn't this crap be punishing you for your bad intentions in a previous life versus a few semesters ago?"

"It's just an expression."

"No, it's not! Karma's a thing people believe in! Not me, but I *am* a fan of personal responsibility, and you *swim* in that."

"I do not."

"Kira. Yes, you do. It's not easy to admit you've been awful to people—we all do it, but hardly anyone admits it and tries to stop. You could have kept being mean or selfish or what the hell ever you were doing, but instead you've found your way back to who you were before all that. You're the kindest person I've known, and I've known a *lot* of people. You can't just decide to be that out of the blue. It's who you are. Who your parents missed and wanted back."

She would not look up. "You'd be amazed how much your personality changes when you stop drinking before noon," she said.

"I bet."

"I need a tissue."

"Okay." I grabbed the whole box from the teacher's desk.

"Where is everyone? I've never seen it not filled with randos sketching and stuff."

"They'll be back after lunch. They're scared of me in here crying."

"Listen, we have a chance to do for Katiana what your parents did for you."

"Send them to another state?"

"Your parents said *no*. They brought you here to get you away from the noise and out of the spiral. They parented the shit out of you! Katiana doesn't have anyone to say no to them. No one else is going to be the goddamn adult in this situation, so we have to do it. Come on."

"I'm too tired."

"Well, I'm not. I'm fed up. Aren't you?"

She held a giant wad of tissue to her eyes and reached out to touch the white paint. "Yes."

"Good! Stay that way. Let's go."

The principal's desk was bigger than it needed to be, super ostentatious, but I was grateful to have its weight between us. Her nameplate, at least, was understated. *Principal Barbara Langford*. My sweaty hands were leaving prints on my jeans. Here I sat, on purpose, in her office, a white woman in her forties, hair parted in the middle and up in a bun. Standard blouse-and-jacket combo. Terrifying. Kira and I in wingback chairs, facing her.

Kira wasn't thrilled, but most definitely she'd had experience in principals' offices before. She spoke first. "It's been going on since last year," she said, quiet but at least out loud.

"Well, that's quite a long time." The principal smiled. "What made you decide to say something so late in the game, Kira?"

Blaming Kira already. "Wait," I said, startling myself. "Shouldn't Tiana and Katrina be here, too?"

"I can hear what Kira has to say without Tiana and Katrina in the room. I don't pull students out of class without a valid reason."

"This *is* a valid reason. They've been after her since she got here: They've destroyed her homework. They painted over this mural. . . . Shouldn't they have to explain why?"

The principal glanced at her desktop screen and found my name. "Muiriel," she said. "I appreciate your concern for your friend, but you will not dictate the terms of this meeting, young lady."

I sat back, stung. Nothing shuts me up faster than a *young lady*.

"They should be here," Kira said.

The principal sighed. "Girls, I have known Tiana and Katrina since they were in kindergarten. This is a tight-knit school, but the students here are welcoming and kind, including and especially those girls. Now, our island community may not be what you're used to, where you're from—"

Where you're from?

My hackles raised, and Kira sat up and forward, both hands on the giant desk.

"We are a fourth-generation island family," she said, her voice loud and steady. Her eyes were. Lit. Up.

Yes.

"Well," the principal said, "but you are new to this school, and we don't—"

I held my breath, waiting for the Classic White Person Line: *But where are you* really *from?*

"I am *from* this island," Kira said. "My family built this island. This is my home. We are not new. We belong here. I belong here, and I need help to get Tiana and Katrina to leave me alone."

I wanted to stand up and applaud.

The principal turned and sat there reading her computer screen. She wouldn't even look at us. She jotted something on a Post-it note and walked out, leaving the door wide open. We heard her voice low, talking to the secretary.

"Um," Kira whispered. "What the . . ."

"Should we stay?" I whispered back.

"I think so? This is weird. I hate it!"

"She's probably hoping we'll leave. Let's just . . . sit."

So we did. Kira pulled out her phone. "I'm telling Elliot what's up; I don't know if he's even seen the mural yet." She sat and typed, and I wondered whether I should tell Sean where we were. But was that too weird and clingy?

Why hadn't this happened on our group lunch day?

We sat there for close to twenty minutes, getting more and more nervous, and then out in the reception office, another voice.

"Okay, then, let me talk to her. Where is she?"

Kira and I looked at each other.

Francine?

"Muiriel," she said, breathless and in her chicken jeans and her raincoat, the ones she wore to clean the coop. Her *not planning to get out of the car, I'm just dropping you off* outfit. "Kira, what's going on? Are you okay?"

The principal came in, dragging a third chair for Francine.

"Thanks, Barb, I'll stand."

Barb?

Francine really did know everyone on this entire island.

Barb smiled. "So," she said, "the girls and I were just having a conversation about friendship. About how sometimes it's not as easy as we'd like it to be. Now, ladies, I know it's hard to believe, but Francine and I were both teenagers once, and I think we could tell some pretty harrowing stories about times when maybe there was a squabble or a misunderstanding between our gal pals. Am I right, Francine?"

Francine turned to Kira and me, puzzled. "Are you two in a fight?"

Kira groaned and brought Francine up to speed—the bullying, the sculpture, the mural.

Francine put her hand on Kira's cheek and squeezed it, near tears, and then she turned to Barb. "Where are Tiana and Katrina? Why aren't they here?"

"Francine, I'm not pulling innocent students out of class for some she-said/she-said nonsense; the friends can work it out on their own."

"We are not friends," I said, more to Francine. "They ruined the mural; they do weird manipulative shit all the time. They're why Kira isn't in art this semester; I was in the room when Tiana smashed her sculpture."

"*Language,*" Barb said sharply. "You *saw* Tiana do it? You watched her do it on purpose?"

"I was in the room; she pretended it was an accident—"

"And you watched them paint over this mural?"

Kira looked down.

"Did anyone see them do any of these things?"

"I was in the room," I said again. "Please just ask them."

Barb sat back in her swivel chair. "So, you girls would like me, with no evidence whatsoever, to punish Tiana and Katrina, just because you say so—is that right?"

What had I done? Poor Kira. This was a horrible idea; she would hate me for this.

"Barb," Francine said, "come on. I know Muiriel; I've known Kira all her life. Look at her—she's asking for help. They're telling the truth. Let's just get Tiana and Katrina in here and figure this out."

Barb shook her head.

"Then why did you call me?" Francine said. "Did you call Kira's parents? More to the point, did you call Tiana's and Katrina's parents?"

"No, I called *you* because I see here you are Muiriel's guardian, and—"

"Foster mother," Francine corrected.

"Right," Barb said, "and so I thought, as a foster parent, you could give me some insight about certain patterns of behavior that might shed some light on this situation."

Francine was genuinely perplexed. "Patterns of behavior? I don't know Tiana or Katrina well enough to know their . . . patterns."

"No, Francine, it's . . ." Barb smiled and glanced at the computer. "I'm seeing *Muiriel's* school records are . . . There's a lot of starting and changing schools midyear, and I'm wondering if the reasons for her erratic school attendance might explain her behavior today."

Color rose in Francine's face like a rash. "Girls," she said in a tone I'd never heard her use, "wait by the door." I grabbed Kira's hand and we moved fast. Francine went to the desk where Barb sat, hands folded tight. "Muiriel's *behavior* today was coming to you for help, to ask you to help Kira. How *dare* you—"

"Francine," Barb said, "you know Katrina and Tiana are both very overwhelmed with academics, and that can cause stress—"

"I'm sure they're very busy," Francine said. "The thing is, I don't give a shit. I want them off my girls' radar *now.*"

Warm, happy tingles prickled my scalp.

"Kira!" Now Elliot came running in the office, also breathless.

If it wasn't so tense and awful, this would have been an exciting afternoon.

"The grass!" he said.

Oh, Elliot. Jesus, now Barb would think we're selling weed. Kira looked miserable.

Elliot held up his camera. "Time lapse! I set it for one frame per minute on the grass boxes in the classroom, all through the night until seven this morning. The mural was in the shot."

Barb's face kind of lost some color.

"I'm so sorry," he said to Kira. "We'll re-create it; I took a million pictures. They're all here, and every frame of Tiana and Katrina painting over it." He smiled brightly at Barb. "I'll email them to you. Is it Barb dot edu?" Then back to Kira: "Oh, and I almost forgot—these are for you." He put a winter daisy bouquet in her hands. Kira dropped back into the chair, beamed up at Elliot, and then turned, smiling, to Barb.

"So, Principal Langford," she said, taking off her cardigan sweater, all calm confidence and wicked tattoos. "Let's talk patterns of behavior."

My hero.

I surreptitiously pulled my phone from my bag.

You will not believe the shit going down in Langford's office.
Wish you were here.

Sean responded immediately.

Are you okay?

Very.

Francine came to where I stood, leaning on the doorframe. She put her arm around my shoulders for one strong, tight hug. "Still mad?" she whispered.

"Furious."

"Good."

"You have your phone?" Francine called out over Tony Bennett's overwrought rendition of "Winter Wonderland" the afternoon school let out for winter break. "And your house key?" I held up both for her to see, finished emptying the dishwasher, and went back up to the bedroom to put on more of the lip gloss Kira had given me as an early Christmas present.

"Hey," she called up the stairs. "Your gentleman caller is here!"

I raced down the steps and stopped. "Oh," I said. "It's just you."

"Hilarious." Sean kissed me and then stepped back to take in my jeans and new blue sweater attire. "You look beautiful," he said. "Wear a heavy coat."

"Back by midnight," Francine said.

"Back by—oooh, midnight?"

She smiled. "Midnight."

It was a winter solstice miracle; Sean's mom existed. And I met her.

"Muriel," she said, "call me Sarah," and she hugged me right there in the doorway. She wasn't quite my height.

She pulled me into the kitchen, where she poured us hot cider and apologized for having to leave in a few minutes for an avalanche-rescue-protocol class in Seattle, which, whatever that was, cemented the notion that she did indeed have my dream job. "Sean's told me so much about you; Salishwood is counting their blessings you showed up."

"I'm counting *mine*," I said. "I love it."

She beamed up at Sean, his same beautiful smile. Short dark hair, elfin features, jeans and a blue plaid flannel. Off-duty park ranger style.

"Okay, so listen. Francine tells me you're aging out in August, and—"

"Mom," Sean said. "Seriously?"

Her face fell. "I'm sorry! Oh, Muriel, I didn't mean to—"

"It's okay." I laughed. "Sean, I *am;* we can say it."

"But—"

"Dude. It's cool."

He shook his head at Sarah. "Why is this the first thing you need to talk about? Can we ramp up a little slower; she'll be back again. I hope."

My toes tingled.

"It's *not* the first thing, but it's related, and I'm leaving in like five minutes, so I wanted to make sure I got to tell her—"

"Sarah," I said. "Tell me."

That warm smile. "Muiriel. There aren't a lot of women park rangers."

"I know."

"Sean says you have the makings of an excellent one."

"Well, I mean—"

"Rangering requires a bachelor's degree; Sean says you don't plan to go to college, and I wondered if it was because you're aging out."

"Oh my God," Sean whimpered, and held on to the kitchen sink.

I turned around to look at him. "You've been talking a lot about me."

"He talks about you *all* the time," Sarah said. "Listen, here's the thing: extended foster care. Have you ever considered it? Or is it a totally stupid idea? Because you could go to school, and—"

"Mom!"

"It isn't stupid," I said. "Just not possible for me."

"Why?"

"Mom, it's five after, you're going to miss your ferry, and we'll be late to our thing." Sean stood by the door with her coat and a backpack.

"All right, I'm off," she said, and went to pull her coat around her small frame. "It was wonderful to finally meet you, Muir— may I call you Muir?"

"Yes, please."

"Sorry if I overstepped. It's just—life is too long to not spend it doing something you love. Also, I'm sick of the Park Service being such a sausagefest. We need you." She took her pack from Sean and kissed his cheek. "See you Monday, love you, and I'm sorry I embarrassed you, but I did give you life, so let's call it even. Good night!" And she was gone.

He stood sheepishly, hands in his pockets. "I am so, so sorry," he said. "I shouldn't have told her all of that; it's your life and not my business, and definitely not hers. . . ."

I went to him and pulled his hands free. "I have no interest in ever being a mystery to anyone, ever," I said. "If I said it to you it's your business. Your mom is a ranger, so now my life details are official National Park Service business. Dream unlocked. Where are we going?"

On the north end of the island was the Puget Sound Reserve. One hundred fifty acres of part-pristine, part-manicured forest and field and ponds. A family of logging moguls had produced a nature-loving, environmentalist son who bought the land, lived there in a manor house overlooking the water, then died and gave it all to the public to protect and wander at will. The sky was nearly black on this longest night of the year, and past the entrance gates, beneath a giant tulip tree dripping with white lights, people were assembling lanterns.

We joined the group of maybe fifty people, mostly Francine-aged but also some little kids and a few old people, to pour rice into a jar, twist a wire handle around the top, and stick a candle in the rice, where it stayed still and upright.

"Genius!" I said.

We all gathered beneath the tree, and a guide said, "Welcome to the winter solstice walk, you lucky few who got tickets in September. Sorry it always sells out so fast, but a small group keeps the magic . . . magical. Stay on the path, please no talking, and if we're lucky, we'll hear some owls. Maybe even our resident foxes."

"September?" I said.

"I had high hopes. Happy solstice," Sean whispered.

My knees went goosey.

In a wobbly line in the cold dark, we followed the candlelight on paths through fields, into dense forests, and best of all, along the shore of a pond full of frogs and night birds floating sleepily. The bobbing line of tiny golden starlight in the jelly jars reflected in the black water.

Past the pond we continued to a wooden bridge, voices of some school choir kids in the dark singing my very favorite winter song, even though it talks about Jesus and his insatiable need for gifts, "In the Bleak Midwinter."

"I can't take it," I whispered. "I think I might pass out."

"It's too dark to faint, keep it together!" he whispered back.

"Shhhhh!" The old people in front of us turned to scowl.

"Hey," he said, quieter, "what is extended care?"

"It's a super unromantic thing to talk about on a candlelit walk."

"Got it."

I took his hand and pulled him off the trail. "I'm nervous. I want to give you your present now," I whispered.

"You're *nervous*? Is it a box of snakes?"

"A box of . . . what mall are you shopping at?"

"I don't know! What kind of present makes someone nervous to give?"

"And your first thought is snakes?" I pressed a small wrapped package into his hands.

"Oh, Muir," he said, holding his lantern over the brass compass I'd taken from my pillowcase bag that morning. "Are you sure?"

"I am."

"Because I love it. So much."

"You do?"

"It's just like Muir's. You honestly don't need it?"

"I'm getting better at finding my way. I thought, maybe, you could carry it for me."

He kissed me, and the golden lights passed by us in the dark. "God, I love winter. Pitch black and it's only six o'clock. We really have till midnight?"

"Midnight."

He looked up in the moonless sky, stars scattered like glitter. "My whole life on this island, and this is my first solstice walk."

"My whole life *anywhere,* and it's my first. Thank you."

"Thank *you,*" he said, holding the compass in both his hands. "I promise if you get lost, I'll come find you."

We stood and shivered, eyes on the sky. "Sean. Is your mom really gone until Monday?"

"Yes."

"Oh," I said. "Really."

✶ ✶ ✶

I carry with me a brass compass I wish I did not need, but this, Joellen says, is the rub of dependence born from fear; a snake eating its own tail.

Joellen gave me Muir's *Wilderness World,* so it was sort of her fault I started walking away from every house she put me in the moment I arrived, just to feel the familiar outside. But also there was a third-grade teacher who bears some of the responsibility.

This teacher, as the seasons changed, was not really into holiday celebrations but was obsessed with examining axle tilt. She was psyched about every living thing experiencing light from our sun but in many different ways, depending on where we lived on Earth, and on the time of year. The stars we slept beneath in Seattle were not the stars over children in China or Australia. Our winter was not Brazil's winter.

I loved this. I loved it *intensely*.

Winter holidays are different in every foster house, but *axle tilt*. That is magic we all live beneath, whether we feel like it or not. I could walk outside and see the light and stars of each season, every celebration, the same way each year. Tradition, no matter where I lived or with whom.

In the very beginning, the calls to Joellen about moving me to a new house came from the parents, not me. Outside, searching the spring or autumn sky to find the constellations on the worksheet my teacher gave me, I accidentally walked far and for long stretches of time, never scared because outside was familiar; I couldn't be very far from wherever I was supposed to be. By the time Joellen came to get me, I'd have been walking nearly two hours, past shops, through neighborhoods and into parks, up and down the hills of streets and homeless encampments, along the waterfront and the fish markets. I was never *lost*. I just wasn't sure the way back to each house.

"You have to ask first," Joellen pleaded. "Tell them where you're going."

Except I wasn't going to a place. I was walking to be walking under the sky and the sun and the stars.

"It's okay," I said. "I'm always somewhere."

She found me, for the third time in as many weeks, at the ferry dock watching seagulls float in the circus colors of the black water reflecting the light of the giant Ferris wheel beside the city aquarium. Too much light to see many stars, but autumn was on its way.

"Muir," she said, sitting beside me. "We need to figure this out."

"Okay," I said, beside her on the splintery dock wood.

She put a thing, small and cold, into my hands. "You need to learn to use this. Keep track of the time, use a map, and you'll never be late or lost. Can you promise?"

Little brass compass. I held it to the sky, aligned with the dim stars that made Cygnus the Swan, tilting south.

I did not take the compass from any house or from anyone. It was a gift, though gift status does not justify keeping a thing. *Need* can, if the need is true. I wish I didn't need my compass. I wish I had a sense of true north anywhere in me. I can walk forward alone and never be scared; it's going back to each house that gets me lost, every time. I can't ever find my way home. That's what I get for being born rootless.

* * *

At eleven-fifty-three I walked quietly into the house, relieved Francine was still up, so I didn't wake her.

"Was it wonderful?" she asked, Terry Johnson snoozing beside her, bathed in Christmas-tree light and, in a welcome break from Christmas music, the TV light from *Antiques Roadshow.*

"It *was,*" I said, a little more obviously indicative than I'd intended, and sat beside her to pet the sleeping cinnamon roll.

"I'm glad," she said. Then she turned down the TV volume. "Do you have everything you need?"

"For what?"

"You know." She nodded. "For dating."

"For . . . *oh*."

"Sorry, I know, but it's my job, I have to—"

"Yeah, yeah, of course—"

"Because if there's a particular brand or something—"

"Francine!" I could not help it, I laughed, and Terry Johnson got up and left.

"This is serious," she said. "Just tell me and I'll buy them."

"Oh my God, okay, thank you, moving on . . ."

"Muiriel."

"Yes, I know." I collected myself and coaxed Terry Johnson back up to my lap. "Believe me. I'm very detail-oriented and obsessed with securing my eminent exodus, and I'm not going to TMI you here, but trust me. I have what I need."

"And he's also—"

"Oh, Francine, I am not good with actual conversations or human emotions. Can we please use hand puppets to talk about this?"

"You think it's a picnic for me? Good Lord, the one thing you don't act like a sixty-year-old woman about. Here, put this pillow on your face and just say yes or no. First, do not use off-brand condoms. Do you have good, expensive ones, and would you like me to go to Costco and just leave a box in the bathroom for you?"

I could not believe this conversation was happening.

But I was also kind of relieved it was happening.

"Yes and yes," I said, muffled, from behind the pillow stuffed in my face.

She paused. "Wait, yes to what?"

"Please go to Costco!"

"Okay, great, good, see? This is progress! Now, are you on the pill, or do you want to be?"

"No. Maybe? Is it expensive?"

"Not necessarily, we can look at your insurance and what you might have on your own later, and we'll figure it out. Okay?"

"Okay," I said. *Right, like I'll be able to afford health insurance. Good one.*

"Okay."

"Can we be done with this now?"

"Yes, for now we can be done." She took the pillow from me and tossed it on the armchair. "See why I only ever had little kids?" She turned the TV volume back up.

"Francine."

"Mm-hmm."

"You believed me today. At school. Without proof."

"Your word is proof."

Wow.

"Between you and me," she said, "Tiana's and Katrina's moms are both 'bride at every wedding, corpse at every funeral' type gals. If you know what I mean."

"Yikes."

"People make a whole lot of excuses for bad behavior when they're related by blood, and that's not love. That's not family. That's narcissism."

"I'm sorry," I said.

"For *what*?"

"That I got you in the principal's office. I'm sorry that because of me, now Barb thinks you would bring someone bad into the school. We got them *suspended*. Will all the parents hate you now because of me?"

She looked at me. "Never apologize for someone else's igno-rance. You are not responsible for that, ever. Understand? I told you, Barb is . . . let's just say we're not working with the top brass there. If anyone hates me because some spoiled brats finally got a well-deserved consequence, then great, hate away. I was humiliated when Barb said that nonsense about you, about your *record*. I wanted this to be a good school for you."

"It *is* good, I swear. I'm used to people saying what Barb said. But I don't go around making trouble in school ever, you know that, right?"

"You didn't make trouble—you got something done. You know I've read your file; you're a ghost with good grades."

"I've never . . . I don't do that. Principals never even learn my name; I'm always gone before they know I'm in their school. But, Francine, those girls were vicious to Kira. No one was going to do anything about it."

"I know."

"And I've never had a friend for so long, in one place."

"I know."

"But I don't want to be trouble for you."

"*Trouble?* Listen to me. I am so proud of you I can't stand it. You are a good person. A brave person and a true friend to Kira. Maybe now, for the first time, you're having some battles. It's because you're living a life, with people who matter. Nothing causes trouble more than that."

Terry Johnson shifted in my lap.

"I want to hug you now," I said. "Okay?"

She laughed. "I appreciate the warning."

I leaned over Terry Johnson and put my arms around Francine's soft shoulders.

"Muir, are you crying?"

"No," I said, wiping my tears on Terry Johnson's blanket. "It

253

was just a really nice night," I said. "Thank you for letting me stay out late."

"Well, it's good you enjoyed it, because after tonight you'll probably develop an eye infection from rubbing that filthy dog blanket on your face and you'll wake up blind."

"It's not filthy," I said. "It smells like Terry Johnson."

"Exactly."

"He's a little bear. He smells like the great outdoors. John Muir had a dog like Terry."

"Did he really?"

"Well. It was his friend's dog, Stickeen."

"*Stickeen?* What kind of a dog name is *that*?"

Terry Johnson and I exchanged a *look*. "Muir borrowed him to explore Alaska together. He had to make little leather booties for Stickeen's paws to protect them from the ice and snow. He was a super-lazy dog; he wouldn't help hunt, he was stubborn. Played by his own rules."

"You hear that, Terry Johnson? You're probably related."

I yawned. "Well, I think I've hit my limit," I said. I got up from the couch and headed toward the stairs.

"Hey," Francine said. I stopped and turned. "Kira brought a present for you. I put it in your room."

"Thanks." I took the steps slowly. Tired. Happy.

Upstairs, the room was glowing warm with even more Christmas lights Francine had strung on all the walls while I was gone. I stood and held my hands up in the colors. What a thoughtful thing for her to do.

For me.

On the dresser was an odd-shaped package wrapped in butcher paper and tied with twine.

A little version of the Terry Johnson sculpture. A perfect likeness.

The lights blurred through my tears, and I set him on the bed-side table where I would see him first thing every morning.

I picked up the stack of clothes from the dresser top, opened a drawer, put them in, and closed it.

* * *

I carry with me, when I can find it, a pack of Fruit Stripe gum.

Grocery stores in spring are the best-smelling places on the planet for a kid. For a kid that is me. Stores are smart, all the candy is on the low shelves, and I loved nothing more than touching and holding the slippery bags of jelly beans and smelling them through the plastic. Bulk-candy aisles were even better. I lifted lids on bins of gummy bears and sour worms. But best of all were the jelly beans right there, unwrapped, fresh and sweet and shiny. Little gem beans with scent so specific. I loved it so much.

The hardest part about learning to sleep in a new house for me was how the house smelled. For the most part, they were all clean, and some of them were amazing, the air inside full of Febreze or fabric softener—just, every house smells like itself and in the dark and quiet, most times the scent is there to anchor you to where you are. Nothing kept me awake worse than lying in the dark, thinking, *Is that eucalyptus? Menthol? Is there a gas leak and we're all going to die? Where is the window in this room? . . . Will I be able to get the other kids out the window in time— Oh man we're on the second story. . . . Do I drop them down in the bushes or will the fire depart-ment bring one of those giant circle trampoline things? . . . Those look fun; I hope I get to jump down on it. . . . But what if I aim wrong and land on the driveway? . . . Wait, does this house have a driveway or do they park on the street—no, that was two houses ago. . . . And* then I'd hear birds singing and the light in the room was gray and brightening fast—up all night just in time to get up and zombie off, bleary-eyed, to school.

One Easter in fourth grade, I think, I had a really good basket. People donate things for kids in foster care, and every kid in that house got chocolate bunnies (solid, not hollow) and marshmallow Peeps and sidewalk chalk and bubbles and about a million things of jelly beans. I put my face into the plastic Easter grass and just inhaled. The other kids laughed, and I did, too. I mean I was *huffing* Easter candy. But it gave me the best idea.

Jelly beans in my pillowcase. They smelled so sweet and good, so familiar, that I slept all night straight through. It was heaven. Until the ants came.

I walked to the store every day after school, smelling my way up and down every candy aisle, searching for an alternative, but nothing smelled enough like jelly beans that wouldn't also necessitate another visit from an exterminator. The poor mom. Those ants were relentless and everywhere; I needed something sugarless that was flat and could maybe stay packaged but still smell good.

John Muir must have had such a terrible time sleeping in a bed inside a house after so many years outside in open-air Yosemite. For the worst of winter, he built a cabin for himself on the valley floor but over a flowing creek, so that it ran free right in the middle of the floor and out the back. What a cold, clean scent. What a sound to sleep to, rushing water splashing over a stone creek bed, right there beside him. Maybe it drowned out the pain of his unbrushed teeth and gums.

Gum. Flat, wrapped, sugarless.

I ran to a register where the kid bait waited to drive parents insane and picked up a pack of every kind of gum. I pressed them all to my nose and breathed deep until there it was: Fruit Stripe. Thick, compact packaging with lots of sticks of sort-of jelly-bean-scented, paper-wrapped perfection.

Every new house after was broken in with a first-day tradition: long walk for the lay of the land, and along the way a duck into a store for my Fruit Stripe.

New pack every couple of weeks kept me sleeping through each night.

Consistency. As a sleep aid, highly underrated.

Eighteen

EASTER SUNDAY AT SALISHWOOD was unexpectedly glorious, mostly because the sun was out again. Sean and I, still and forever happily Natan-free, guided groups of families on walks in the woods, where we spotted fledgling birds and baby squirrels and even fox kits. Spring babies. When the morning sun had burned the mist from the forest floor and rose high above the trees, we helped kids find the eggs we'd hidden earlier, consulting a map to keep track in case some got left behind. I watched them root around in bushes and up in trees and beneath rocks and wondered—worried—if Zola was still home. If she was happy.

Before I'd left for Salishwood that morning, Francine gave me an Easter basket full of chocolate eggs and jelly beans. "You're still a kid for another few months," she said. "My last. Indulge me."

I loved it more than I let on.

"Hey," Sean called, walking fast toward me. "Look who I found!" And from behind him, Zola ran screaming toward me.

I knelt down and let myself hug her for real.

"I missed you," she said into my shoulder.

"Are you still home?" I asked.

She shook her head. My heart sank. Back with the bad-penny lady.

"But I have a new social worker. Guess who?" She smiled, *huge*.

"*No!* Joellen?"

She nodded and whispered in my ear. "Joellen says she's trying to see if I can live with my grandma, so I can still see my mom sometimes."

"Would that be good? Do you want that?"

"*Yes.*"

"Well, listen, no one will work harder to make that happen than Joellen. She'll do everything she can."

"I know."

"Things okay at the house?"

She shrugged.

"Is she remembering to take you to swim?"

"Sometimes. Will you help me find eggs?"

"I know where all the best ones are." And we searched in the forest while I worked to remember her life was out of my control and to not lose myself in worry for her. I could not rescue Zola or any kid. I was barely going to be able to save myself.

When the eggs were found and the afternoon warm, she waved from the bus window, and I smiled and, flying in the face of common sense, blew her kisses.

In the late afternoon Sean walked me to Francine's house. "That kid loves you," he said.

My head hurt.

"She's not home anymore," I said. "I'm not supposed to tell you that."

"It's in the vault."

"I feel guilty."

"About?"

"Leaving her? That I'm here and she's back with this woman who isn't the best. Not the worst, either, just . . ."

"Not great?" he said carefully.

"Not great." I'd never been so worried. Or more to the point, let myself admit I was worried. About Zola. About anyone.

Sean took my hand, and we walked. He didn't tell me not to worry. Didn't tell me it wasn't my problem. And I knew if I'd said one word about launching some scheme to go to the city and rescue her, he would have either gone along with it or found a way to do it right.

"Thank you," I said.

"For what?"

"Everything. Nothing."

"You're welcome?"

At Francine's house I used my key and called out to Francine, who did not answer. "Want some water?" I asked Sean, on the porch taking his muddy shoes off.

In the kitchen I froze.

On the floor, half of him under the breakfast table, Terry Johnson lay still, eyes open, in a pool of vomit.

"Francine!" I lifted Terry's head, held his face in my hands, and looked into his eyes. *"Sean!"*

"No car, she's not here— Oh *no.*" He knelt beside me. The vomit was sparkling, shiny bits of colored foil reflecting light. Wrappers. "Chocolate," he said.

I'd left my Easter basket on the table.

I choked back sobs and pressed my fingers through Terry's

scraggly fur to feel for a pulse in his neck. Sean listened near his snout.

"He's breathing," Sean said. "Barely."

"We have to make him throw up again, how do we make him?"

"Here." He tossed his phone to me. "Google it, I'm calling the vet."

"The number is on the fridge." One hand on Terry, the other thumb-typing, I called Francine first.

Where is she?

Her familiar ringtone ("White Christmas"—all year long) came from her phone on the sink beside the refrigerator. I Googled *dog poisoned* and read about pouring hydrogen peroxide and water down Terry Johnson's throat.

"Are his gums gray?" Sean asked. "The vet says pull his upper lip back."

Gray. I nodded through sobs.

"Okay," he said, trying so hard to stay calm. "They say be really careful but pick him up, because we need to go. Now."

"Terry, wake up. . . ." My chest heaved. No car, how would we get to the vet? "Sean, call your mom!"

"Not home."

"Kira!"

Sean scribbled a note to Francine and snatched a blanket from the couch, wrapped Terry Johnson like a baby, and three minutes later Kira barreled in a cloud of dust down the driveway in her mom's car.

I held Terry Johnson on my lap in the blanket, and Kira blew through every stop sign and one red light. I jumped from the still-moving car to race through the doors of the only emergency vet on the island. I passed Terry with trembling arms in his blanket burrito to the waiting vet technicians, who rushed him away through swinging doors. I stood, all of me shaking now and breathing hard, until Sean and Kira were beside me.

"Sit," Kira said, and Sean brought me a clipboard of paperwork to fill out: address, emergency contact, Terry Johnson's age, his weight, last vaccines given.

"Dogs are so dumb," Kira said, her hand on my knee. "But they have iron stomachs. My grandma's dog ate a diet made almost exclusively of his own poop, and that guy lived to be fourteen. Terry Johnson will be fine. He *will*."

Sean stood beside me, his hand stroking my hair. "Is that *true*?" he asked Kira.

"Mine, too," the receptionist said, leaning over his desk to pass a box of Kleenex to Sean. "Upside is I never have to clean the yard; downside, you do *not* want her licking your face."

"This is chocolate," I sobbed. "It's *poison*. I poisoned him."

"So is poop," the receptionist said. "If he was breathing—he was breathing, right?"

"Barely!"

"Takes a lot of chocolate to kill a dog. Try to relax."

The door opened. Francine walked in, looked at me, and put her hand to her mouth. "Is he *gone*?"

"He's with the doctor," the receptionist said.

"Francine, I'm so sorry, it was an accident—"

Sean brought her a chair, and she sat beside me, unable to speak.

There was a giant bag of jelly beans on the receptionist's desk. It would always be the smell for Terry Johnson now, the smell of his last day.

I had gotten so used to the clean smell of Francine's house. Of the soap she used on the sheets and towels; it made me sleep better than I had in years. I liked it so much.

This is not about you, I brain-screamed. *Stop crying and take care of Francine!* But the harder I tried to stop crying, the more I thought of Terry Johnson curled beside me in bed, keeping me company, waiting for us to come home, making sure I was never lonely.

How many kids had Terry Johnson known? Had they all loved him? Did he love them all? Did he love me?

What had I done?

Francine's eyes were closed.

I closed mine, too.

Francine reached for my hand and held it. "Are you okay?" she whispered.

I burst into fresh tears.

And then the doctor came out.

In the late-afternoon sun, standing on Francine's porch, we said goodbye to Sean and Kira. Francine hugged them, hard. "You saved us."

We watched them drive away, and then sat on the porch and watched Terry Johnson make his careful way through the damp grass, gingerly lifting every paw before carefully stepping on it, licking water from the grass. Still woozy, but he would recover completely.

"I left it on the table," I said. "I wasn't thinking. I'm sure Joellen can find me a place this week; you don't have to worry. I'm . . . Francine, I am so sorry."

She stared at me, beside her on the porch steps. "If I didn't know you better, I'd guess you were being dramatic, but you've been in too many placements for that."

"I can call Joellen tonight," I assured her.

"Muiriel. I love that dog. But he is a *dog*. You are a person. And I am the person who bought the chocolate and handed it to you as you were getting ready to go to work; it was an *accident*. You did nothing on purpose—we'll both remember better next time, and let's congratulate ourselves on surviving Christmas—there was a ton of chocolate lying around then, too, and nobody died. Come on. We're not *that* bad."

"But—"

"Look at him! He's perfectly fine. Even if he hadn't been, it would *not* have been your fault, and for God's sake, I would never kick you out. Don't you know that by now?"

The words I understood, yes. But what she was saying; that no matter what I did, she wasn't going to let me go? I could stay until I was done, even if I killed her *dog*?

It had been such a long time since I'd wanted to stay anywhere. With someone.

"Do you have kids? Your own?" I said, breaking my *Do not ask the foster parents personal questions, especially if you like them* rule.

"I do not," she said.

"What did you do before you retired? Before you fostered?"

"Well," she said, "I was a pediatric nurse."

"No way."

"Oh yes. I loved it. I worked at Children's in the city. And then I was about to turn twenty-five years old, and there was this cardiologist from San Francisco. We moved to Seattle, got an apartment together."

"But did you— You didn't want kids?"

"I wanted kids desperately. He said he did, too, though it never was the 'right time' for him. But I loved him. So I waited, and when I was thirty, we got married; we moved back here to the island, and I thought, *Well, now's the time,* but still he wasn't ready. I loved him some more, and I waited and waited some more, and I woke up one day and I was forty years old. And he woke up that same day and told me he had changed his mind. He didn't want kids. Or me. And he moved back to San Francisco."

"Francine."

"I'm not proud; I can tell you that. Here's the thing: don't ever put the needs or wants of a grown adult over yours if it's something as elemental as wanting children. It's a real *gave him the best years of my life* mess. Could have become a Miss Havisham up in here, but I get too bored."

"Unbelievable."

"Led me to fostering, though, which I loved. Still love."

"Did you ever see him again? After he left?"

She shook her head.

"That's— You would have been a really good mom. You *are* one."

"Well, thank you."

"Do you want to Facebook-stalk him? Tell me his name; I could help you."

She laughed.

"I get that," I said. "'The best years of your life' thing. Happened to me."

"Oh, sweetheart." She smiled. "Don't think like that. Your best haven't even started yet."

"No," I said, disbelieving that the words were coming out of my mouth but feeling, even as I said them to this woman who kept showing up and *standing* up for me, a weight leaving my heart. "Mine was over before it started. I waited for someone, too, and I didn't know I was doing it. I liked them so much I stayed with them too long, until it was too late. They took the best—the *only*—chance I had."

"Chance for what?"

I could not say the word. Not after a lifetime of insisting I did not want it, believing the story of how brave and smart I was to avoid the snare of its trap, swimming all my life against the current determined to drown me.

But then Terry Johnson stretched and blinked in the sunshine. Francine moved my hair out of my eyes, tucked it behind my ear, and said, "You don't have to talk about it." And I was suddenly so tired.

Swimming is exhausting.

* * *

I carry with me a toiletry kit. The star of the packing universe.

Memory, as a substance, is definitely water. It either evaporates completely, or it gets soaked into the brain sponge until the sponge gets squeezed by some unexpected *something,* and then the water spills everywhere. A lot of times, the something is photographs. People insist they remember intricate details of a moment because they've seen a picture of the family dog they never met—*I swear to God I remember we were at the lake because the dog was with us and I remember him, his name was Biscuit! He smelled like dirty pennies!*—when in reality Biscuit died before the person was even born. Or there's the thing where people hear stories from other people's lives, and the stories get repeated over and over and the water is absorbed into another sponge and then you've got people fighting over whose memory it truly is.

I don't have any photographs from when I was little, except the ones Joellen sometimes took and put into my file. And I am not with the same people year after year to hear the same stories over and over, sloshing our memories around in one another's sponges. All to say, I feel like I can safely rely on the accuracy of the memories I do have being truly mine, which for the most part move forward in long stretches of an uneventful life. A cold, slow-flowing river.

Except sometimes my memory is an ocean.

What I don't remember, Joellen tells me, is that when I was born I was super hard to place because of the meth. But the hospital got me clean, and when I was a year old, a couple picked me up in California and brought me to Seattle. I was free to be adopted, no parental rights to fight about, and the couple told Joellen they wanted to adopt, they wanted *me*.

I don't recall the move, but I remember the man and woman. I know I called them Mom and Dad and I was their only child. I remember Joellen came to visit me each week. I remember preschool and the house; I had an upstairs room with a window, and I could see water. I had a bed and stuffed animals in a wicker basket and clothes in a dresser and a closet. I remember the dad taught me to tie my shoes and the mom showed me how to lick a stamp and mail a letter, and I took baths with a toy ferry that had cars in the hull you could take out; I lined them up on the edge of the tub and stayed in the water until my fingertips wrinkled, and I remember the dad read books to me every single night.

I remember my fourth-birthday cake from Baskin-Robbins (mint chocolate chip ice cream and chocolate cake), and I remember the next day we ate leftover cake while the woman and man whom I called Mom and Dad explained to me that Joellen was coming to get me for our weekly visit, but that this time, Joellen was taking me to a new house, where I would meet lots of new siblings and new parents. They helped me pack a duffel bag of clothes, and the woman said, "Look, I got you a present. This is called a toiletry kit. It has all your soap and shampoo and your toothbrush right here all together with a nice handle—a place for everything, and everything in its place."

Joellen tells me in retrospect it made her nervous, the way they kept putting off my adoption. But they were so good to me, she says. I was so happy; I was so comfortable. She let me call them Mom and Dad because they insisted they were going to adopt me. But still they just kept . . . waiting. For something.

In my file, Joellen's notes say simply, *Foster mom pregnant.*

I was a last resort they put off committing to while there was still hope they could have a *real* kid, brand-new, in the original packaging—theirs. One who shared their perfect DNA and so, therefore, deserved a family more than me. They kept me long enough to decimate my best, only chance to ever have a family, just in time for me to become "unadoptable," and then they put me back in. They did not love me. They set me adrift.

Joellen says when she came and got me that last day, she took me to a park by the water and that it took her nearly forty-five minutes to get me to stop crying.

I don't remember that part.

✳ ✳ ✳

"They put you back in *after* you turned three?"

Francine understood.

Well past my prime. I was four years old. In the often mind-bendingly insane world of foster care, three is not a magic number. Three is a dismal number; it is the age after which a foster kid's chance of finding parents plummets statistically to *unadoptable.* Not that it's illegal to adopt a kid that age—it's just incredibly unlikely after that. Mathematically. I was more good evidence.

"They told Joellen adoption was their last resort, but now they didn't need to, and even if they did, they wouldn't have time to take care of me once their own baby was born."

"*You* were their own baby."

"I was a placeholder."

"The purpose of adoption is not for parents to 'find a kid.' It is for children to find parents. If they didn't understand that, they shouldn't have been allowed anywhere near you."

Amen.

Terry Johnson looked at us then, from his hiding place in a patch of tall grass and daffodils. He made his careful way to us and looked up expectantly, asking to be lifted.

"Well," Francine said, "you dodged a bullet."

"That's what Joellen says."

"And adoption, if it's the best and only option for the child, is a wonderful *first* resort."

"Joellen says that, too."

"Joellen is right."

I scooped Terry's sore little body to my lap, and Francine held his paw in her hand.

"My poor baby," I said. "What would your mommy have done without you?"

"Lucky us," Francine whispered loudly to him. "What would we do without our Muiriel?"

That night I pulled a clean T-shirt from my suitcase and saw that some things I hadn't worn in a while were getting wrinkled, crowded with the pillowcase of shame, which I held for a moment, feeling the weight of the things inside, and then shoved back in, beneath my shoes.

Not a big deal to just put some more clothes in a drawer. Below the one with the new clothes. In the bathroom, I put my shampoo in the shower, my soap on the sink.

Just for convenience's sake.

Nineteen

IN JANE'S SALISHWOOD OFFICE on the last Saturday in April, she sat on her desk and did not fire me, which I'd assumed she'd been trying to do, only delicately. Getting rid of Natan couldn't have been fun for her family life. Our interactions, and hers and Sean's, still stayed politely professional. Just the way I liked it, but less touchy-feely than I think she preferred. I'd assumed my days in the forest were numbered, and the thought of losing this dream—though unpaid—job kept me awake most nights and broke my heart, but instead she said, "What are you planning to do after graduation? Where will you be?"

I wished I had an answer better than *I will be in Seattle, which is too expensive but is the place I know best with viable job options, trying to cobble together as many part-time gigs as I can while I search for a room to rent, so to sum up: I will be in the world testing out survival techniques, trying to not be homeless.*

"I'm asking," Jane said, "because two of our master's candidates are graduating, leaving room in the budget for a paid position—part-time, no benefits, but overtime on weekends. Any chance I could convince you to take it?"

"Excuse me," I said. "What now?"

Kira set an entire cake, white and fragrant, on the kitchen table before Francine and Sean and me. And four forks.

"Does a part-time job with no benefits really warrant an entire cake?" I asked, already reaching for my fork.

"It does when it's this job," Sean said.

"If," Francine said, "it's a job that does *not* interfere with a person's finals or torpedo her GPA in the last month before she graduates from high school, then yes. That is entirely cake-worthy."

"Francine," I said. "No potential employer is going to look at my GPA. If I have a diploma, that's all they'll care."

"Okay, but colleges do, and—"

Kira stabbed her fork in the cake. "I'm defusing this tension by saying, in no way to deflect from Muir's amazing job, that I have been accepted to the University of Washington and I am going there in the fall instead of back to Southern California, and I am embarrassed because it is partly because I am too scared to leave home yet, so I am going to stay here and ferry in to school every day. The end."

"Oh, Kira," Francine said, rushing to get champagne glasses from the cupboard.

I hugged Kira, still in her chair and trying to eat cake.

"Let's go smock shopping," I begged. "Please can we get you a beret, and will you wear scarves all the time now?"

"UW is not the Sorbonne. I think there's a strict jeans-and-T-shirt policy. And my personal anti-scarf agenda."

"Kira, don't be embarrassed," Sean said. "I'm glad you'll be here. I will, too."

I turned to him. "You *will*?"

"I got my letter from UW. But I also got the Salishwood spot."

"You people can't drink yet, right? Gah, mother of the year, here . . ." Francine was frazzled with happiness. "Milk, we'll have milk. This cake is giving me hyperglycemia."

"Sean," I said, "what the *hell*? This is the best day!"

Really letting myself admit that I care about people I liked may have been hard when my heart broke with theirs, but *this* part— getting to be overjoyed when they were—I could see how normal human emotional attachment could get addictive.

"You're going to be a national park ranger. You are going to wear the uniform and live on a mountain! *You. Guys.*" I hadn't had milk and cake in years. It felt like being five years old at a birthday party. Like everything was starting brand-new.

Kira went to Blackbird, and I walked Sean to the road.

"Why didn't you tell me before?" I said. "About UW? About Salishwood?"

"Because I wanted . . . I was waiting to see."

"See what?"

"What you were doing. Where you would be."

I stopped walking. "But I don't know where I'll be."

"You— Did we not just celebrate you getting an actual job at Salishwood? Won't you be here?"

"I can't live on that, I can't stay here—maybe I can ferry in from Seattle for it, but I'll need to get another job near where I'll live. Maybe two more."

He stood and just looked at me. *"How?"*

"I don't know."

"You *have* to know."

"I don't."

"Seattle is more expensive to live than here. Why can't you live here? Just stay."

"But there aren't jobs that pay enough or that have benefits here."

"This is nuts. How are you going to—"

"I'll figure it out. I will. I don't want to think about it anymore right now; I'm too happy."

"But—we graduate in, like, six weeks. You'll be eighteen in three months. How can you not—"

"Sean," I said, hard. "I am the one aging out. I *have* thought about it; it's all I *ever* think about, every minute of every day for the past ten years, but no amount of *thinking* will change the fact that it's happening—this is how it happens. I've done what I can to make it easier, and now I just have to let the clock run out, so please can you let me, for just this one afternoon, think about how happy I am for my friends? How happy I am for me. That I have a job I love that I might be able to keep if I can find another one to support it? Please."

"There has to be another—"

"Okay, now I'm *begging* you. Stop." I kissed him goodbye, and he walked down the road, and home.

Back in the kitchen Francine sat with Terry Johnson on her lap at the table, a new habit since Easter. "Everything okay?"

I sat down. "I get impatient with people," I said.

"Do you? I haven't seen a lot of that."

"I did just now."

"Well."

"I will never understand why people think they know my life better than I do. I get tired of explaining things over and over."

She nodded.

"Am I stupid?"

"Of course you're not."

"I don't know what else I can do. I've tried so hard to do everything right. I move forward constantly; it's all I do."

"I know."

"I'm not lazy; I don't just sit around waiting for the world to be good to me, I don't depend on anyone else, I have to take care of myself; I know that." My eyes were burning. "What was I thinking? I can't take this job." I sat at the table, head in my hands. I felt Francine sit beside me.

"Yes, you can! You love it; you have to take it."

"I can't be in two places at once. The ferry is too expensive to be commuting every day."

"Then stay. Stay here."

"Francine, come on." Terry Johnson jumped off her lap and clicked across the linoleum floor to ask for a treat. "He needs his nails trimmed," I said. "I'll do it tomorrow."

"Muriel. Do you want to go to school?"

I pulled Terry Johnson up on my lap. He growled.

"I have five hundred dollars in a checking account and a part-time job with no benefits. I have no insurance, no credit, no permanent address, no car, and a phone *you* pay for with the money the state gives you, which ends the moment I turn eighteen."

"That's not an answer. Are there things you think you want to do for work that might need a college degree?"

"I don't know." I did know. But did we have to go over *again* why school was impossible?

"The state will pay your tuition. Community college lets you transfer directly to a university, and you can still work a part-time job. You have excellent grades and teachers love you, you can apply for financial aid and scholarships, you have work experience, volunteer hours up the wazoo, personal and professional references; use my address; I'll put you on my phone plan. Next."

"Tuition is pointless if I can't pay rent. Loans ruin your life. I can't owe anything to anyone. Ever."

"Loans let you get an education so you can get a job to pay the loans back."

"In theory."

"Okay, yes, but—"

"I'm not your problem," I said. "I'm mine."

"You are *not a problem.* You are an infuriating person, and you damn well know that in Washington State Joellen can apply to get your foster status extended until you're twenty-one years old. You keep your health insurance, tuition is paid for, or I can cosign for loans and you can stay in one place rent-free. With me."

"You can't do that."

"I can. I will."

"Francine . . ."

"Or, I could adopt you."

The air left the room. And my lungs.

"Muriel. There are people all around you now who wish you would stay. Not to trap you or hold you back, just—you need to breathe. You need time in one place to be still and quiet so when it's time to go you're *really* ready. You'll be on your own for the rest of your life, three more years is nothing—but it could make everything possible for you. Let us help you. Let *me* help you."

I pushed my chair back and put Terry Johnson on the floor.

She promised. She said she wouldn't try to adopt me. If I stayed all year I would be done, her last kid and my last foster parent, released from care and free to go. *She promised me.*

"Muiriel."

"I think I need to go rest for a while. Is that okay?" I did not wait for her to answer. I took the stairs two at a time and without thinking or understanding why, I slammed the door shut. My first door slam.

All my life I'd listened to kids do this. Slamming doors are birdsong in a foster house—always there, a kind of background music. The attic was warm. Stifling. I climbed on the bed and shoved the window open wide. Down on the lawn, directly below the window and the bat house where they dropped their poop, always oddly shiny from digested iridescent insect wings, was a crowded patch of the most beautiful wildflowers I'd ever seen. Lavender, cosmos, impatiens, ranunculus.

Grow where you are planted.

I rage-cried, as quietly as I could, into a pillow that was clean and smelled like the lemon detergent Francine used once a week for linens. Every Friday. A familiar, happy scent I had begun to look forward to. Comfortable. Warm. Safe.

I cried harder and slammed the window shut.

Twenty

THE SUN WAS NOT YET ABOVE the trees when Sean walked up the Salishwood road and found me drinking lukewarm tea on a boulder beneath the trees.

I'd left before Francine was up and walked nearly five miles of trails already. "Hey, paid employee," he said, and sat beside me. I leaned against him.

"Sorry I mansplained your own life to you."

"I never heard a *Well, actually,* so I'll give you a pass. This time."

"I'm being selfish. I want you to stay."

"I would stay if I could."

"You would?"

"Of *course* I would. This island is like living in a snow globe. It's disorienting. You, and Kira, and Salishwood, the forests. The *toast.*"

And Francine.

"So . . . okay, I'm confused. Are those good or bad things?"

"In theory they're good."

"Okay."

"In reality, I will never get to live in a place this beautiful, in a life so full of all this . . ."

"Muir, I hate to break it to you, but you do live here. You live here and you work here and we don't want you to go. Everyone wants you to stay; everyone loves you. I love you."

My heart went still.

"Look up and away and around and anywhere but at me all you want, but if I love you that's *my* business. I know you don't owe me anything back, and you don't have to respond at all. It's just the truth. So."

For now.

No one, in all my life, aside from Joellen, ever told me they loved me. He was right. I could not look at him.

"And come on, a snow globe? If you need to be miserable, replay the greatest hits of Natan and Tiana and Katrina—throw in some of Barb's racist bullshit and mope all you want—just *stay*. Please."

"I can't."

"I don't— What about what my mom said? What about the foster extension—you could stay with Francine until you're twenty-one?"

I put my head in my hands. "I just want to walk. I want to walk all day, every day in the woods alone. Why isn't *that* a job?"

"It *is*," he said, brightening. "That's a wilderness ranger. Like a forest ranger but . . . in the wilderness. Without a gun. If you had a degree in environmental science they would be begging for you. There's wilderness in the Cascades, and the Olympics. . . ."

I put my head on my knees. "Francine wants to adopt me."

"*What.*"

"Yeah."

"She said that? Out loud?"

"Yes."

"But—you're an adult."

"Yeah."

"I don't— Can she do that?"

"Yes. So I can stay. With her. And go to school."

"You can adopt adults?"

"Sean, keep up, yes."

"And she'd be your, what, legal guardian?"

"No, she would be my legal mother."

I dug in the dirt with a stick.

"Do you like Francine?" he asked quietly.

More than I could ever admit or express properly.

"Muir," he said. "I don't understand why this is bad."

I rubbed my tired eyes. "Did you depend on your dad?"

His brow furrowed. "Of course."

"Will you ever be the same with him gone?"

"Oh man . . . please tell me you're not trying to live your entire life never depending on anyone ever because they might leave or die."

"Too late. I already did."

"Well, that's not our fault!"

"It's not mine, either! You think I like feeling every day like I'm walking a fucking tightrope, one misstep and I'm dead? You think it's been fun feeling like that every day since I was a little kid?"

"Of course not, that's not what I— I mean, we're here, we'll catch you. We're *right here.* Also I have severe acrophobia, so this metaphor is making my hands sweaty."

"How can you be a ranger with acrophobia? That's stupid."

"Muir. We're here. All of us."

"Yes," I said. "You're here *now.*"

"What about our motto? *Life is fucked* and you know that better than anyone, but I know it, too, and I'm glad I didn't not love my dad in case he dropped dead, because when he eventually did, I had years of really great memories. I had my mom, so I survived, and so will you. We are here, not everyone leaves, sometimes things turn out right. Why would it be so bad if Francine adopted you?"

"A million reasons."

"A *million*? Really."

"You don't get it."

"I know I don't get it, I'm begging you to please help me understand."

"Well, to begin with, this country was built on stealing babies from their mothers. White people did it to indigenous people, and they still try it; slave owners sure as fuck did it; white people still adopt kids from other cultures, name them Tiffany, and pull that gross 'We don't see color' crap. The Catholic Church said poor moms and single moms are 'immoral' so they stole their babies and gave them to rich Catholic couples, and then *Georgia Tamm* . . . that bitch stole kids and straight-up sold them. People still do it, and it's just— Adoption isn't always the happy cure-all people pretend it is."

Birds sang in the clean, cool air. What a gorgeous morning to feel so crappy.

"Muir," he said. "I can't ever know how hard every day has been for you, every hour, your whole life. I would do anything to be able to go back and make it right for you. It's insane; it's unfathomable, every kid and parent who was so screwed over. I wish— I honestly understand adoption isn't a magic answer for any of it; I get that. But I mean—were you stolen?"

"I don't— She couldn't keep me, she didn't have the help she needed. Or maybe—okay, she might not have wanted to keep me, she maybe didn't even know she was pregnant; none of it matters. It's all beside the point; I don't want to be someone's legally obligated anything. I can't be trapped. I'm not here to be kept until I'm an inconvenience."

He looked so sad. "Francine would never do that to you."

"How do you know?"

"Because . . . she wouldn't. She doesn't want to trap you; you could never be an 'inconvenience.'"

"You don't *know* that. I won't survive if I let her—if I stay and get used to her taking care of me—it's already happening! The food and house and she sticks up for me, she's . . ." My throat was burning. "It won't work out and I'll be dependent and unprepared for life alone and I'll be heartbroken because I love Terry Johnson so much. I love him. I'll be so lonely without him. I love him, I do. . . ." He put his arms around my heaving shoulders.

"I know you love . . . Terry Johnson. Terry Johnson knows you love him. Trust me. Terry knows you're not able to tell him. Terry Johnson understands that better than anyone. Terry Johnson has never wanted to adopt anyone before you. I know, because I would have heard about it. Terry Johnson just . . . loves you."

I tried hard to stop crying.

"I'm not trying to convince you to depend on anyone. On me," he said.

"Too late."

"Do you believe I love you?"

I wished he would stop saying that. I wished he would say it again.

"I believe you think you do," I said.

He stood up.

"Muir, I'm not going to let you— I know my own mind and

my . . . I'm not just going to walk a million miles in the forest with you, and have a bunch of great sex with you, and want to tell you before anyone else whenever something good or bad or hilarious happens, and watch you eat toast and jam every day, and put up with my jealousy for the obsession you have with goddamn Terry Johnson—who's still pretty indifferent to me, when all I've ever been is good to that guy; I helped save his life and still he barks at me—and I know I can never know what your life has been, but I want to know what it is now and what it will be. And you can't know mine, but I'd never blame you for that because you want to and you try so hard and you know what? I lied. I *do* want you to depend on me. Because you *can*. I want to take even the smallest part of this weight you carry every second, I want to take apart how every adult in your life has screwed you over and replace it with me doing right by you. And so does Kira. And so do her parents. And more than anyone, so does Francine. She wants to be your family and make it so you are never alone, and you can go to school and be a wilderness ranger or whatever the hell you want to do or be, because she knows you could be anything, and so do you. She wants to help you have the life you deserve, and I think you should let her because the only reason she wants it is because she loves you and, okay, maybe that is selfish, but the thing is, she loves you for *you*. She didn't expect to, but there it is, with no agenda, nothing wanted in return. In fact she can't help it and life would be easier if she didn't but it's too late now and it's making her sick to imagine you leaving. *She loves you.*"

He grabbed his water bottle and walked away, fast, to the lodge.

Then my heart wasn't still at all. Now it just felt broken.

"So you're *not* really sick? Or you are and pretending not to be?" Kira demanded, arms crossed, standing beside my Blackbird table where I sat sulking over tea and toast. "Because you look not great. You look like you've been crying."

"I have."

"So you *are* sick."

"I feel awful. I told Jane I was sick so I could leave, but I'm not, like, flu sick."

Her arms relaxed. "Okay."

"I'm sick of being mad."

"Maybe you should go home and sleep?"

"Not home," I said. "Francine's house." I put my head on my arms.

Kira sighed. "Okay, now your hair is in your tea. You're a mess."

"I don't care."

I heard her sit in the chair across from mine. "Muir."

"What."

"Muir."

I lifted my head. I forgot sometimes, because she was so kind, and sometimes so hurt and vulnerable, how fierce her appearance could be when she needed it to. Ears pierced, all tattooed, dressed in black from her boots to her shredded tank top, hair up and away from the stern look on her face, now so familiar, unwilling to put up with my bullshit. Not content to let me suffer.

My friend.

I kept my head up. "Francine wants to adopt me."

Kira sat back. "She *does*?"

"Yes."

"How do you know?"

"She offered."

"She did not."

"She did."

"Well," Kira said. "That is . . . I mean. Can't say I'm not surprised, she's never . . . Doesn't mean you have to let her."

"She promised she wouldn't."

"I know."

"No one ever keeps their promises. Ever."

"Okay, but isn't this one more like, *I promise I'll never take you to Disneyland, oops, I guess we're going—surprise!*"

"No," I said. "Adoption isn't like going to Disneyland. At all."

"I'm sorry," she said. "I just wish . . . it could be."

"Kira. She *lied* to me."

She put her hands on the table. "Or maybe she just really likes you and wants to be your home to come back to, no matter when or where you go?"

I glared down into my tea.

"What?" Kira said.

I shook my head.

"Oh, all right, I get the silent treatment now? Muir. *Muiriel.*"

I sat.

She stood. Untied her apron. "Hey," she called into the kitchen, marching behind the counter. "I'll be right back, I have an emergency." She tossed her apron onto the glass pastry case, grabbed her wallet, and stood beside me. "Let's go," she said. "Now."

"I'm not done with my tea."

She got a paper cup and lid, poured the tea in, and held the door open.

"I'm only going because I feel like it," I said as I stepped out into the sunshine.

"Oh, I know," she said, and dragged me to the bus stop.

The late-spring morning was cool and bright at the trailhead to the bonfire beach. In the trees at the path we had walked with Sean to the water, I stood now with Kira in a clearing before a long stone wall, shaded by a low wooden roof, curved like ribbon, beneath the words *Nidoto Nai Yōni:* Let It Not Happen Again.

Photographs and words were embedded in the wood, black-and-white images of Japanese American women and men and children, teenagers at the high school, families and homes and pets and farms and shops. Pictures of people living what looked like a beautiful, happy life.

The sun was warm on my back and I read the posted notices from the US government, the word *Japs* again and again. Japanese American citizens, Kira's family, suitcases in their hands, dressed in layers of their best clothes, even elegant hats, waiting on the dock, armed white soldiers lurking beside them and in the periphery. A tiny little girl in a wool coat smiled in the arms of a white soldier wielding a huge gun. A young mother held an infant, both visibly tagged with numbers, not names. Grandmas and grandpas, mothers and fathers, and siblings rounded up while their neighbors watched. Ripped away with virtually no warning from their homes, farms, beloved pets, and friends. Gone.

Then photographs from the camps. From Manzanar. Razor-wire fences and gun towers in the desert, keeping the families imprisoned to appease white America's rabid, racist fear. The American government betraying its own people, handing out gold stars to Kira's great-grandmother, to all the mothers of dead sons, killed while fighting for the America that put them in this prison.

I stood, mesmerized by the faces of a group of teenagers. They looked like my age. In the yard at Manzanar, in the dust and dirt. Smiling. Friends or cousins or siblings, but together. And rising behind them, above the tower and the shacks and razor wire, away but not far in the desert, I recognized Mount Whitney, the highest peak in all the continental United States and, if you start walking in Yosemite Valley, the end of the John Muir Trail.

One more cruelty. Imprisoned beneath the freedom of that mountain, its soaring beauty turned to a looming taunt.

We walked to the water's edge, where the dock once stood, where Kira's family was marched at gunpoint to a ferry that took them away from home, to an unknown future. Today the water sparkled, quiet and calm.

"I didn't get any artistic tendencies or talent from my great-grandmother," she said.

"You did," I sighed. "It's not debatable; it's an established fact. You are an artist."

"I didn't *inherit* it from her," she said.

"Those birds are works of art," I said. "That she didn't make art before or after has nothing to do—"

Kira shaded her eyes from the sun. "No, I'm not *related* to her. Not by blood. None of us are."

I blinked in the light from the water. "Not related to who?"

She sighed. "Muir. Keep up. To my great-grandma."

"Why not?"

"Because my grandma was an orphan. My great-grandparents adopted her."

I stood, blank-faced. "She wasn't a baby? In the camp?"

"She was. Look, I wasn't ever going to go into all this if you were going to be gone the second you graduated, and I'm sure as fuck not here to be your Wise Asian Friend who drops the fucking

287

ancient mystical knowledge about the beauty of family or some shit, and yes I admit bringing you here was a bit dramatic, but if Francine . . . Look. This whole situation is getting stupid, and I need you to really hear me."

A carload of people pulled into the parking lot and walked to the wall, talking quietly and taking pictures.

I sat in the grass beside the water, my chest tight. Kira sat beside me.

"When the internment started, the government searched all the orphanages for Japanese kids," she said. "If a baby had even one-eighth Japanese blood, they were taken to Manzanar, to this makeshift orphanage called Children's Village. Something like a hundred babies and toddlers and little kids. My grandma was born with a deformed left hand, which apparently freaked out her parents, who left her at a Catholic orphanage in Oregon, and that's where she was rounded up before her first birthday and sent to the prison camp because Japanese orphan babies were totally a threat to national security."

"Obviously," I said.

She smiled. "Right? My mom says a lot of Japanese adults back then considered orphans part of the *Burakumin,* which is like *untouchable.* So when the war ended, most of the orphans were either sent back to the nuns or adopted by white families. But not my grandma."

"Why?"

She shook her head. "Don't know. My great-grandparents' son was still alive, fighting in the war, so it wasn't like a mending-a-broken-heart, lost-child thing. All Grandma ever said was that Great-Grandma and Great-Grandpa saw her playing in the camp one day, chasing birds in the dirt in a fenced-off area cordoned with razor wire and they just *liked her so much.*"

We turned to look over our shoulders when the family at the wall laughed. They were speaking Japanese, the kids all had flowers that they placed on the narrow ledge beneath one of the embedded photographs.

"Muir," Kira sighed. "I never wanted to be all, *Oh, I understand all about adoption because some people I never really knew adopted my grandma decades before I was born.* I can never know your life, I would never pretend to, but none of us can know anyone's but our own, and I know *you* now. So does Sean. And Francine. And be pissed about this all you want, but we wish you would stay."

Variation on a theme.

"Did you and Sean talk about this?"

She frowned. "About what?"

"Me. Staying."

Her eyes went up and back. "You know, we have our own lives. You are not the sun and moon—we don't have time to ruminate constantly on your life plans. *Of course we talk about this shit!* Don't you get it? Francine has had probably a hundred kids live with her, kids she adored, and she had them with her when she was a lot younger and could have been a, like, energetic, run-around-the-park type of mom, and she has never once brought up adoption. Ever. I will never say any of this was *meant to be,* because I think that's a bullshit concept and it's also gross and disrespectful to your actual mom, and it's just a total lie. But what I am saying is . . . sometimes people turn out to be the ones . . ." She paused. She blinked fast.

I moved closer, right beside her.

"Saving me from my asshat ways wasn't the only reason my parents came back here to live," she said. "And the Suquamish would rightfully be all *Whatever, bitch* to hear me say this, but for lack of a better way to express it, this is our home. We belong here. My family belongs here." She opened her wallet and pulled out a folded piece of lined notebook paper, the blueprint material for all her masterpieces. "Here," she said. "This is your tattoo."

"You said to never start. You said I'll get addicted."

"Well. Yes. But at least you know a good artist. It was going to be my next, but I want it for you." I unfolded the paper.

Black ink, simple, languid script, a beautiful, single word.

Gaman.

From the bird-pin shoebox.

"To bear the seemingly unbearable with patience and dignity," Kira said.

I turned to her, my friend, who more and more I could not imagine being without.

"Kira, I can't. This is you. This is your family."

"Yes," she said. "It is."

* * *

I carry with me a paper price tag.

In a thrift shop once I found a pair of shoes. They were brand-new, not a mark on the soles, silver strappy satin sandals with a kitten heel and tiny rhinestone buckles, Value Village tag: $20, *and they were my size.* The label stitched to the arch read *Prada.* They were unlike any shoe I had ever owned, and I knew I would never have a reason to wear them, ever. Too special for jeans. But I saw them, and I loved them.

I held them to me and skulked around the aisles. Had anyone

else seen them? Maybe I could wear them to a dance. Maybe I would wrap them in tissue, save them for if I ever got married one day. My whole month's allowance for one pair of shoes I would never wear, but, oh, perfect diamonds-in-the-rough of off-brand Crocs, skanky worn-out running shoes, and dirty Converse, beautiful and perfect and waiting to be found by *me*.

Or maybe not.

Too good to be true.

Someone bought these shoes brand-new for a crap ton of money, and then changed their mind and dumped them here. Why?

Blisters? They trip you up and let you fall? If these shoes truly were so special, so good, they would not still be here, waiting for me to find them. Someone who deserved them, who knew their true worth and had reasons to wear them, would have found them and taken them home by now. It was too good to be true.

I put them back on the shelf but kept and carried the paper price tag with the rest of the blackbird nest. Most nights when I can't sleep, I lie staring into the dark and think about those shoes.

* * *

I was honing my avoidance skills like a petulant first grader and feeling more sorry for, and sick of, myself every minute.

I was tired. I'd managed to not interact with Francine the night before and woken up to a note from her about an early-morning doctor appointment, my lunch made and waiting in the fridge, and five voice mails from Joellen that I was choosing to ignore. They were there on the phone, her voice probably waiting to tell me I should let Francine adopt me, and why wasn't this my dream in life, and what was wrong with me, why couldn't I just give in.

Once at Salishwood, early, I checked in with Jane and then

literally hid in the trees, atop the granite boulder, to avoid talking to Sean. The buses pulled in, and then:

"*Muiriel!*" Zola came running and scrambled up the boulder to me.

"Zola! What is *up*, miss?"

She held on tight as always but was unusually quiet. I left her alone about her mom, asked her nothing about where she was living.

"Should we go look for fox poop?" I said instead.

I held her hand, and we walked to meet the rest of the kids at the trail. Spring was finally warming into summer. Deer and rabbits and snakes were out and about in the forest. Rain left the soil and trees and seawater clean and alive, a relief to breathe it all in. Sean led the hike and left me alone to be the jerk I insisted on being. I let myself be occupied with the forest and with Zola all the way into the woods and back out, until we came into the clearing at the lodge, and Zola dropped my hand to wave at someone small with unruly, curly hair who was talking to Jane.

"Muir," Zola squealed, "look! Why is she here?"

"Don't know." Zola waved and ran to her, and Joellen turned and saw me, and she smiled. All my life until this island, the only person in the world always happy to see me come into a room. I walked fast to her, didn't pretend to not be happy. Zola turned actual cartwheels in the grass.

"Joellen, watch me!" she yelled.

"Whoa," Joellen laughed when I threw my arms around her. "Are you hugging now?"

"What are you doing here?" I asked. "Do you have another kid on the island? Sorry I didn't listen to your messages yet. Can we have lunch before you go? We could go to Blackbird and get toast. Francine's at a doctor appointment, but she'll be back. What are you doing here, why didn't you tell me you were coming . . ." Joellen's smile was fading fast, and I finally saw she was not alone.

A uniformed officer stood behind her, near her.

"Oh God," I whispered, "what is it?" She pulled me aside.

"It's—it'll be fine," she said. "He just needs to ask some questions. . . . It'll be all right. Call me when you're home, and I'll come by on my way off the island, okay? Muir? Okay?"

"Jo. Who is he here for?"

"Honey, please don't worry, call me later." She squeezed my hand and walked back to Jane and the cop.

I turned myself around in a cold panic. Where was he; where had he gone—

"Muir." Sean. Beside me. "What's with . . . is that a *cop*?"

Just when I needed him, exactly where I wished he was. Again.

"I guess," I said. "What is he—city? Sheriff?"

"How would I know?"

"Is it about Natan?" I whispered, hoarse. "Did he press charges for assault? Am I going to jail?"

"No! What are you— Who's your friend with the hair?"

"My social worker."

His eyes were wide. "*Joellen?* Crap . . . it's like meeting my in-laws." I did not return his smile. "Catch me up here—she didn't tell you she was coming?"

"*No.* I can't believe this is happening. I'm going to jail."

"Why would you even— Muir, you are *not* going to jail. Just hold on."

Exactly what I needed him to say.

We stood and watched Joellen talk to the cop, then Joellen went to Zola, still turning cartwheels in the grass. *Thank God,* I thought. *Comfort the poor kid. Those are probably anxiety cartwheels.*

Then she took Zola's hand and led her to the cop.

"What the—what is she *doing?*"

Sean and I sat on the wooden picnic bench and watched Joellen kneel beside Zola, who nodded and shook her head at the cop's questions.

"Wait," I moaned. "Someone is dead. Her mom. Oh God, Zola." I couldn't stand it. I went to her and stood behind her and Joellen.

"Muiriel, honey—"

Zola's head whipped around to me, her eyes pleading. "Muir, I didn't do it. Tell them I didn't."

"Is someone dead?" I whispered to Joellen.

"No," she said, full voice.

I turned to Zola. "Honey, what didn't you do?"

"Miss, I'm going to have to ask you to step back, please," the cop said, and stepped nearer to Zola.

I could see his badge. *Seattle Police.*

"She says I stole something," Zola said, pulling my arm. "Jewelry, a bracelet or something. I never took anything— Muir, help me."

Time slowed to zero.

What did you do to get put in foster care? She doesn't know how good she's got it. They all steal.

"Miss," the cop said to Zola. "We're talking to *you* right now, and only you."

"Who said that, Zola?" I asked her. "Who said you stole something?"

Sean was beside me again. "What is it?"

"Joellen, tell them!" I turned to the cop. "This child does not steal; she never would."

"Miss, I'm going to need you to back up."

"She just fucking told you she didn't steal anything, didn't you hear her?"

"Muir," Joellen gasped. I nearly did, too. Had I just said *fuck* to a police officer? My breath was shallow. Surrounded by people, outside in the sunshine, still I was terrified. But *Zola*.

Francine's voice was in my head. *Your word is proof.*

"What house is it?" I asked.

"I can't give you that informat—"

"*Our* house," Zola said. "The one you and I lived in. I'm with my grandma now; I haven't lived at that house in such a long time. I didn't take anything!"

Oh, god. The police-happy Allen wrench house.

"Joellen," I said. "You know that woman. Whatever she's missing, she probably lost it, or she's wearing it right now."

"Muir," Joellen sighed. "Please, just let him do his job."

I turned to the *officer*, a bland-faced, fully uniformed white guy who looked not much older than me, gun in a holster on his hip. He got on a ferry to come to this island and interrupt a class field trip, to take down a ten-year-old black girl for a petty theft she didn't commit, accused by a crabby white lady who couldn't be bothered to put Zola's once-a-week swim class on her calendar, who called me a "bad penny" when all I did was keep her house clean and help her remember to take her stupid hypertension medication, because she had the *world's worst memory*.

"That woman we lived with, she once spent half an hour searching her car for her phone—using her phone flashlight."

The cop nodded. "My mom's done stuff like that." He offered me his hand to shake. "Officer Irvin."

I nodded but did not touch his hand.

"Okay," I said. "Now picture a sixty-year-old woman with four foster kids in rotation who does that shit on the regular. Tell her to look for whatever she's missing in the sofa cushions: that's where she keeps the TV remote and most of her important tax documents. Zola didn't take anything from that house; she just wanted to get out of there and go home."

"Can I?" Zola asked. "Can I go home now?" She watched the rest of the kids lined up to get back on the school buses.

"What can I do?" Sean whispered near my ear.

I could not watch this happen. Zola was too young; they were going to ruin everything for her. "Jo," I said, low, "what did she say Zola took?"

"Bracelet," Jo whispered. "Gold."

Zola stood beside Joellen, holding her hand. Terrified.

Blood thundered in my ears.

"Sean," I said, "take my phone. Call Francine. Tell her to come home. Tell her I stole a gold bracelet from a foster house and there's a police officer here to search my room. Tell her I need her."

They all stared and said nothing. Joellen, Jane, the cop.

Zola.

My whole life of careful perfection, my future, gone—and I couldn't have cared less.

Twenty-One

I USED MY KEY AND OPENED the door. Terry Johnson got a whiff of the cop and nearly twisted himself into a pretzel, barking and nipping at him. I picked the dog up and lifted his ear to whisper *please, calm down.* He wiggled and whined, but I held him tight. Poor Francine. All I ever brought her was trouble. Now a cop was in her house, and she wasn't home. Was this even legal?

Zola still clung to Joellen. Sean was gone; he'd convinced Jane to take him home for his mom's car, and he went looking for Francine, who was not answering her phone. I grabbed the grocery pad from the fridge and raced to scribble out a list.

"Miss," the officer said, hovering at the bottom of the stairwell. "I need you to stop what you're doing and—"

"Am I under arrest?"

"No, but—"

"Then hold *on.*" I could not believe the words coming out of my mouth. To a *cop.* Neither could Zola. Or Joellen. They sat nervously together at the kitchen table, and my terrified lungs refused to let me get a full breath.

"Muir," Joellen whisper-begged. "Don't do this to yourself. Let him go through the motions. Just do what he asks, we'll clear it up, and it'll be over."

I didn't believe that for a second, and it pissed me off that Joellen did—and that for the first time, the very worst time when I needed her most, she was scared. She was supposed to be in charge; she didn't get to be scared. I slapped the list I'd written on the table in front of her, and, Terry Johnson still tucked under my left arm, I got Zola some crackers and juice. "Don't worry," I whispered to her. "Everything is going to be all right. Do you trust me?"

She nodded.

"Good. I trust you, too." I spoke near Joellen's ear. "Call her. Call that woman right now and tell her to check every one of the places I've written here. Tell her I said to try. She'll find her fucking bracelet."

She looked up at me—her fear shifted to join my anger. Thank God.

I stood tall as I could, and faced the cop. My stomach turned at this scene, Zola surrounded by all of this stupidity, my anger and protection of her coming off horribly white-savior-y, but *fuck*. Zola was a *child*. She needed to see herself in me, in another foster kid taking charge, not being helpless. Because adults were failing her. *Again*.

"Let's go," I said, pretending hard I wasn't terrified, and started up the stairs.

But there was a knock at the open front door. "Muiriel," a voice called. "What's happening?" Kira's *mom*. And Kira, in her Black-bird apron. And Sean.

Kira's mom strode in, assessed the situation, came straight to me, her arm around me holding Terry Johnson. "Tell me what to do," she said, glaring at Cop Irvin. I shook my head. "What's happening?" she asked Joellen. "What do they want with Muriel?"

I exhaled. I was safe now. Sean and Kira stood beside me. *My* people. My people's *mom,* assuming not the worst of me but that I was being wronged. Here to protect me. Zola smiled up at Sean with a tiny bit of hope.

"What the actual F?" Kira whispered.

"I don't know," I whispered back. "But you're here. So it's going to be okay."

"We just need to let this officer take a look in Muriel's room," Joellen said. "It won't take but a minute." Her words were calm, disjointed from their anxious, high-pitched delivery.

NCIS island justice. I could not believe this was happening.

"Does he have a warrant?" Kira's mom asked, moving to anchor safely at Zola's side.

"Seriously, what the shit is going on?" Kira asked, low.

I spoke quietly. "They think Zola stole something from one of our placements, because a white lady says she did, which Zola abso-fucking-lutely did not; I'm buying time for Joellen to clear it up."

Kira seethed. Sean was stone-faced.

My stomach burned, but I could not let them do this to Zola. I would *not.*

Then a sickening moment of realization:

The striped pillowcase. My blackbird bag of treasures. All of it stolen. John Muir was right all along: I should have kept nothing, no attachment to things. Carrying those worthless things really was going to ruin me.

Zola looked through the chaos to me. Kira's mom took her hand.

"Hold on, Zola, we are going to fix this together, all of us" I said. "Stay here with Kira's mom. Joellen, *call that woman.*"

She picked up Francine's landline.

Sean took my shaking hand for a second, then I held tight to Terry Johnson and started up the stairs to my room. "It's up here," I said to Cop Irvin, who hurried to follow me, with Kira and Sean right behind him.

"Muir, you don't have to do this," Kira's mom called up the stairwell. "I wish you wouldn't. We should wait for Francine."

"Mom, she's got it," Kira yelled back to her.

I set Terry Johnson on the perfectly made bed. Everyone crowded around in the room that seemed much smaller now.

"Wait, hold up!" There was another voice in the kitchen, pounding feet on the stairs, and then Elliot stood with us in the room, breathing hard, his camera safely, perpetually in his hands.

Amazing.

"This is unacceptable," Cop Irvin said.

"I'm just here to document," Elliot said. "Seriously, pretend I'm not here. Go. Muir, I got you."

Kira smiled.

I went to the dresser.

Please, Joellen. Do not let me down.

I moved and spoke as slowly as I could, buying Joellen as much time as possible, while still in total disbelief that any of it was happening in the first place. We were all starring in a filler episode of *Dateline* where the producers forgot there was supposed to be a crime and instead booked an overwrought, forgetful lady being peak white at Zola's expense.

"Let's see . . . gold bracelet . . . okay, well, these are my three books. And here," I said, my voice small and scared to death, "have a look in the drawers. There are eight shirts, five pairs of socks, three pairs of pants, and two skirts. Kira helped me find those because I wanted to look pretty for a boy I like." Sean looked like he was about to cry. Elliot took pictures of the drawers. Of me. Of the cop. Of the room full of people around me: *Portrait of the World's Most Boring Crime Scene.* "Shoes I sometimes keep under the bed. I have three pairs. Write that down—are you writing it all down?" Cop Irvin shined a flashlight into the drawers, moved things aside.

And then, out of all other options, I hefted my suitcase to the bed. "This will just be some more T-shirts and my toiletry kit. Some things from the kit are in the bathroom, but most of it is in here. Toothpaste, tampons, you can take it all with you to the station; it's all I've got."

Downstairs, one more voice. Terry Johnson barked. Sean picked him up and whispered something into the top of his scruffy head. Terry growled but let Sean hold him.

Footsteps on the attic stairs, and Francine stood in the doorway, small in her jeans and sweater, her eyes first to me, then to Cop Irvin, his hands on my suitcase to open it.

"Don't touch that suitcase," she said.

"Ma'am, I'm Officer Irvin. And you are?"

"I am Muiriel's mother."

"Foster," I said reflexively.

"Foster mother," she said, and came to me. "Sweetheart, are you okay?"

I nodded. "But please don't leave."

"Of course not," she said, then she turned Cop Irvin. "What

is going on here? What information could you possibly need from this girl?"

"This young lady says she's in possession of stolen property, so I am conducting an investigation. Just doing my job, ma'am."

"So am I. You listen to me," she said. "You cannot separate your actions from their context. This child is not a thief. Zola is a *baby*. She is not a thief. I want you out of my house. Now."

Warmth flooded my hands and heart. "It's all right, Francine," I said. "Everything will turn out right."

Cop Irvin opened my suitcase, pulled the blackbird bag of useless crap from its place beside my shoes, and emptied it onto the beautiful handmade quilt. A quilt for a kid in foster care.

"What am I looking at?" Cop Irvin asked.

"My life," I said, surrendering to humiliation. "I took these things. I carry them with me from house to house."

I stepped apart from everyone, my heart thudding and shamed, and watched this cop rummage through my secret treasures, searching for anything of value. No one said a word. Cop Irvin held up something shiny. "What's this?"

"That is a thimble," I said, barely audible.

He tossed it back on the bed. "Okay. And this?"

"Sobriety coin. From when I got off meth."

Cop Irvin frowned. "Okay. This?"

"A key."

"To what?"

"A Christmas closet."

He looked around the room.

"No, in another house. For gift wrap and a plastic Santa and lights."

"Why?"

Nothing and everything.

One by one these worthless things, my only worth.

Library card. Fruit Stripe gum to help me sleep. Dollhouse dollhouse. Paper price tag for the beautiful shoes I wish I'd bought. Paper Dixie cup, my very own.

Zola's Allen wrench.

At last, he picked up the empty pillowcase, turned it inside out, and shook it.

The Red Rose polar bear. Cop Irvin picked it up, tiny and white and lonely.

"No, wait," I said. I took it from him and put it in Francine's hands. She held it like it was the most precious jewel in the world.

"Muriel," she said, looking around the room. "You put some clothes away. You unpacked."

"A little," I said.

And then, its entrance right on cue, through the open window a bat flew in.

Cop Irvin ducked and swatted. So did everyone else, except for Terry Johnson and me. And, of course, Francine.

"Keep your pants on, my God!" she shouted, and stood on the bed to shoo the bat out with her bare hands. She rolled her eyes at Cop Irvin. "Little hairy thing with wings," she said. "Get ahold of yourself."

That woman, barehanding a possibly rabid bat; she was mine.

"Francine," I said.

"What is it, sweetheart?"

I could not say.

She put her arms around me, and I let her. "I'm so tired," I said.

"I know," she said into my hair.

"Francine," Joellen shouted from downstairs, "do you have speakerphone on this thing? She found it; she found the bracelet!"

Joellen. Thank God. All my life she has never let me down.

"For Pete's sake," Francine sighed. "It's a rotary dial phone."

She started out of my room, then turned. "Let's go," she said to Cop Irvin, and led him back down to the kitchen, her warm hand squeezing mine on her way out.

We stood alone in silence.

I gathered up the things I'd carried for so long, back into the pillowcase, and sat on the bed. Sean took the bag from my clenched hands, set it on the dresser, and put Terry Johnson on my lap.

"Be careful," Sean said. "He's a delicate creature." And he sat beside me. Then Kira on my other side, and Elliot beside her.

"Does that *happen*?" Kira asked. "They call cops on *little kids*?"

I nodded.

"That is . . . ," Kira said. She took my hand. Elliot gave me a tissue.

Sean petted Terry's head, his free arm firmly around me.

Nothing more. And it was everything.

"Joellen," I shouted, "can Zola come up here?"

"Here she comes!"

Then footsteps on the stairs, and I held my arms out to Zola as she flew up onto the bed with us.

"I'm Zola," she said to Kira and Elliot, and offered them her hand to shake. "It's like *Charlie and the Chocolate Factory*," she said. "Bunch of old people in a big bed together. Is this what you do for fun?"

"Yes," Sean said. "Yes, it is."

"Muir," she said. "I told them I didn't take it."

"I know you did. You told the truth, and a lot people are afraid of the truth. But you have to keep shouting it until someone hears you. Make them listen. Your mom hears you, and your grandma. And I do. I always will."

She nodded. "Who is this?" she said, reaching for the Terry Johnson sculpture on the bedside table.

The real Terry walked across everyone to investigate Zola.

"Oh, it's you!" she said, and rubbed the real Terry's ears.

I put the sculpture back on the table.

"My prized possession," I said. Kira tried not to smile.

"Oh, here." I reached in the pillowcase and put the Allen wrench in Zola's hand. "In case you get lonely."

"You don't need it anymore?"

"No," I said. "I don't think so. Not anymore."

When everyone else was gone, Francine made us toast. She put the polar bear on her own bedside table, and we sat on the porch steps, watching Terry Johnson eat grass in the yard like a very small cow.

"Francine."

"Hmm."

"That foster mom blamed Zola because she was the only black kid in the house."

"I know," she said. "Joellen is reporting her."

"How did you know?"

"Because she's a middle-aged white woman, and so am I, and I know we are very often the absolute worst. When you are a middle-aged white woman, never forget to call your brethren—sisteren—out on their shit. And your own."

"I won't forget. Barb was doing it to Kira, too. But Kira shut that shit down."

"Oh, Lord. See what I mean? Every damn time."

"Did that cop even need to be here?"

"No," she sighed. "But they can't ever get to you without going through me first. No one can. And they *won't* get through me. Do you understand?"

"I do."

"Do you trust me?"

"I want to. I think so."

"Okay then."

"I'm not . . ." I watched Terry Johnson jump after a moth. "I'm nervous. I have *friends*."

"I know."

"I have a job walking around a forest with little kids. And I have Terry Johnson. And you."

"Yes, you do."

"I feel guilty."

She frowned. *"Why?"*

"No one else gets out like this. Other kids don't deserve it less because they got in trouble, because they don't have a 'perfect' record, because someone abused the crap out of them. It isn't fair. It doesn't happen."

"Okay, then *do* something about it. Don't waste your energy wallowing in guilt. Take this one time things turn out right, go to school, figure out who you are, and work to change the legislation. Or work in social service, be a judge, run for office, or you know what? Be a foster parent. You would be a *really* good mom. Guilt never fixed anything. Hard work fixes shit all the time."

Exactly the right thing. Every single time. How was she doing this?

"Will Zola be okay?"

"She will," Francine said. "We won't let her not be. Joellen is with her. I'll keep track of her—you can help me. She's with her grandma, her family is fighting for her. She isn't alone."

My heart sped up. "Francine."

"Yes."

"Do you think it means I'm dead inside that I don't want to find my mom?"

She *looked* at me. "Of *course* not. Where are you getting this garbage?"

"Am I wounded?"

She squinted like she couldn't see me well. "*Wounded?* How?"

"Like, am I ruined because I was left alone? Will I ever know how to be a good person who loves other people? Is it too late for me?"

She stayed close beside me. "Oh my," she said. "Someone has done a number on you. Look at me: No one has any right to tell you how you feel, to feed you such ridiculous lies. You aren't wounded; you are not broken—you are a human person with human feelings and emotions including sadness and loss, which are perfectly normal and need to be felt, and worked through, not obfuscated by bullshit pseudoscience that some grifter invents to write self-help books and make money off vulnerable people. Repeat after me: People can be dickheads. Go on, say it."

"People can be dickheads."

"People can be wonderful."

"People can be wonderful."

She smiled.

"That's it?" I asked.

"Well. Basically. Trust yourself. You know the truth."

"What does *obfuscate* mean?"

"To cloud. To confuse. To *lie*."

"Francine."

"Yes, sweetheart."

"I feel old."

She sighed. "I know. It's been a long day."

"No," I said. "*Old*. Like I skipped childhood. Like I've already lived a whole life."

She nodded. "Because you *have*. You need to rest."

"I'm worn out. I feel useless."

"You could never, in a million years, be useless. You are a precious jewel, don't you know that?"

I could not look at her. "I think I'm scared."

"Of what?"

I tried to swallow, and forced myself to tell her the truth. "I won't make it on my own."

She took some hairpins from her pocket, stuck then in her mouth, and pushed them one by one into her messy, familiar bun. "Twenty years, a hundred or so kids, and I've loved them all, but I can tell you I've never worried that one wouldn't be with me the next Christmas. I'm worried now."

Me too.

"Stay with me," she said.

"I can't."

"*Why?*"

"I'll be trapped," I choked out.

"What does that even mean? Home is just a soft place to land in between adventures, or trouble, or what the hell ever. It's a harbor, not an anchor. Be brave, see the world, every forest and mountain, and know you always have a safe place to rest and come back to. Muir, you can't see the paradigm if you're in it."

"I don't know what a paradigm is."

"Forest for the trees. You've been telling yourself this story for so long, that you can't depend on anyone in the world but yourself, and yes, you come rightly by it, and you've kept yourself alive that way. But try to see outside that story, and for God's sake, don't let fear lie to you. Joellen is here, just like she's always been. Your friends are here. I'm here. A home doesn't have to be a trap. Muir, I don't feel sorry for you. I just love you."

"I can't," I said.

"You *can*. I'm here now."

"You're too late."

I lay down on the porch then, my head on her knees, and cried.

"I'm so tired," I sobbed.

She did not talk. She patted my hair and gave me tissues from her pocket. Such a mom thing, tissues always at the ready.

"I don't care how bad your last therapist was," she said. "We'll find you a good one, and it will change your life. Okay?"

I nodded into her knee. "What if I grow up and decide I do want to find my mom?"

"Then I'll help you. I'll do everything I can, and we'll find her. Or we won't. Either way, I'll be with you, because as long as you're breathing, nothing is ever too late. I don't want to hear you say that again, understand? We do not talk or think that way in our house."

Terry Johnson was worried. He sat on Francine's lap to lick my face.

The Salish Sea was salty in the evening air. The flowers beneath my window nodded in the breeze beneath the flitting bats. I sat up.

She moved my hair off my face. "Oh! Oh, I forgot, I have something for you. I need to . . ." She got up and went in the house.

Terry Johnson whimpered but stayed with me.

"I don't know, man." I rubbed his ears. "She's *your* mom."

She came back out, sat on the steps beside me, and said, "Lift your hair up."

She put something cool, a delicate gold chain, around my neck, and fastened it.

The chain.

"Kira brought it to me a few days ago," she said. "She'd gotten it almost all the way untangled, her mom worked on it, even Sean tried. Poor Kira, she was embarrassed to ask me for help; she wanted to do it for you by herself. I promised her I would get it free, and so here you are . . . early birthday gift from all of us."

I touched the cool links of the necklace, perfect and strong and whole. All this time, all those hands, still not broken.

There is not a fragment in all nature, for every relative fragment of one thing is a full harmonious unit in itself.

For the first time in so long, my racing heart was warm and calm. *Happy.* I put my arms around Francine and hugged her tight. "Should we take Terry Johnson for his before-bed walk?"

"Let's," she said. "I'll get him leashed up."

Because that was the routine in this house. In our home.

"Together, please, we have to smoosh. Oh my God, you people are hopeless. *Closer,* so we can see the 'Muir.' " Kira held her phone out as far as she could, but the four of us—Sean, Elliot, Kira, and I— were not going to fit in the frame with the entire text of the carved sign at the entrance of Muir Woods.

"Just let me take one of you guys," Elliot said, camera, as always, at the ready.

"No," she said. "We have to all be in it; I'll get it."

Early-morning coastal June fog swirled around us, floating ghostly into the trees. My whole body buzzed with anticipation.

"I told you, we should have brought a selfie stick," Elliot said.

"No way." Sean stretched his arm from the weird position he'd been holding it for the picture. "No nonessentials; the key to a well-packed suitcase is not organization. It is *simplicity.*"

"Be still, my heart," I sighed, and fell into his arms.

"Get a room," Kira said, but smiling. "Excuse me," she called to a woman pushing a stroller. "Could you take our picture, please, under the sign? So all the words show?"

"Love to!" The woman took Kira's phone and immediately began art directing, producing major eye-rolls from Elliot. "Okay, let's go boy-girl-boy-girl. You there, Tall Guy, let's see some crouching. . . . Good, okay! Tattoo Girl, you look great, chin up a little. . . . Beautiful! Hiking-Shorts Guy, left arm behind you, perfect, and you . . ." She looked past the screen to me.

Being unremarkable has been the hallmark and savior of my existence. There is no tactful way to describe invisible.

"Happy Girl," she said. "Yes, *you.* Move right beside Hiking Shorts. I love it. Okay, now everyone say, *Muir National Monument National Park Service Department of Interior!*"

Best. Picture. Ever. All four of us blank-faced, together beneath the entrance sign of the final stop on our graduation road trip to California, approved by Kira's mom and dad, Elliot's mom and dad, Sean's mom, and mine. My Francine.

Luckily the art director held her finger down and took a burst of, like, twenty-three pictures, so we also have one where we're all laughing, holding on to each other. Happy.

"That poor kid," Elliot whispered as the art director strolled away with her baby. *"Honey, put your face in the cake.... Pretend you're having fun—no, not like that...."*

"She's an artist," Kira said. "You should understand her pain. Getting you three to cooperate the rest of the summer will be my grand oeuvre."

We were her living art project. Every day since graduation, every place we'd been, she was collecting leaves, jars of sand, rocks, pamphlets, pieces of string. These things she carried with her from each place to take home and, with Elliot's photographs, turn into something beautiful.

Only months before, travel for any reason, let alone for sentimental pleasure or adventure, was a dream I could never have imagined. Losing a penny of my small savings to frivolity was the death knell of my survival alone in the world, but now I could breathe. I could let some money go, work to replace it, maybe even graduate from college. Because I could live in one home. Francine's and mine. Our home. At least until I turned twenty-one.

Or maybe forever. For now, three years to breathe was a miracle.

Already plans were in place for Yosemite in July, to walk the valleys and climb the mountains my Muir loved and kept safe. Sean was in charge of packing for our partial John Muir Trail *saunter.* He wanted to walk with me, he said, on the path where he and his mom found a way to keep his dad in them for always, and learned to live without him.

Then Kira would join us at the trail's end to gather together at Manzanar, where her family's roots were embedded in the desert, roots that grew into the strength that kept them together and alive, and brought them back to their island home.

Our family stories. And we began, at her and Sean's insistence, with mine.

"Muir, look," Kira said. "The collection is begun." We stood together beside Elliot and scrolled his camera through the cordons of what Kira had christened our *San Francisco Muir Trip*.

All of us and a random NICU nurse Kira procured, smiling after a tour of the neonatal unit and a lunch of mac and cheese and lime Jell-O in the hospital cafeteria, everyone pointing at me in front of the *John Muir Medical Center* sign.

Sitting together on the front steps of John Muir's house in Martinez, where he tried so hard to live with his wife and daughters, aching until, because they loved him so much, they set him free to wander alone in the wilderness, his only true home.

Sean, Elliot, and me on a blanket at Ocean Beach, watching Kira surf wave after wave, the happiest I'd ever seen her, which made me the happiest I'd been.

And now, the best for last. The redwood grove Muir rescued from destruction, safe here beside the wild California coast.

Sean held my hand into the grove of trees towering nearly three hundred feet, most of them five hundred years old, the oldest over a thousand. We walked together in silence and near darkness, the giants obscuring weak, overcast sunlight. Mist collected in our hair, dripped from the ferns on the forest floor, and from the redwoods' needle leaves and cones.

We came to a bend in the trail where a park ranger spoke to a group of enraptured tourists.

"The coast redwood, *Sequoia sempervirens,* may grow up to three hundred eighty feet tall, so you might assume its root system would be as deep as it is tall. In truth, the redwood's roots are very shallow, which leaves them vulnerable. Alone, a sequoia may not survive to maturity. But together in thick groves, their roots spread and intertwine, even fuse together, giving them strength to withstand the forces of nature. Together they thrive in swift winds and floods, and grow taller than they ever could alone."

The ranger led the tourists around and past us, still rooted on the trail, staring up into the redwoods, now alone together in silence. We stood in the cool air, this boy I love and my friends and I, beneath a sky warming gold as the sun found its way through the clouds.

"Are we ready?" Kira asked.

"Yes," I said. "Let's go home."

Author's Note

My daughter asked me to write this book. She was born into foster care and lived in three foster placements before we met. She's too young to remember, but who she is now was shaped by how her life began and continued within the foster care system. She said she never read a book about a life she recognized, which, according to her, meant less "people being molested all day and setting the house on fire" and more "a person getting used to new houses and people and everyone isn't perfect or evil but sometimes there's happiness." A wide pendulum swing, but I got her point.

The memoirist Mary Karr says, "Write less about how you suffer, and more about how you survive." Still, this story was not mine to tell. I did not grow up in foster care in America. I was never orphaned or separated from my birth family or adopted, and I hesitated to write a story that was not my own. My daughter became increasingly annoyed and said, "I'm not asking you to write your story. Write mine. Listen and I'll tell you."

If it is true a writer is a professional listener and question asker, the resulting narrative depends solely on whom she is asking and listening to. For this book, the voices I listened to were those of the kids actually living in or aging out of foster care.

I also listened to my daughter. I listened to friends and family members in the foster care system. I exchanged mail with former foster youth and read their stories. I asked, and listened, and wrote, and my daughter's story became part of someone else's, and another someone's. And after a long while they all became Muir's story.

The kids I listened to have known great joy. They have suffered and survived. They are the experts on their own lives, and they understand that the purpose of adoption is not to procure children to fulfill an adult's desire to be a parent; that the intended purpose of adoption is to find parents and families for children who need them. They know there are adults who genuinely believe the lie that foster care is where "bad kids go" and who also refuse to acknowledge the brutal and violent history of child stealing in America, which is racially, economically, and religiously motivated.

The kids I listened to said orphaned and fostered children are human beings, not "gifts" for adults; they are not "lucky," and they don't owe the world, and every remotely nice adult they meet, a debt of genuflecting gratitude by default. They said white parents have no right to erase the identity and heritage of children of color. They understand that every human is entitled to have at least one adult they can rely on, and every child is entitled to the truth of their own experiences and emotions, their own lives. They reminded me that orphans in films and books are routinely depicted as evil or "troubled" or defined only by suffering, or they are supernatural or ridiculously angelic. The kids I listened to explained to me that for a child, losing a family, losing parents in any way, is traumatic, and that a child's joining a new family is not some purely magical, meant-to-be scenario simply because it brings the foster or adoptive parent joy. The voices of adults, well intended or not, overwhelmingly drive the myopic, adult-centric false narrative of foster care and adoption in America, talking over those of the kids in care who are screaming that no one is listening.

My daughter wanted a hopeful, happy ending, and so I gave that to her. I gave that to Muiriel. Muir's story is fiction, not meant to represent the norm of every, or any single, foster adoptive story. But it was born of truth from honest voices, and I am grateful they let me listen. I hope I listened well. I hope we always will.

If you want to learn more about foster care in America, these organizations reliably amplify the voices of former and current foster youth and make life better for families and kids in and aging out of foster care. I owe them an immeasurable debt of gratitude.

agingoutinstitute.org

firstplaceforyouth.org

mockingbirdsociety.org

treehouseforkids.org

Phoenix Ashes: Former Foster Youth Voices Community:
facebook.com/PhoenixAshesVoices

Acknowledgments

First and always, thank you to Melissa White, agent, editor, writer, the best good fortune I've known. To Folio Literary for having me in your home—gratitude doesn't even come close.

 To Chelsea Eberly, who always finds the true story in a bird's nest of thousands of words in as many drafts: you are magic.

Thank you to my editor, Jenna Lettice, lover of Teddy Roosevelt and John Muir, whose talent for storytelling, rivaled only by her patience, spot-on instinct, and wisdom, brought this book to life and made it sing. You were meant for this book; the best parts are all you.

Eternal gratitude to Caroline Abbey, Casey Moses, Stephanie Moss, and everyone at Random House Children's who read, edited, designed, or otherwise touched this book. Thank you for making Muir's story happen. Special editing gratitude to Barbara Bakowski, Erika Ferguson, and Patricia McHugh for keeping the narrative from wandering too far into the wilderness.

Thank you for answering my millions of questions: Charles Nelson III, PhD, professor of Pediatrics and Neuroscience, Harvard Medical School, and research director of Boston Children's Hospital Laboratories of Cognitive Neuroscience; and Harold Grotevant, PhD, Rudd Family Foundation Chair in Psychology and director of the Rudd Adoption Research Program at UMass Amherst.

For your devotion to improving the lives of former and current foster youth, thank you to Treehouse and the Mockingbird Society in Seattle, Washington, and to Amy Lemley and Deanne Pearn, who created California's First Place for Youth. Thank you also to Phoenix Ashes: Former Foster Youth Voices community, for your brave commitment to making the truth known.

Thank you to my favorite social and adoption workers and foster and adoptive families, who shared inspiration, stories, and truth: Rebecca Frasier; Joellen Pinter; Lisa Hllavay; the Neuse family, Sarah, Alex, and Mac; Sarah Nelson and the Cargillova family; Litza Johnson and Bernadette; Paul Pierce; Joer Amirez; and DJ.

Thank you to the authors—and my dear friends—Catherine Nguyen, Caitlyn Flynn, Martha Brockenbrough, and Nicole Ching. And most especially to my sister, Christine Kiekhaefer, who introduced me to my daughter.

Heartfelt gratitude to the many generous people who shared their families' experiences surviving the internment of Japanese Americans, especially the storytellers of the Bainbridge Island Japanese American Exclusion Memorial Association and the Bainbridge Island Historical Museum; Delphine Hirasuna, author of *The Art of Gaman: Arts and Crafts from the Japanese American Internment Camps 1942–1946;* and Renee Tawa and Sheila Kern, for their reporting on the Manzanar Children's Village, "Childhood Lost: The Orphans of Manzanar," for the *Los Angeles Times.* Thank you to Mary Woodward, for your family and your beautiful book *In Defense of Our Neighbors: The Walt and Milly Woodward Story.*

For inspiration and accuracy, the docents at the John Muir National Historic Site in Martinez, California. Thank you to Connie

Walker for educating me about Canada's Sixties Scoop and residential schools, which used adoption to devastate indigenous lives. Deep gratitude to authenticity readers Nata Guterson and Celia Connor.

For help with Terry Johnson, thank you to Gretchen Landon, Dr. Julia Mulvaney, Dr. Evan Crocker, and the entire team at Mercer Island Veterinary Clinic. I love you all so much, and so do Henri and June and Henri's left ear.

Love-filled gratitude to my librarians, especially Linda Johns of the Seattle Public Library, Sarah Abreu at MIHS, and the staff at the Bainbridge Public Library, my home and writing refuge.

Special thanks to Victoria Irwin and Karen Maeda Allman for immeasurable kindness.

Love and grateful devotion to the supportive early readers and hand-holders: my Café Verité coven and my Bainbridge writers, who gave me a new home: Dawn Simon, Jennifer Mann, and Suzanne Selfors. Thank you also to Bainbridge Island's BARN for writing support and space.

Heartfelt gratitude for time, reading, and kind words to Deb Caletti, Jo Knowles, Martha Brockenbrough, Holly Cupala, Jeff Zentner, Kathleen Glasgow, and Joy McCullough.

Thank you to Georgia Hardstark, Karen Kilgariff, and Steven Ray Morris for saving me from myself.

To my family: you are, as always, on every page I write. Unless I say it's not you; then it's probably not. My older daughter, Julia J. K. Rizzle Neal. Tim and Vickie Longo, the Falletti family, Kathy and James Clark, the Temmermans, and the Kiekhaefers. Sarah Sydor, unending love. James, Henri, and June Longo, for daily writing assistance. Thank you to my Fair Oaks family: Joe, Dan, Dan's Joe, Deanne, Beth, Aaron, Merete, Barbara, Karen, Lucy, Corey, Jeff,

Amy's Jeff, Patrick, Poe, and my sisters Lisa, Brianne, and my very own Analise Langford Clark. I would be alone without you.

My father, Fred Belt, who would have loved this one.

My dad, Robert Irvin, who loved them all. Who is in every word, always.

Deep respect and gratitude for every former and current person in foster care, and to you who let me listen to your lives, who helped me to tell Muir's story; though it will never be enough, all I know to say is thank you. Thank you. Thank you.

Tim Longo Jr. For walking me into the forest, for your love of the wilderness and of John Muir. And me. And REI. But mostly me.

And to my own brave truth-teller: Cordelia Elanor, the reason for this book, the reason for it all. Always.

About the Author

JENNIFER LONGO is the author of *Six Feet Over It* and *Up to This Pointe*. Her storied careers as a playwright, elementary school librarian, preschool teacher, and literary associate at San Francisco's Magic Theatre prepared her for the most humbling fortune of her life: being a foster and adoptive mother. Jennifer holds an MFA in Writing for Theatre from Humboldt State University. She lives on an island near Seattle with her husband and daughter and writes about writing at her website.

jenlongo.com